THE DESCENT OF MAN

UNBRIDLED BOOKS

THE DESCENT OF MAN

KEVIN DESINGER

Unbridled Books

Copyright © 2011 by Kevin Desinger

First paperback edition, 2012
Unbridled Books trade paperback ISBN 978-1-60953-069-3

The Library of Congress has cataloged the hardcover edition as follows:

Desinger, Kevin.
The descent of man / by Kevin Desinger.
p. cm.
ISBN 978-1-60953-043-3
1. Life change events—Fiction.   2. Self-actualization (Psychology)—Fiction.   I. Title.
PS3604.E7586D47 2011
813'.6—dc22
2010047172

1   3   5   7   9   10   8   6   4   2

Book Design by SH • CV

First Printing

FOR MARIANNE

THE DESCENT OF MAN

 truck with its lights out idled in the street. White steam pulsed from the tailpipe and drifted off, but the truck made no sound. From our bedroom window I could make out the motionless shapes of two men on either side of the truck, facing each other. They both turned toward our house, but I was able to step back before they looked up to the second floor, where I stood in the dark. I recalled having been awakened by a clank like you hear from a distant game of horseshoes, but not why it had drawn me to the window. Marla slept on, but she can sleep through anything.

When I peered out again, both figures were standing together on the near side of the truck. They were studying our car. Even after I realized that the sound had come from a piece of steel striking the pavement, an element of disbelief kept me from piecing together what was happening. My sleepy forty-year-old brain plodded through the stages of cognizance, from seeing to understanding. In college philosophy I had learned the difference between *immediate* and *mediate perception*. Immediate: *two guys*. Mediate: *I recognize them* as *two guys*. The first is simply the mechanism of my eyes discerning shapes in the visual field; the second is my brain making sense of the shapes. Both stages happen at the speed of thought—the first perhaps even faster because it happens before thinking interferes. Either I'd skipped the next class or we hadn't covered a third stage of perception (maybe *making sense of the action*), but it took what seemed like forever: *Two guys are stealing our car.* The fourth stage, let's call it *self-awareness*, quickly followed: *I'm standing here like an idiot watching two guys steal our car.*

I pulled on a pair of jeans, a work shirt, and my running shoes. Almost as an afterthought I woke Marla. There was enough light for me to see her sit up and rub her eyes like a little girl.

"What time is it?"

I grabbed the handset of our cordless phone from the nightstand and pushed it into her hands. "Call the cops! Two guys are stealing our car."

She reached for her bedside lamp. I said, "No light!"

Now fully wakened by the urgency in my tone, she forced the phone back on me. "*You* call the cops." Then, "Why are you dressed?"

"I'm going outside to get the plate number of their truck."

"No, you're not!"

"I want to make sure we get these guys."

"Jim, please. They might have guns."

She had a point, but I gave her the phone again. "If the cops get here in time there won't be anything to worry about." I felt around in my nightstand drawer for the notepad and pencil I keep there and slid them into my shirt pocket. Then I said, "Keep away from the window."

As I slipped out the back door my hands felt strangely empty, so I detoured to grab a two-foot length of old galvanized pipe from a pile of plumbing scrap I kept meaning to recycle. The pipe made me feel safer, but I also felt an unfamiliar anger. This was a new experience for me, even in our modest neighborhood, where rashes of break-ins occurred now and then but were quickly stopped, and where our middle-aged Camry was about the nicest car on the block. The pipe felt natural in my fist.

Our neighbors to the left are tidy people who don't own a dog, and I was able to find my way easily and quietly across their backyard and around the far side of their house to the street. There's a street-light two houses down on the near-side parking strip and another farther up the block; otherwise it's porch lights. I started across the street, glancing toward the two guys breaking into our car. They had their backs to me.

Keeping behind the parked cars, I worked my way toward the idling truck. I could see through the windows of the cars, but not well enough to read the plate number. The truck—which I could hear now, its engine's deep, covert burble—had both doors open a foot or so, maybe to provide a quick exit if the thieves had to abort. One of them was in the driver's seat of our Camry, and the other was leaning over the half-open door. I kept moving up the sidewalk until the truck was between them and me. As I crouched down, gripping the corroded pipe, my anger grew as if it were being released at a mo-lecular level into my hand. It spread up my arm and shoulder and concentrated in my chest.

Something in the Camry broke with a loud snap, and one of the car thieves swore. At the same time something in me snapped too. Without thinking I crossed the few feet of open street and slipped into the cab of the truck. I placed the pipe on the passen-ger seat, pulled the shifter into "drive," and hit the gas. The truck lurched up Juniper. I couldn't bring myself to look anywhere but the street ahead. I shut my door, then made the long reach across the bench seat to close the passenger door. Keeping my eyes on the road, I felt around on the dashboard for the headlights switch and pulled it on. The cab smelled like a riverside tavern: cigarettes, sweat, mildew, and beer.

A rising sound of sirens triggered a tightness in my chest, as if the cops were after me instead of the car thieves. I pulled on the seatbelt shoulder strap and tried to keep calm, to drive as if this were my truck. My arms were shaking, and the tightness spread to my stomach. Flashing blue and white lights came into view, and a cop car rushed past me faster than I'd ever seen a car travel on a residential street.

The light at Fulton let me into heavier traffic heading west toward the river. I didn't want to cross the bridge into downtown, so I took a side road near the railroad yard and eventually entered an unfamiliar industrial area. It was randomly lit in yellow and brown tints, deserted as the moon. Half a mile later I realized what had happened: *I had taken a vehicle from two car thieves at the same time that they were trying to take ours!* I couldn't decide whether it was irony, poetic justice, or just dumb luck.

I slowed alongside a stretch of hurricane fencing with railroad tracks on the other side and found myself laughing convulsively. The only thing that kept me from choking on this strangely gripping laughter was when I finally thought about the cops talking to Marla, working their way around to a question that should have occurred to me earlier: *And where is your husband now?*

At this thought I accelerated and cranked the wheel hard to the right; the truck dove into the ditch, collapsing the right front fender and killing the engine. The impact caused the pipe to roll from the seat to the floor, and at the same time my chest hit the horn, which gave a weak bleat. Then everything was still.

I pulled out my handkerchief and began to wipe my fingerprints off everything I had touched. My hands had the adrenaline shakes, so I worked with care. Covering my hand with the handkerchief, I turned off the lights and ignition and let the keys drop to the floor. Then I picked up the length of pipe and tossed it onto the road.

Stepping down from the cab, I rolled my ankle on a stone the size of a softball. I grabbed the stone and slammed it onto the hood of the truck. The sound was satisfying in a primal way. Shouting with each blow, I swung the stone again and again, leaving a lot of dimples but no real damage. I hurled the stone over the hurricane fence, then picked up the pipe and went after the windows. They exploded into tiny, glittering cubes. I got all four: front, driver's side, back, and passenger. Then around again for the mirrors and lights. When I stopped, my tension was gone.

I stood back to look at the damage and recalled my interest in the license-plate number, which was why I had gone outside in the first place. Now I might be able to use it to learn the owner's name and address, and maybe his criminal record. Feeling for my pen and notepad, I walked around to the back of the truck and found the license plate in its bumper recess behind the tow ball. Then I realized that the registration papers—if I could find them—would be even better.

I went over to the passenger door and reached with the handkerchief through the broken window to open the glove box. Sure enough, inside was a tire warranty envelope holding several folded sheets of paper. I took it all. After wiping my prints from the glove-box lid, I folded the envelope and shoved it into my wallet pocket. I picked up the length of pipe and started walking toward home but stopped before the first curve for one last look. There is a deadness to a vehicle with no glass. It seemed likely that the truck belonged to the thieves, but if not—if they had been cruising around in something stolen, something that couldn't be traced back to them—I could see how I might be held responsible for it ending up in a ditch, all battered up.

Around the curve and another hundred yards up the next straight stretch, I came to a vacant lot surrounded by thick brambles. The narrow gravel entry crossed a culvert half choked with silt. Using the pipe, I poked my handkerchief deep into the culvert, and then, with a two-hand hurl, I sent the pipe rotating into the brush at the back of the lot. Now only the envelope tied me to the truck.

There was enough ambient light to illuminate some of the vacant lot, though most of it was dark. The gravel was strewn with bottles and pieces of wood and rusted metal. I found a scrap of plywood the size of a cutting board and slipped the envelope beneath it, then left the lot and started again for home. I had no idea whether the cops would think I was a good guy or a bad guy. Perhaps, like myself, they would have a mixed opinion.

A couple miles from home I started jogging. I had to work up a story for the cops, and it was becoming apparent that my running—my *having run*—could only help. If nothing else, I could say I was worried about Marla. Which was true. And this concern might tip me toward being a good guy, help me atone for abandoning her in the first place, then making her wait so long for my return.

I opened up and ran hard. My feet found a rhythm, but there was nothing natural about it. I ran until my side began to ache. When I stopped to catch my breath, my pulse pounded in my face. My clothes were damp with sweat. The stitch in my side receded, and I started walking again.

I didn't want to admit to Marla that I had taken the truck. It had been foolish and impulsive, and nothing in her sense of social order allowed for such an act. She would be torqued that I had disappeared for *whatever* reason; I should have stayed and called the cops and let things take their course. This is why civilized people pay taxes and have insurance. The premiums and deductibles are small prices to pay for protection.

But this is a male quandary: If we just stand there and watch we feel like idiots; but (depending of course on what we do) we can also feel like idiots for having acted. There might be a narrow window of involvement that can keep us from feeling like idiots, but in the moment we can't know whether our course of action will make us appear heroes or fools.

Approaching Fulton, I started jogging as if on my wake-up run. I wasn't wearing sweats, but you see this now and then, guys jogging in their street clothes. While the light was red I ran in place, trying to appear concerned about keeping my heart rate up, working on my breathing. At this ridiculous hour. It must have been two or two thirty. Well, you see this too, the lone jogger at night because his job has him on an odd schedule.

Any situation offers choices (this being part of my explanation to Marla), and I was tired of hearing about guys stealing cars and taking a slap on the wrist for it. If the courts couldn't solve the problem, maybe it should be up to the citizens. I knew this argument had holes in it—vigilantism being the most obvious—but maybe holes were good; maybe they would distract her from my having been gone so long.

I was in our neighborhood, a dozen blocks from home. I still couldn't figure out why I had taken the truck. Usually I make the right decision—the *civilized* decision—but between sneaking closer to look at the plate number and finding myself in the truck, I'd had a glitch in my decision-making process. Maybe this was the way to look at it: I had followed an instinct because none of my self-preserving or ethical governors had been activated. In this sense taking the truck may have been the natural thing to do.

I wondered if there was something in me, perhaps in all guys, that sparked bad decisions and got us into trouble. Something that ten thousand years ago had gotten us *out* of trouble but over the ages had become obsolete and, as we became more civilized, illegal. The call of the wild. Tapping the feral side of the brain. *Eliminating* the brain.

I had been gone a long time. An hour? No, probably not an hour but longer than a half hour. Let's say forty-five minutes. I should have been gone five minutes total and gotten back before the cops arrived. I was forty minutes late and not home yet.

Walking faster again, I wondered what had happened to the thieves. It didn't seem possible for them to have taken our Camry—they hadn't gotten the engine started before I'd driven off in their truck, and the cops had come so soon afterward. Most likely they had tried to get away on foot.

What if they had eluded the cops? I looked up the street and saw a hundred hiding places. But no, if the car thieves were still at large, cop cars would still be in the area.

It bothered me to think I might have destroyed an innocent person's vehicle. Maybe their insurance would cover them for the loss. But if I were held responsible, given the situation and my clean record, perhaps the worst that would come of it would be some kind of fine and probation (basically a slap on the wrist). The owner of the truck would collect on the insurance, minus the deductible, which I would gladly pay. In fact, I would insist.

I was at 40th and Juniper, looking two blocks down toward our house. All was quiet. Still, I didn't want to be seen arriving from the direction in which the truck had gone, so I trotted over to Cedar, then turned west, paralleling Juniper until I was behind the Ferguson house, which faces ours. Their garage and fence blocked my view, so I continued up to the next corner and turned toward Juniper; a moment later I was home.

It was as if nothing had happened. Our car sat there alone, unlocked. I looked in through the passenger-door window and saw that the ignition switch cover had been torn away.

This was when I came up with my story for the cops. It would be the truth up to where I had been on the far side of the street, maneuvering into position to look at the rear plate. And then one of the guys spotted me, and I panicked and ran. I hid for a while, trying to calm down. I didn't know how long (I would explain), but I might have been followed, so I stayed hidden. . . . No, I didn't see what happened to the truck because the guy chased me the other way.

Them: But they say no one chased you.

Me: They're lying.

Them: They don't have any reason to lie . . . at least about chasing you.

Me: Neither do I.

Them: You would if you took the truck.

Me: If I *what?*

I would have to practice my surprised indignation.

.   .   .

I found Marla in the kitchen, calmer than I'd thought she would be. Calmer but not exactly relaxed. She was in her jeans and robe now, leaning against the sink, impossible to read.

"So where did you go?"

I said, "One of the guys came at me, and I ran."

"No, you didn't, you big fat liar. You stole their truck." She was incredulous and amused but definitely torqued. She said, "I stood there and watched you, okay? You stole the truck, so again, where did you go?"

"I told you not to look out the window."

"And I told you not to go outside. The next thing I know you're stealing a truck!"

"It wasn't stealing."

"Are you kidding me? In what world?"

I said, "You're right. I'm sorry. I just drove." I looked down, trying to work out how to tell her what had happened. A glint of light on my wrist caught my eye—a crumb of glass riding among the hairs. I picked it out and dropped it into the wastebasket beside the refrigerator. I said, "I didn't have a plan. When I realized the cops would ask where I was—" I suddenly saw the distinction between the three phrases *the truth, the whole truth,* and *nothing but the truth.* I would tell her the truth, and nothing but the truth, but she wasn't getting the whole truth. The problem was that I would have to wing it in terms of what I kept from her. I was too disorganized to have a plan, any more than I'd had a plan when I'd taken the truck. It had been a mistake not to brush myself off, shake out my clothes and hair for bits of glass from the windows. But this brings us back to our quandary: If we wait until we've thought of everything, we don't do anything. I would still be standing at the staircase window, now staring at the space where our car had been parked.

"Well," I said, "I drove it into a ditch and hustled back here."

"You drove it into a ditch." She made two fists as if holding a steering wheel, then shoved them forward and down. Her words were a statement, but the gesture was a question.

"I know. It was a full-moon thing."

"It's not a full moon tonight, Jim."

"That's the *kind* of thing it was. Did you tell the cops?"

"Please. I may have fallen off the turnip truck, but I didn't land on my head. I told them I was afraid to go to the window, but I heard the truck drive away about the same time I heard the sirens."

"Did they get the guys—the car thieves?"

"Yes. One cop came back and said they got them right away. He didn't mention the truck, but I'm sure the thieves will speak up about that. I mean, come on, Jim, you stole their truck with them standing three feet away! And don't you *dare* tell me the best defense is a good offense." She cut herself off. "Incidentally, I like the story about you running away. It explains why you were gone so long. The cops—actually, it's a Sergeant Rainey who is running the show—he told me to call him as soon as you got back. He wants you to look at some photos, I think. He called them throw-downs. Instead of a lineup."

"But I didn't really see anything."

"Even so, I'm sure he wants to hear from us."

"Okay, make the call. I'll stick to the running story for now."

"Which is good because it's clear that you have been. Which might have saved your bacon with me." I acknowledged the serious half of this last remark with a nod.

She pulled a business card from the pocket of her robe and started punching the buttons of our phone. I went to the front door and looked out the window to the street.

She said, "Sergeant Rainey, please." She waited, then told me they were patching her through. I listened, trying to let things flow. I had

to quit trying to control everything and also to quit acting impul-
sively. I resolved to behave somewhere in the middle. Marla said, "Hi,
Sergeant. He's home—my husband is home. . . . Oh, I'm sorry, this is
Marla Sandusky—you caught the two—yes, the Camry on Juniper. . . .
Sure, I'll tell him." She listened for a moment. "He said one of them
came after him, and he . . . That's right. . . . Well, he was hiding." After
a longer pause, she said, "No, just the Camry. . . . I have a bike. . . .
That's right, or the bus. . . . Sure, we can do that."

She hung up and said, "He wants us to go down to the station. A
patrol car is coming by."

"Good, because our car probably won't start."

"He knows. The guys trashed the steering thing where the key
goes in."

I rubbed my face, wishing we were done. "I suppose it has to be
tonight."

"He said it's about the throw-downs, but I think he's bothered by
how long you were gone. If you didn't take the truck."

"I was planning to say I was chased."

"By a *fourth* guy?"

"A third guy."

"We have the two they got, the one who drove off in the truck,
and now the one who chased you. Even three seems like a stretch."
Then she said, "Wait. If you're planning to say you didn't see the guys,
how can you say one of them came after you? I mean, if you picture
it, how would it work?"

"If I'm hiding, maybe I just *think* he followed me." Then I said,
"No, because that would still mean I saw him start after me."

"No, no, that could be good. You're all nervous about being out
there, and you hear the scuff of a shoe, and you skedaddle. They see
you go. and the guy in the truck panics and takes off, leaving the

other two. So no one really has to chase you." I warmed to her in a way I never had before; she was taking my side after what I'd done, even after I had lied to her about it. It's hard to tell how a person will behave until the situation arises.

I said, "But why do the cops want *you* down there?"

"I wonder too. Maybe he wants to check our stories against each other."

"That's what I think."

She said, "Then we're agreed that I stayed away from the window?"

I left that one alone.

"Oh, please," she said. "Do you really want to workshop who committed the bigger crime tonight?"

It was true: She had looked out the upstairs window; I had taken the truck. I still didn't think of it as stealing, but it was by far the bigger offense.

She frowned and pointed at me. "Hold it. You saw the guys when you went downstairs. I mean, between you and me right now, you saw more than a truck. When you first woke me up, you said you saw two guys."

"Just shapes, no faces." When she hesitated, I said, "Really. Just the truck in the street and the shapes of two guys by our car." The only part of it I didn't want her to know about was how I had pounded on the truck.

She studied me briefly, then said, "Okay, you lie about taking the truck, and I lie about looking out the window. We won't recognize anyone in the photos, and that should be it."

"The timing again?"

She said, "If you got back right after the cops left, that's half an hour. We can say we went out to check the car, and then we had something to drink before we called in, which should help with the time gap. I mean, he said to call right away, but that doesn't mean we did."

It hit me how much clearer her thinking was than mine.

I said, "What about the neighbors?"

"The neighbors?"

"Did they see anything? Did anybody come out?"

"The whole block came out. Stacks was first, of course, that chest of hers heaving dramatically. We had quite the crowd. But then the cops got the guys—who tried to hide in Barky's yard, big mistake—and ran them down to the station, and everyone went back to bed. I doubt anyone saw you come back. Which reminds me, where do we say you ran off to?"

We looked out the window to the street where the truck had been. I still didn't regret taking it, but I didn't feel very secure about it either.

Actually, I think I was feeling regret; I just wasn't ready to admit it, even to myself. I said, "The truck was aiming right, so I would have run left."

She said, "Which is good. It's where you came back from, if anyone happened to be looking. So if you ran that way, then up the next block . . ."

We looked left down Juniper for a moment, then turned toward each other and said in unison, "Fred Jackson's garage!"

ergeant Rainey looked as if he were the principal of a grade school and I was the tenth consecutive kid to be marched into his office. Or I felt like a naughty boy being marched into the principal's office, and Rainey seemed weary of me at first glance. He gave me a frozen-faced, I'm-watching-your-pupils-dilate-so-don't-lie-to-me look, and all I could think about was the lie I planned to tell. Tapping his pencil against a notepad on his desk, he invited me to sit.

"Let's see, here. You're a wine steward in a sandwich shop?"

I nodded.

"And your wife is a schoolteacher. You live in a house on Juniper and park your Toyota Camry out front. Why don't you tell me what happened tonight."

I gave him the truth until I reached the part about getting close to the truck. Then I said I heard one of the guys make a move toward me, so I ran down the block, took a right at 37th, and kept going until I holed up in Fred Jackson's garage, about two blocks away. I told him

I hid in the corner behind the boat—Fred's aluminum drift boat—and I took a piece of firewood from the stack along the back wall, and if I heard anyone coming I planned to beat on the boat and yell for help. I found it surprisingly easy to invent the details. But then it occurred to me that I had made a mistake because of how closely this version paralleled what had really happened—me beating on the truck with the length of pipe.

Rainey said something I didn't catch.

"I'm sorry?"

"That was your plan?"

"Actually, I was in a hurry." I laughed, and it surprised me. I had a lot of nervous energy. It's amazing how worked up you can get over lying on record to the cops, even when it's not your only thrill of the night. This was different from driving away in the truck because it was face-to-face. And I couldn't react to the adrenaline rush by beating on something and roaring like a prehistoric galoot. A pressure was building in me—made worse by the sense that I was a suspect in the disappearance of the truck—and I had to just sit there and maintain the restrained demeanor of modern man.

I said, "I didn't have what you might call a plan."

"Did you see any of the thieves?"

"Only shapes."

"How many?"

"At least two."

"No, I asked how many shapes you saw, not how many you think might have been there." This was when I realized I still didn't have my story straight. He said, "It's *my* job to figure out what happened. All I want from you is your side of it. So again, how many car thieves did you see?"

"Two."

"And the one that came after you?"

"That was later. Not a lot later, I mean, but I didn't see anyone right then. I was looking at the truck."

"Still, in your story, one of them came after you."

"Actually, it might've been a noise, like a scuff. It happened right after something broke in the car. There was a snap, then this other noise, and I ran."

"But in fact, you didn't see anything."

"I think I panicked. In fact, my wife—"

Oops. Why bring her into it?

"What about your wife?"

"Oh. Well, I was telling her what happened because I was gone so long, and it made sense to her that I ran. I wanted to see the license plate of the truck, but when I got close, I got scared. I mean, they were right there, and it was so quiet." He watched me. I said, "Actually, I might have made the noise that spooked me. My wife doesn't think I'm very brave."

It's interesting how often you can use the word *actually* when you're making it all up, when nothing you're describing is actual.

"Were you carrying anything?"

"What do you mean?" I was worried that he had a witness, one of our neighbors perhaps, who had seen the whole thing—including me carrying the pipe into the truck. Was he just riding out my version to see how far I would go? *Well*, I thought, *I'm in this far.* Also, I still felt I was one of the good guys, an ordinary citizen trying to protect what was his.

He said, "Did you have a weapon?"

"We don't keep guns in the house. When I was hiding, I found a piece of firewood, but that was more of a—you know, something to pound on the boat with."

"In Fred Jackson's garage."

"Yup. I mean, yes." I cautioned myself, *Don't get too comfortable.* Then I realized I was making mistakes because I was too tense, not because I was too comfortable. The middle part was missing, the kind of relaxed you get when you're in a serious situation but innocent, and telling the truth. I was close to what Marla calls the church giggles, where the tension alone can make you explode with snickers at notions that normally wouldn't spark a chuckle. If I got any less comfortable, who knew what pumpkin-seed remarks might be pinched out of me?

"What's funny?"

"Nothing. I didn't know what it would be like, is all."

"What *what* would be like?"

"This."

"Did you hear the dog go off? The one they call Barky?"

I felt certain that a loud dog could be heard from two blocks away, but when you put me in the back of Fred's garage, I wasn't so sure.

"Barely," I said. "It sounded like a million miles away."

"Is that the dog's real name?"

"It's what we all call him. He's got a hair trigger, and then you can't shut him up. His real name is Jeeves."

"Jeeves."

"I know. They missed by a mile with that one."

"Yeah, but with dogs you can't be sure."

"They could have named him Stupid. You figure that out right away."

He scribbled on his pad, then sat back, took a deep breath, and sighed.

"Okay, Mr. Sandusky. Mr. Jim Sandusky." He was consulting his notes, holding the pad at arm's length. "I think we're about done here, but I want to say something off the record." He set the pad on the table and looked at me. I waited for him to move the pad to a drawer or turn off a tape recorder, some indication that "off the record" was anything other than a mental construct.

Eventually I said, "Okay."

He said, "I'll be honest here. There might be repercussions if you took the truck. But if you were to tell us where to find it, you would get your life back in pretty short order."

I recalled my last look at the windowless, battered wreck.

He watched me with a slight smile for a moment, then said, "I do like the idea of you taking it." I leaned forward, and he raised a hand. "I'm not saying you did, but a timid guy like you seeing two thugs stealing your car, and somehow you end up in their truck, angry as hell, stomping on the gas, your eyes as big as baseballs . . ." He peered at me through his hands, which were miming binoculars, then sat back and looked at the pad. "But no, we'll accept your story as you told it. Officially it doesn't have any holes—no gapers, anyway. Believe me, the cops don't care whether or not it's true."

After a moment he said, "If you stole the truck, right now you would be wondering how to read me. You'd be asking yourself if legally I can say I don't care if you stole the truck—and by legally I mean whether it would hold up in court if I used it to trap you into confessing. You would also want to talk about it, not have to worry about the phone ringing with me on the other end saying we found a partial print on the parking brake and we need you to come down for more questions."

I said, "Makes sense."

"That's good," he said, nodding. "Neutral." He paused, but I couldn't tell if it was for effect or a real pause. What I could tell was that, in spite of what he had said when he'd set down the notepad, we weren't nearly done here. I kept quiet, waiting for the rest of it. He said, "And partly you're wondering if we would go easy on you, maybe even let you off, if you were to confess right now."

He leaned back and sighed. "Well, Jim, I can't help you. I could swear on my grampa's pocket watch that this really is off the record, but the more I said it the less you would believe me because I'd say the same thing either way. Obviously, if you took the truck, you'd have to play it as if I'm trying to smoke you out. That's your *disposition*." He liked that word. "Which is interesting, see, because now you're assuming I'm lying, and I'm assuming you're telling the truth. It sounds like I'm not, but believe me, I am. Which is the opposite of what usually happens at this desk." His *believe me* was beginning to sound like my *actually*.

But the man had an interesting mind. And to be honest, I wanted him to admire me for what I'd done: *I had taken their own vehicle right out from under their noses!* I also wanted him to see how I had to lie to keep the law, which was too general to appreciate the special circumstances of this situation, from treating me like a criminal. In a way it made us equals. And adversaries.

He gave a conceding nod. "You say you heard something—sure, that could do it, turn you back into a timid guy." He didn't seem any more convinced than I was. He flipped through his notes for a moment, then thumped his index finger on one of the pages.

"But *someone* took that truck. If it was you—if you sneaked out of the house and made it across the street and moved into position, and then somehow you jumped into their truck and drove off—that doesn't make any sense either. No one does that. I mean, no one would *do* that. It's just as likely that an alien spaceship beamed you and the truck aboard and then for some reason kept the truck and dropped you off somewhere nearby. And now you're sitting there with some kind of probe up your ass. You are a first-class head-scratcher."

He looked at me for a moment. "From your side of things—I know it's late, but give me a second here, let me work this out—you say you ran. Which is what you would normally do, and now you're uninteresting. But it's also what you would *say* you did, if you took the truck." It started to seem as if he would simply talk until he had everything figured out, even the details of my conversation with Marla. And it probably showed on my face. I was sitting there waiting for this absolute stranger to say, "You probably lied to your wife about stealing the truck, and then I'll bet she leaned back against the sink and told you she watched you climb in and drive away."

I mentally focused on what I recalled of Fred Jackson's garage, its door stuck open all these years, the drift boat that had never seen a river and probably wouldn't until it belonged to someone else, and the firewood stacked against the back wall. I tried to imprint the image on my brain so that it would be the only thing Sergeant Rainey found when he got that far in there and started rummaging around. In order to get away with the lie, I would have to become the lie.

I said, "We're still off the record?"

"Sure."

"Were they in their own truck?"

"We believe so."

"But why? Why would they do that?"

"Well, think about it. They're driving around at two in the morning, perfectly legal. They stop in the middle of the street—not so legal, but hell, a hundred newspaper-delivery people do that same thing every morning of the year. So they're stopped in the street, they get out and look in the window of someone else's car—they might flashlight the interior or test the handle to see if it's locked—questionable but still legal. It's when they try to get in that they leap the fence. See, they've been committing the crime all along, but this is when they're committed *to* the crime. Now, if you go back and put them in a stolen vehicle from the start, they're bustable all night long. Roll through the wrong stop sign and get nailed for grand theft auto."

"So what happens now?"

"I want to hold them for a few days for resisting arrest, which might put them on the defensive. It won't last long, but it's worth a try. Eventually they'll start thinking about what happened to their truck."

"Do they think I took it?"

"That's the real question, and frankly, I don't have an answer. We asked about a third guy ditching them, and they gave us—I mean they *each* gave it because we had them in separate rooms—the big ol' Bob Hope double take like they really didn't know what we were talking about. There wasn't a third guy."

"But that doesn't mean it had to be me."

"My point is, if they suspect you—if they think they're being run through the court system by the guy who stole their truck—they're going to get hot. Irony is lost on people like this. And let's not forget, they know where you live. Now, if you were to drop the charges and make a show of good faith by paying for the ignition repair out of your own pocket, this might be the end of it."

It felt as if dropping the charges would be the same as admitting that I had taken the truck. Finally I said, "I'm not sure what to do, so let's go ahead with it."

He turned in his swivel chair, which groaned as if similarly disappointed by my decision. "Oh, boy, that's not what I wanted to hear. And I probably can't change your mind?"

"Why do we keep letting guys like this off the hook?"

"You know where it could go, don't you?"

"No."

"All the way."

"By 'all the way' you mean to court? Lawyers and newspapers?"

"No, I mean one of them might try to kill you."

I was glad Marla wasn't there to hear this. He said, "We can't hold them forever, and just a *whiff* of guys like them causes cancer in guys like you. Think of yourself as a slice of bread, and they're a can of Drano. After they come in contact with you, all that's left is a puff of smoke and little crusty bits. So if they start phoning or following you around—if this goes nonboring—I want to know about it."

He watched me. I acted like I was thinking. I wanted to show that I wasn't shaken by his words, but I couldn't think of anything to say. I didn't want him as an adversary, especially if one of these guys went "nonboring" on me. I hated not being able to help him figure me out.

He said, "They saw it, by the way."

My heart sank. "Saw what?"

"The truck, an older beer-bottle-brown Ford, was seen a few blocks from your house. The two officers in the first patrol car mentioned it later." To no one in particular he said, "We missed the boat on that one too."

He picked up the phone and punched three numbers.

"Franklin? Rainey. Are those throw-downs ready?" He nodded and said, "That's right." He waited, then said, "On your way, could you stop in on Stevens and get the wife? I want her here too."

He hung up and said, "We have some shots for you to look at."

"What kind?"

"They're instead of a lineup. It used to be we'd put you in the room with that big window you see in the movies and trot out a row of guys. Now we show you photos."

"It would be better if you showed me silhouettes."

"Yeah, well, we can't use those in court."

"I was just saying—"

"I know, but we're back on the record. Our little heart-to-heart is over."

A moment later the door opened, and Marla looked in. Behind her a cop with a manila envelope said, "This is the place. Go on in there and take a seat."

Rainey said, "Stevens, did Franklin hand those shots off on you?"

"I guess he did."

"Well, that's not important now. Let's see what we got."

Stevens approached the desk and patted his midsection, which had pretty much the normal swell for a middle-aged guy. "I can always use a walk, Sarge. I don't mind."

"Either our little alpha up there stops trying to take over or I'm going to march him by the ear into a cold shower." He took the envelope from Stevens and thanked him.

Stevens looked at Marla and me. "You want a coffee? Soda pop?"

We said we were good. He looked at Rainey, who put up a hand. Stevens pointed at Marla, said, "Thanks for coming in," and closed the door behind him.

Rainey said, "He'll make some kid a wonderful grandfather."

Marla said, "Yes, he's nice." I could tell she'd missed his point.

Rainey emptied the envelope onto his desk and pushed a dozen photographs toward us. "Just go through and take a good look at each face."

I gathered up the shots, and Rainey said, "Come on, Jim. You have to share. Your wife was at the scene too. If I turn you loose and my boss asks me if both of you looked at the shots, and I say no, he'll make us go through it again. So each of you, look at the shots, and we'll be out of here in no time." He looked at his watch. "Believe it or not, I have to get some sleep too."

I laid out the photos and pretended to study them. I gave my full attention to each before moving on to the next, recognizing none of the faces. Marla looked at each one but paid less attention.

At the end we looked up, and Rainey said, "Nothing?"

We shook our heads.

"Well, I've taken up too much of your time." He pushed back from his desk and stood. "You know what I'm going to say, but I'll say it anyway. You have my card. If you think of anything else, give me a call."

I stood at the bedroom window and said, "What did they do?"

Marla joined me from behind, sliding her hands under my arms and interlacing her fingers across my chest. She pressed her mouth into my shoulder as we looked down at our dead car beside the curb. The police cruiser that had dropped us off had left a while ago. It was four in the morning, and the world outside was as still as a painting. The session with Rainey had me sleepless, my head buzzing from the verbal tennis match. Marla can sleep anywhere for any length of time, and I could tell she was exhausted, but she stayed up with me.

She said, "I don't know. I stayed by the phone like a good little girl."

I bumped her pelvis with my butt. "Come on. It must have been strange. What did they do?"

"They just stood there like it was okay for their truck to leave without them. Like it wasn't theirs." After a pause she said, "Which, I mean, did you think about that? What if it wasn't theirs?"

"There wasn't a lot of thinking going on for a while. It was only after I wrecked it that I figured anything out. But Rainey said these guys won't drive around in stolen vehicles looking to steal another one." She accepted this with a nod. I gave it a moment before asking what had happened next.

She said, "Well, you took off in the truck, and the one in the street walked a short way after you, then just stood there. The other one jumped out of the Camry, and they kind of barked at each other, and suddenly they both ran up the street, which was when I heard sirens. I went downstairs and met the cops at the sidewalk. Two more cop cars went by without slowing down, lights going—no sirens on those—and the neighbors started showing up. I told the cop who questioned me—that guy Stevens—that I stayed by the phone and didn't see anything. I'm pretty sure he believed me."

"That's good because Rainey didn't even pretend to believe me. He said he didn't care, but I'm pretty sure he thinks I took the truck."

I was looking down at our car, trying to picture it—trying to imagine any earlier activity out there at all. Marla dropped her arms down around my waist, holding my belly. I'm self-conscious about the softness of my midsection when it's relaxed, but tonight for some reason it seemed okay that I was showing signs of middle age. I was doing better than Stevens, though not by as much as I would have liked.

She said, "Are you in trouble with him?"

"Rainey? I don't think so. I believed him when he said he didn't care. In fact, that might have been the only truth told tonight." Even this wasn't true because he had certainly been telling the truth when he'd said the situation might go all the way. *Nonboring*.

She said, "You were so smooth. It was like a dream, especially from up here, not being able to hear much of anything. At first I didn't think it was you . . ." she was picturing it, "because you were on the other side of the street, and I didn't see how you got there. And mostly you were in the shadows and behind the parked cars, sliding along. But then you were right across from them, and I almost pounded on the window to distract them from seeing you. Then you were inside the truck, and it moved up the street, and you were gone."

"Not the brightest thing I ever did."

She gave me a warm squeeze, and I was reminded that I'm not very good at seeing myself through her eyes. Then she gave me a different kind of squeeze and said, "You shouldn't have left me here like that."

"I know. I'm sorry. That's one of the things I figured out on my way back. I shouldn't have taken the truck either, but leaving you alone was worse. I still like the idea of getting the plate number."

She brought a hand up and patted me on the chest. "And I still like the idea of letting the cops handle it."

We stood there for a while.

I said, "On my way home I realized the car thieves wouldn't be hiding as I walked by because the cops would still be in the area, looking for them. Then it occurred to me that the cops should still be looking for me."

"I told them you were probably hiding. Rainey asked if I was sure you didn't take the truck, and I said you would never do anything like that. Then he asked me for like the third time if I looked out the window. He said it seemed more natural for me to want to see what was happening—with you out there and all—but I told him I was afraid they would look up and see me."

"That guy figures stuff out like lightning."

"He told me they probably wouldn't chase you—they would want to just get the hell out of there. And all I could do was stand there and think how ..."

"Stupid the whole thing was?"

She said, "I was going to say risky. How unlike you it seemed."

"Okay, but it felt pretty stupid."

"I'm not sure I'd—"

"I mean the kind you spell with two *o*'s. Stoopid."

She said, "The same two *o*'s as in 'boob'?" She pressed against me.

"Exactly. I'd never do it again. That I can promise you."

Rainey's warning about the possibility of repercussions flitted through my head again, as it had been doing about every five minutes. I concentrated on the idea, tried to make it real, but it wouldn't conform. It remained abstract, along with my hiding out in Fred Jackson's garage, how aspirin works, and the grassy-knoll slant to the JFK assassination.

After a long silence she said, "Someday you'll have to tell me why."

"Why I'd never do it again?"

"No, why you did it in the first place."

"Someday I may know myself. Bubba factor is my guess."

"You, my dear, are underendowed in the bubba department. I'm guessing midlife crisis."

"Well, it's better than growing a ponytail and buying a Corvette."

She laughed. "No, it's about the same."

"Actually, I think I went prebubba."

She gave me a kiss behind my ear. "Men shouldn't waste calories on thinking."

"Underendowed," I said, shifting my shoulders and hips to create more contact with her. "You know what that kind of talk does to me."

She slid her hands back down over my belly, then lower. "Yes, I do."

CHAPTER THREE

'm the wine steward at the Franklin Heights Deli. I started off hating the title because it sounds pretentious. *Wine steward.* We're not a cruise ship, and I don't wear a uniform. When I had business cards made up, the woman—I'd guess she was just a few years younger than me—got out a form and asked what my job title was. I said, "Wine guy." Her pen stopped.

"Wrong."

"What do you mean, 'wrong'?"

She stared at me through her Elvis Costello glasses and said, "Look at it." The space was still blank. "You have to capitalize something, and you can't capitalize 'guy,' like 'Wine *Guy*,' unless . . ." she pointed at me, "what if you don't capitalize *anything*, like an e. e. cummings poem?"

She was making me feel a generation older, the way body piercings do.

I said, "I thought about 'Wine Manager,' but that makes it sound like I'm trying to keep from calling myself a wine steward."

"Plus it's too corporate. How about 'Wine Czar'? You could wear one of those hats—"

I said, "'Wine Steward' is sounding pretty good about now."

She gave a matter-of-fact nod. "I think you just have to face it."

So my card says I'm a Wine Steward. It's a fussy term, and it's fussy of me to make such a big deal of it. My only defense is that we're talking about two different kinds of fussiness. People whose jobs allow them to dress casually for work often poke fun at those who have to wear a suit, but most of them work as hard to achieve that casual appearance as the suit people do to spiff up. Fussy-casual. That's me.

The Deli is John Harper's operation—he owns both the building and the business—but he lets me run my end of it pretty much however I want. The only part of my duties I don't like is that when it gets busy I have to help with the lunch rush. I like immersing myself in one thing and resurfacing on my own—like waking up without an alarm. But just about every day around noon, when the line at the ordering counter gets long and I'm not taking care of a wine customer, I get called over to scrub up and ladle soup or throw a few sandwiches together. It's not that bad, and, as they say, labor is good for the soul. My real point is that if this is the worst of it—having to fix a dozen lunches for familiar customers—I have a pretty nice setup.

John let me choose my computer when he took me on, and he hired someone to help me design the wine page of our website. The only part he got serious about was the money. I was to assume we would be audited every year. I must have given him a puzzled look because he said, "Keep perfect books. I would rather go broke than get in trouble with the tax man."

I make all the wine-purchasing decisions, work out the pricing policies, and set up the displays. He tells me when he needs something done a certain way, but if he offers a mere suggestion I'm free to ignore it. Owners can be too hands-on, making them difficult to work for, but John delegates well and keeps focused on the big picture. Still, trusting a quarter million dollars' worth of stock annually to someone who previously worked only one year in a supermarket wine section has got to be tough, even with his Eastern philosophy. I think he saw where I was headed in life and, because it would in turn help him, helped me get there.

We first met in the aisle of the supermarket. I was sitting on a case of wine, drawing up display tags—weekly markdowns, Parker ratings, and how this or that had wowed 'em at whatever wine show—when I felt someone pause behind me. Asking if I can help often drives off the timid shopper, so I simply turned, offered him a nod of acknowledgment, and kept at my work with the colored marking pens until the tag was done.

When I turned again, I found a man in his comfortable fifties, head tilted, studying me. His shopping cart was half filled with romaine lettuce. Nothing but the lettuce. He saw me notice and smiled.

I said, "May I help you?"

He looked around at my wines. "Yes, by coming to work for me."

"Come again?"

"You like your work, I like your work, I would like you to work for me."

"I'm pretty comfortable here."

"Obviously, but is that it? End of story?"

"I think so."

"But you don't know what I'm offering."

He had a point. Somewhat defensively I said, "We have good benefits here and good pay, and I get along with my manager, which is huge."

"That's because of your work."

"I couldn't say."

"It's because of your work." He was sure. "I can top what you're getting here, both in pay and benefits. I would be your manager, and I think we would get along."

"I don't think so. I mean, yes, maybe you can offer something better, and maybe we would get along, but I don't think I want to change. I just got things where I want them here. And I have seniority, which I would have to give up."

He chuckled. "No, you'd have seniority. That I guarantee." He pulled a business card out of his shirt pocket and said, "Well, I shouldn't push. When you're ready to swim, you'll let go of the dock." He handed me the card. "My name is John. It might be worth your while to drop by." He looked around and said, "Less of a *corporate* feel where I am."

I glanced at the card as a courtesy before putting it in my pocket.

He said, "And think about what you said just now, about having things where you want them here."

I honestly believe I would have let the matter drop if he hadn't added that last remark. I chewed on it all evening, about what it had taken to organize the wines on the shelves and make up a Rolodex of contacts at import companies and distributors. Eventually I realized that the difficult part of organizing the wine department was complete, and though I got great satisfaction from having succeeded in this regard, I felt a certain disappointment in knowing that I would be coasting from now on. If I were a character in a comic book, I would have said in my superhero voice, "My work here is done," and flown off into the sky in search of another wine department in distress.

As it turned out my flight would have been a short one. The address on John's card was just eight blocks west, a shoebox lunch stop recently closed due to illness in the family.

. . .

On my lunch hour the day after John gave me his card, I walked down to the doorway of the shop. Construction had begun, but, seated at the dozen or so tables, now more tightly grouped back by the cheese and cold-cuts display case, faithful customers were having sandwiches and soup.

I found John at the far front corner of the shop, where the window facing the street met the bricks of the west wall. He was talking to a man in a white shirt with rolled-up sleeves, an architectural drawing open on the floor between them. When John saw me, he excused himself and came over, and the drawing rolled up toward the other man's foot.

"I want to show you something," he said. "If you have a minute."

"I have forty-five minutes."

He led me back outside and over to the front window of the law offices that took up the remaining two-thirds of the building on the far side of the brick wall. There was no furniture inside, and no people. He said, "I just bought the rest of the place. After we get the trusses installed I'm removing this dividing wall. But see that door over there?" He was starting to light up like a storyteller about to divulge a magical secret. "That's where you come in." Centered on the far wall was a door to what might have been a low, narrow storage room.

"That's an entrance?"

"No, but it would be yours."

"It looks like a supply closet."

"It's a staircase." He was almost gleeful. "Down."

I said, "To the basement?"

He said, "Not the basement. The *cellar*. It's where the *good* wine will live. Do you currently have a room where the good wine lives?" He seemed to know that a cool storage area was the only critical lack at the supermarket. Without a cellar, I (or they) would never be able to acquire any truly special wines. To have—to possess and store and eventually sell—to *handle* truly great wines is, for some members of my world, more important than anything. I looked at the door to the cellar and suddenly felt that in my current situation I was little more than a box-boy.

"I'll have to talk to my boss."

"I can help you with that too." We went back inside, where he pointed toward a table back beside the lit doors of the beverage cooler. There was my boss, manager of the supermarket, involved with a large, awkward sandwich. Sometimes our city has a small-town feel. He was in mid-bite when he saw me, so he indicated with his head and sandwich together to come over.

I sat across from him. "Hi, Bill. Did you know I would be here today?"

He wiped his mouth with a napkin and said, "No, I eat here all the time. Their meatloaf sandwich is a work of art. But I thought you might at some point. If you take his offer I'll need you for two more weeks."

It turned out that John had been talking to him for a month, hoping to win me away from the corporate scene with no hard feelings.

Before I went back for the second half of my supermarket shift, John handed me a wine box half filled with catalogs and a pad of art paper. On the first page was a loosely accurate sketch of the law-office wall with the enclosed staircase leading down.

"Start with that and draw me some shelves for wine. You get the whole west wall just as I've drawn it, from the front window to the beverage cooler in back, all the way to the ceiling. And think of the top of the cellar staircase as storage space. If you would like, we can put in one of those library ladders that slide along a track. Make it work, and make it handsome. And keep a record of your hours—this will be overtime, mind you, part of your professional day. Try to have something for me by tomorrow or the next day. It doesn't have to be an artistic masterpiece, but be accurate with the dimensions."

I agonized over it because my first choice was so expensive. I finished drawing by the end of the first evening and spent the second evening just staring at it, thinking about how much it would cost and how John might take the news. I would be fired before I was hired. Still, I left everything as it was. When I went in, two noons after he had handed me the assignment, he looked over my work, referring to the catalogs where I had bookmarked them. Finally he said, "Looks good." Just like that. I wanted to hug him.

He went to his office and brought back a check ledger. "How many hours did you put in?"

Because I didn't want to charge him for the time I'd just sat there thinking about the money, I told him just the one evening. He wrote me a check for both evenings. I said, "Wait. You didn't hear me."

He said, "No, it was *you* who didn't hear *me*. I dare you to tell me you didn't spend both evenings on this." When I didn't answer right away, he said, "Thinking is part of the process. Even the big boys sit there and think. Noodle time might be worth more than time of action."

He looked at my drawings again. "You will have a Wall of Wine."
I said, "And you will be broke."
He smiled. "This isn't the biggest risk I've ever taken. I'll be fine."

While it was being built, I came to see that it had been a good move on his part to let me design the shelves. The cost was trivial compared to what he spent on the entire remodel, and he was even less experienced with wine-display particulars than I was. And I'm sure he figured I would be happier with my own decisions.

I learned later that he didn't have as much money as it first seemed. He was generous in certain areas, miserly in others. He kept a copy of Sun Tzu's *The Art of War* on his desk, using it to inform him on business strategies. He said it helped make the correct decision seem obvious.

Along with the wine shelves he also gave me the island, consisting of a series of high, narrow tables made of butcher-block maple, arranged to form a modular bar. There was enough room beneath the tables to store deliveries and have them be out of the way but still close at hand—more than fifty cases could be stacked under the island tables. If you were to order a case of a certain syrah from the Napa Valley, say, and return the next week to get it, you would find it beneath one of the island tables—a box with your name in Magic Marker on the side, along with the arrival date and the price, which would be 10 to 15 percent below the shelf price. I wouldn't have to be present; you could take it to the cash register, and John would ring it up.

Perhaps because of the remodel, some older people with a lot of money started gathering in the late afternoon every Friday, sharing pricey bottles, talking quietly. They sat at three round tables pushed together into a clover shape, forming a private wine-tasting group that we called the Elders. They insisted on paying retail for the wine; in turn John insisted on providing a plate of baguette slices and a selection of cheeses to go with the wines. The Elders (who were far more familiar with expensive wines than I was at that point) made suggestions as to what might be nice to have on hand next week, and I was able to respond with a regular turnover of upper-end vintages. John raised a concerned brow when he saw the first order sheet, which included two cases priced at over nine hundred dollars each. I was able to assure him that all but three bottles of the twenty-four were already sold, putting us in the black before the cases arrived.

He bowed modestly and said, "Student become teacher."

At about this time I formed an open-to-the-public tasting for our regular Friday-evening customers. For my own convenience it ran from seven to nine, an hour past closing. Having people stay past closing turned out to be a good move because it instilled in them an allegiance, the result of feeling privileged to remain after the doors were locked. They took the tasting more seriously than they would have otherwise, which allowed them to make better-informed decisions as to what they wanted for their own cellars. This in turn made them happier with what they bought.

For the regulars each week I would pull six wines of a particular grape of interest from the shelves, trying for a range in price and quality (often not related), and end the evening with a real treat, something from the cellar where I kept the treasures that were no longer in distribution. The cellar bottle was to represent what I thought the other wines were aiming for, the essence of the grape of interest.

At the beginning I didn't charge but left an empty water pitcher near the lineup of bottles for tips. Ones and fives appeared right away, and pretty soon it was just about all fives. The group remained fairly stable, between ten and fifteen people, none of whom were those difficult individuals who insinuate themselves into social events simply to drink for free.

One Friday evening I was pouring for the open tasting when a man from the Elders approached John, who was having coffee with two friends at a table near the cash register. This was where he usually hung out toward the end of the day, relaxing between ringing up folks on their way out and unlocking the front door for them if it was after eight. The coffee was because he didn't drink alcohol—evidently he hadn't had a drop since the first of August 1968, the day he had been discharged from the army.

I'd said, "You must have been about twelve."

"I'm older than I look."

"That's because you don't drink."

"Oh, I don't know. For a while I was way ahead of the game. Now I'm probably about even." He tended to give all the information he was comfortable giving on the first pass. I could see something in his eyes beyond age, maybe evidence of pain he had endured at one time. I had to learn to not ask for details.

The man's voice didn't carry over to where I was, but he talked with his hands, gesturing a couple of times toward the wine shelves. John's hands replied with an assurance that he would look into it. He came over to the regulars and told me there seemed to be a disagreement concerning a certain Leonetti. I said we had a few in the cellar, and if he'd tend to the open tasting I would go down for one.

When I returned, I handed it to him and said it was a hundred bucks. He looked at me, then over toward the man who had asked for it. I told him a hundred was already less than the customer would pay anywhere else. Still he hesitated. I said, "I'll bet you a nickel they won't be bothered by the price."

"These people aren't bothered by price. But a hundred bucks?"

"More than fair." I tapped the label of the bottle and said, "*That's what the cellar is for.*"

He went over to the man and his wife and showed them the bottle. As the husband reached for his wallet, he looked over to me and gave me a small thank-you nod. I nodded in return. John noticed this tacit exchange as he opened the bottle, then went back over to his friends and sat back down to watch the rest. The husband poured a small sample for each of the Elders. They all swirled and sniffed, swirled and sipped, chatted, then did it again. Then the couple brought the bottle over to us at the open table.

I said, "Well, who was right?"

She frowned. "I think we both missed the point with that other bottle."

He turned to her. "And it was a little cool."

"This or the other?"

"The other," she said. "A little dormant. We should have let it sit more."

I said, "Maybe it was the food you had with it."

She said, "Maybe," and the husband just shrugged. It was the temperature.

The wife set the half-full bottle on our table and told folks to go ahead; she hoped it was a treat.

I said, "Are you sure?"

"We have these other wines to get through, and some of us have to drive."

After this exchange my situation with John was secure. Before then he hadn't been clear that in a few years the value of a twenty-five-dollar bottle can more than triple and people will still buy it. Later I pointed out that he wouldn't buy a top-of-the-line Mercedes, but that didn't mean the car wasn't worth the price to someone else. This was another way I got lucky. He was sketchy on selling something at a price he would never pay, and I'd stumbled upon a simple way of making it make sense to him. His understanding had been theoretical—otherwise he would never have hired me—but now he understood it emotionally.

My personal feeling about this whole business is complicated—probably because I haven't worked it out entirely. It begins with the idea that some wines sell for three hundred dollars a bottle, and even though I have a very good palate, no bottle of wine can give me three hundred dollars' worth of pleasure. For some people, however, part of the experience is in the payment itself. It's as if they're giving themselves a gift: *Please, let me take care of that for you, it will be my pleasure.* Paying for it is part of the pleasure.

So I won't apologize for the price of any bottle we carry, and I respect the decision a person makes in buying it.

One day a guy about my age came in, having heard about a Bandol we stocked. He bought a bottle for thirty-five dollars and left. If you calculate how long it might take for him to drive home, open the bottle, and take two sips, this was how long it took for him to phone back.

"I bought the Bandol?"

"Yes."

"How much more do you have?"

"Three cases plus the bottles on the shelves. Maybe forty-four total."

"Cool. How much more can you get from the distributor?"

"Maybe six cases."

"I'll take those too."

"I can't do a discount on this."

"That's okay."

I sold all of it to him for four thousand dollars. It wasn't a mistake, but I wouldn't do that now.

In a narrow sense my job is to sell wine. In a broader sense, however, my job is to have a selection of wines available, to be able to go down to the cellar and return with a bottle, as I had done with the Leonetti. If that same guy were to come in now, I wouldn't let him clean me out. I would retain at least a case and sell bottles out of it one at a time. Toward the end of the case I would treat the regulars to a bottle to show them something special. In this broader description of my job, I was growing into that pesky term on my business cards; I was becoming a Wine Steward.

It's my guess that with any industry, gaining gravity is a self-propagating condition—the better you do, the less energy it takes to continue doing better. It wasn't long before the wine reps from different distributors started calling me, letting me know when they would be coming through with samples of their latest acquisitions.

They usually appeared in the middle of the afternoon, our slow time, wearing either a tweed jacket or the London Fog type of raincoat worn more like a robe, complete with the secret-agent lapels and dangling belt. They'd open what was usually a reinforced nylon satchel and set out samples from different wineries, then politely wait until I finished what I was doing—helping a customer or stocking the shelves. Then we would set out our pads of paper and calculators and over the next half hour work up an order. A few days later a dozen cases would arrive. To the uninitiated I might have appeared to be involved with underworld college professors.

There is something of a pattern to my workweek, but it's not easily discerned, especially when you consider the periodic afternoon drives I make to regional wineries to talk to the winemakers. I don't get to do whatever I want, but it may seem as if I do. Someone of a different moral structure might use this apparent lack of routine to arrange something illicit, but I don't have it in me to cheat on Marla. True, I haven't been tested, but I've never had a wandering eye, and things in general have been so tight with her—even during our crisis—that I can't imagine the circumstances it would take for me to be seduced into any form of betrayal. If this means I lack imagination or creativity, I don't mind. There are worse things to be known for. Worse things to know oneself for.

. . .

The day after the attempted car theft was Sunday, but I called our mechanic anyway. I left a message on his answering machine explaining what had happened. An hour later he called back. Tim is single, lives a couple houses down from his shop, and is liable to work odd hours. I knew when I called there was a chance we could get things going even though it was Sunday. He said if he could find wrecking-yard parts, we would have our car back Tuesday, maybe Wednesday. The thing about Tim is that when he gives an estimate like this—even over the phone without having seen the damage—you can pretty much count on Tuesday being the day. Over the phone he said, "I'm not doing anything right now, and I have a loaner that's not doing anything either. You'd be doing me a favor to drive it around for a couple days."

A short while later I heard a hefty diesel engine rattling out front. It was Tim in his tow truck, maneuvering to hook up to our Camry. He said if I rode with him over to the shop I could sign the paperwork and pick up the loaner. "We're not talking pretty here. It's a mule." It turned out to be a mid-'80s Honda hatchback, after they went from being weightless little toys to having some beef, some actual presence on the road.

Tim disconnected the Camry from the towing apparatus and opened the driver's door to look at the steering column. "These guys," he said, shaking his head. Then he said, "Yeah, probably Tuesday."

On the way home I was thinking about what had led to my driving this unfamiliar car—the entire series of strange events—and toward the end of a string of associations I recalled the envelope in the vacant lot. It would remain there for a limited period. It might be one more day and it might be a year, but at some point the envelope would be gone. Nearing the intersection at Fulton, I realized that I was anonymous in the Honda.

The thing about a loaner is that it's anycar. An owned car has something of its driver's identity because he or she has chosen it—less but still true if it's used. Toyota people never buy Buicks. But a loaner is by definition on hand for use by a spectrum of strangers who have no choice in the matter. Using the Honda as a disguise, I might never have a better opportunity to safely retrieve the envelope.

I felt through the glove box for matches, finding two partially used books. After learning what I could from the papers, I would burn everything. Sergeant Rainey had convinced me that this little adventure might not be over. Whether the threat was from him or the car thieves, I would feel vulnerable in some way as long as the papers were in my possession, which you could say they were, even under a piece of plywood in a vacant lot. When you commit a crime, you replay it again and again. You think about how you might have done things another way. You discover mistakes and omissions. For example, I hadn't wiped the envelope for fingerprints.

I drove around somewhat randomly, checking my mirrors to see that I wasn't being followed. Eventually I circled out toward the industrial area, trying to quell a fear that the cops had staked out the road to and from the wrecked truck in case the person who had taken it returned to the scene. There were no other cars around, and I felt both conspicuous and anonymous in the Honda as I approached the vacant lot. A stakeout seemed unlikely, but I didn't want someone grabbing me from behind, saying, "We knew you'd come back. Your type always does."

Before reaching the entrance I stopped and sat there, trying to determine whether or not I was about to enter another series of stupid decisions. In the end I felt that this envelope was the only physical evidence linking me to the earlier series of stupid decisions; I had to get rid of it. As Rainey might say, I was already committed.

The lot looked different in daylight. The brush surrounding it was denser than I recalled, and the lot itself was larger, about the size of a tennis court. I pulled in tight to block the entrance, stopping so that my door opened into the lot. Now a person would have to climb over the hood of the Honda to get to me. I left the engine running.

The piece of plywood was undisturbed. Still, I half expected the envelope to be gone, but of course it was there. I removed the papers. The top sheet listed the registered owner as Larry Hood.

His last name was Hood. What a joke: doomed at birth.

I tore off a square inch from the corner of the tire warranty and wrote in the smallest letters I could manage, "Laredo," which would put me in mind of Larry but left off his last name because I would never forget Hood. The street address was 1424 SE Condor. I wrote, "14" after Laredo, then below this put "Condor 24," as if it were a football score between two high school teams. The southeast part I would either remember or figure out. I had more space, so I copied the truck's license plate backward, even though I felt sure I could memorize it.

After checking again for witnesses, I wadded the pages individually and piled them like briquettes in the gravel, then lit an edge near the base. I nursed the flame and stayed with it until nothing remained except hot, then warm, then cold black-and-white ash. I chopped this up with an edge of the piece of plywood, stirred it around in the gravel, then spun the plywood over near some other scrap at the back of the lot.

Now the only physical evidence linking me to the wrecked truck was this little stamp of paper, which I slipped into my wallet behind my driver's license. After two seconds I realized that the first thing the cops do when they stop you is have you remove your license from that wallet window, exposing whatever is hidden behind it. I moved the slip of paper behind my library card.

Since the Honda was facing that direction, I decided to risk driving past the truck, just to see if it was still there. I was in the area and still had the anonymity of the loaner, so why not?

When I rounded the last curve and saw the truck ahead just as I'd left it—all empty-eyed and beaten—I stopped in the middle of the road. I couldn't bring myself to approach. It was too real or something, so I sat there, thinking or not thinking, I don't know—nothing I had in the way of thoughts really registered—then I found myself driving in reverse, turned around in my seat with my right arm locked behind the front passenger seat to look fully out the rear window. I veered into the other lane so that I wouldn't surprise oncoming traffic as I backed through the curve. On the other side there was a wide shoulder. I backed onto it far enough to get turned around, then headed home.

I regretted wrecking the truck and beating on it with the pipe. It had been violent and pointless, but now that it was done there was no way to undo it. I've always wondered why people can't block out something terrible they've done, just put it behind them. I can't speak for the others (most of whom I admit were characters from books and movies, with the rare instance in the news of people after years of apparent freedom turning themselves in), but for me even the relatively minor act of totaling the truck was the only thing I could think about. You weave a patch of bright color into the muted pattern of your life, and it's the only thing you look at. Believe me, you can't tear your eyes away.

If my odd series of spontaneous decisions had been part of a movie, I would've started shaking my head when the protagonist ignored his wife's advice to stay upstairs and let the cops do their work.

I'm not sure I would have thought of him as anything close to a protagonist. However, when you're the actual guy, and you're caught up in the moment, everything is different. But after the moment passes it seems impossible to explain this difference to someone who wasn't there, wasn't *in* the moment. The cops, for example. Or a jury, if your case ever makes it to court. Or your wife. Especially your wife.

ine years earlier Andy was still in town. He and I had met in college and hung out together for a few years after getting our business degrees. He had just moved into a large rental house, and his roommates threw him a birthday barbecue one fall afternoon. They had a keg of microbrew and a decent spread of food, and fifty or sixty people showed up. The day was warm, the rooms nicely sunlit, and all afternoon folks circulated between the kitchen and the backyard, with the odd person or couple wandering through the rest of the house to see the layout or use the upstairs bathroom when the one off the kitchen was occupied.

I was single and had been for some time, suffering a reputation among my college friends—and myself—of being alone. My invitation had "Bring a woman!" scrawled across the bottom in Andy's hand. He had this thing about getting me laid, about introducing me to all these different women. I seemed to be some kind of project for him, as if I were gay and didn't know it, and he and I would fight this thing together. Whatever it was, I still liked him. I liked his energy and his sense of humor, and I don't think he ever betrayed me in any sense. (Andy, now that I think about it, was the one to convince me that a degree in business would be more useful than one in philosophy or English literature.)

Anyway, I showed up to the party by myself, went straight to the kitchen to put my gift bottle of red among the other gift wines waiting to be opened, then filled a cup with beer from the keg in the garage. I was still finding my bearings in the crowd when Andy caught my elbow, saying there was this woman I absolutely had to meet. He steered me into the living room, where two women were talking. He stepped in and cut one away from the other as if it were a dance, steering her over to me.

"Jim, this is Suzy. She has the coolest Fiat. It's that shiny little black job out front." He turned us to each other and, with a pivot, led the other woman out of the room. It was surgical, he was so smooth.

I was a little stunned, but I managed to say, "For the record, I didn't have anything to do with this. He knows it bugs me, but he keeps doing it." She just looked at me. I said, "This matchmaking routine." As a final effort I said, "So here we are."

She said, "It was my idea. I saw you when you came in and asked him to introduce us."

"But what about your friend?"

"Her? Not my friend. I was waiting for Andy to find you when she came by and started telling me about her stupid cat. Pretty much of a snore, if you want my opinion."

"Oh. Well, then, how do you know Andy?"

"We met in a bar, had some laughs. Look, how long do you stay at these things?"

"Well, since it's his birthday—"

"He won't mind if we leave. We could always come back." This was the most naked offer I'd ever had.

I said, "Maybe in a while."

"Okay, sure."

We chatted for a short time, but it didn't take. We seemed to be at cross-purposes, and something about the way she had dismissed the other woman kept nagging me. What if I also turned out to be a snore? Perhaps I already had by not taking her up on her offer, not following the hormonal urge to go for a ride in that snappy foreign number out front. At one point she said she was getting another beer and didn't ask if I wanted a refill. Watching her go, I wondered if she would return. I thought, *No, she's gone, you're alone once again.*

I leaned against the back of the couch, sipped at what was left in my cup, and watched out the back window as people socialized on the deck. A moment later the other woman, the one who had been snubbed, returned and collapsed across the cushions behind me in a big dramatic flop.

"I'm not dying," she said. "I'm just tired." Her eyes were closed.

I said, "*Every*body's dying."

Keeping the same exhausted tone, she said, "They should get more sleep." She was speaking to the ceiling, her eyes still closed.

I said, "Okay, so why are you tired?"

"I was burying a cat."

"*Cats* are dying," I said. She leaned up slightly to look at me, then collapsed back. I said, "Sorry. You were burying your cat."

"My *neighbor's* cat." She put her wrist across her eyes. "I have this neighbor who thinks she likes cats. She doesn't, but she's convinced she does. She's chronically confused about who she is, and I guess she thinks it's organic or spiritually healing to like cats, and therefore she does. Two plus two equals four. Only with her it's two plus water equals red. The woman is Dingbat Central. So she has this cat, Steve—has had him for, I don't know, a few years—"

"Steve? She named her cat *Steve*?"

"Sure, why not? Steve the Cat. And he was getting up there, Steve was. Getting old. I never had anything to do with him because I have allergies, but I would watch him out the kitchen window. First he was bouncing up the steps, *boing, boing, boing,* and then all of a sudden he's doing this kind of two-stage push to make it up each step. No pepper. Steve lost his pepper. And now he's dead."

I came around and sat on the back of the couch with both feet on the arm to keep from crowding her. She remained on her back with her eyes closed. If I had wandered off, would she have told this story to the ceiling of an empty room?

I said, "She got him when he was a kitten?"

"No, he was used. I don't know how old he was when she brought him home, but she got him used. I watched him go from a teenager to ancient in four months. And then yesterday I went outside, and there he was on my porch, curled up by the front door like a big dead flea."

I didn't know what to say, so I just said, "Weird."

"That's what I thought too. When it got right down to it, Steve chose to die on a stranger's porch. And Annie—she's the owner, Steve's nutball owner—has no idea what happened. And I have no idea what to tell her. Which is partly why I'm here—so I don't have to deal with Annie. She's going to care, but there will also be a measure of relief, which she in turn will feel guilty about, and there won't be any books to tell her how to deal with it, and on top of that she's confused and delusional and dim-bulbed, born in the wrong century, and it's making me crazy trying to figure out what to tell her."

Suzy chose this moment to return with a full beer. She approached, didn't say anything—just looked at the two of us as if we were a complicated and slightly offensive sculpture—and continued on through the room. I waited a moment, then turned back to the woman on the couch.

"Tell her some cats go off to die alone."

She looked at me.

I said, "Tell your neighbor that some cats go off to die alone. You know, like elephants supposedly do?"

"Yeah, but do they really? Cats, I mean."

"I don't know. I was just thinking that if—"

"No, I got that part, but I want to know if they really do."

"I don't know either, but I doubt it. I think cats are more social than we give them credit for."

She said, "So are elephants, but I think it's also true that they—" She cut herself off. "Wait a minute. It was on my porch. That's not dying alone—alone is in the woods or by a river. *In* the river."

"It was kind of dying alone. An empty porch, right?"

"I suppose. But I'm pretty sure he wanted in."

"Hold it. None of this matters. Suzy doesn't know where he died."

"We're talking about Annie. Suzy's the thing that just walked by with a beer."

"Right. Annie, I mean. I'm just saying you could tell her that cats sometimes disappear for their own reasons. That way you wouldn't have to deal with the specifics, and it might be easier for her to let go of him. In a way it's a lie, but only by misdirection."

"Well, so far she doesn't know anything. She doesn't even know he's dead, let alone where he died, so I can tell her whatever I want, including nothing. I could let her just wander around the yard, calling and calling in her idiot falsetto—well, that's not true because eventually I'd have to shut her up somehow."

"And then you'd have to bury *her.*"

She laughed. "No kidding!"

I said, "So, the deal is, you have to talk to her and you're trying to figure out what to say."

"No, I just want to understand whatever it is I end up telling her."

This stopped me for a moment. I wasn't sure which way to go. I said, "What if you offer it as an opinion, or something you heard: Cats want to die alone. When they know they're about done, they go off by themselves. It doesn't have to be presented as an actual fact. You could say something about how rickety he seemed to be getting recently."

She didn't say anything, didn't do anything. I had no idea where her thoughts had turned. I was thinking that Steve the Used Cat didn't die of old age but instead from kidney disease, or licking antifreeze off the driveway. But I also knew that whatever had killed him didn't matter.

I said, "But why are you tired? It doesn't take all night to bury a cat."

"What makes you so sure?" She sat up with her legs still across the cushions. "You know what? I'm kind of edgy." She rubbed her face.

I said, "I wouldn't say edgy."

"Well, I would. What I need to do is apologize and get out of here. I got about one minute of sleep last night. I don't like being like this."

I came around to the front of the couch. She pulled in her feet, either offering room on the cushion or avoiding contact, I couldn't tell which. I was either welcome or I wasn't. It was the kind of quandary that usually kept me from making a move on a woman. It's part of what had kept me single. But for some reason this time I didn't freeze. I kicked off my shoes and faced her from the arm of the couch, working my feet beneath the cushion. We weren't close to touching.

I said, "So you really spent the whole night planting Steve?"

"It takes longer than you think. Unless . . ." She looked at me.

"Nope. Well, I buried a bird when I was six."

"I trust it was dead."

I pointed at her. "See? You're not so tired."

She said, "Part of the problem was that I had to keep an eye on Annie's house. The way our yards are, I didn't have much choice of where to put the hole." She raised her index finger. "But that's not the whole story. It really begins when I found him on the porch. That's when I started getting tired—yesterday, at seven in the morning."

"Ah," I said, as if this information helped.

She said, "I guess just *finding* dead stuff makes me tired. Anyway, the whole story is, I'm headed to the bathroom for a shower before work and I hear this meowing on the front porch. It's not the happiest meowing—more of a yowl—and I don't want to look. It's seven in the morning, I'm in a robe, my allergies . . . so I take the shower, grab an apple, and I'm on my way out the door when I find him. I think he was asking to come inside, the poor little guy. I didn't open the door, and now he was dead."

"It's starting to make sense."

"What's making sense?" She seemed concerned that I was making fun of her. I wasn't, but the nature of the exchange allowed me to flirt a little.

I said, "The whole thing. Please, keep going."

"So Steve died while I was in the shower." She pushed against the cushion with her feet and scooted backward until she was sitting back against the other arm of the couch, facing me with her knees tucked up under her chin. She wrapped her arms around her legs and stared at the cushion between us. Were we trying to see how long we could go before we had to introduce ourselves? She said, "It's amazing how loose a dead cat is. Like carrying an armload of water balloons."

I nodded as if this were something to consider, but my field of responses felt limited to this nod. I didn't want to ask if she had dropped him. Water balloons.

She started to get up. "This is wrong. I shouldn't be here."

"No, please finish. I'm sensing a payoff."

"Well, it bothered me—everything about it—but I still had to go to work. So I ..." She studied me as if weighing options. "What the heck," she said. "I had to go to work, and I didn't have any experience in this, so I gathered him up in a towel and stuck him in the fridge—the *freezer*, I mean—which gave me a chance to think about what to do with him. I would've used the fridge, but I didn't know if whatever parasites cats have would start crawling around on the butter. Which was ..." she gave a short laugh, "I was going to say it was *cold* of me."

I shrugged. "He was dead. It was a sensible thing to do. Otherwise you'd probably have to throw your food out."

"Okay, I guess you *are* getting it."

"It's an odd picture, but it's coming into focus."

She said, "If you were telling it to me, I would've walked away by now."

"Maybe, but you're tired and edgy, and I'm as fresh as a spring day."

She cast me a dubious glance. "Yes, I think maybe you are." Then she pointed at me. "You know, I could write a pretty convincing horror movie about a dead cat in the freezer coming to life, opening the door, and walking around on its hind legs with this hideous yowl. All day I was picturing a hundred different versions of this, starting with the freezer door opening. And last night I waited until dark and went out into the backyard and started digging. I dug as deep as I could, two feet, maybe three ... wait." She held her hands apart. "Three feet is pretty deep, so probably two. Especially when you're digging quietly, *and* watching Annie's windows. So then I put this ... well, his fur wasn't frozen, it was kind of wet by then. Which was another mistake—I had the evidence right there beside me. I should've left him in the freezer until I was done digging. But anyway, I set this mostly frozen cat in the bottom of the hole and filled it in. And now there's this leftover dirt. How do I explain *that*?"

"It's what happens. It's part of digging and filling in a hole. Even if you don't add anything, like a cat."

"I mean there was a *lot* of leftover dirt. Like I'd buried a Great Dane."

"You have to tamp it down as you fill it in, or you're going to get leftover dirt." I was trying to be reassuring.

She said, "You mean I should've jumped on the dirt on top of Steve? Whether he was frozen or not, I don't think I could have done that."

"Of course not. It's just a thing about holes. You could scatter the leftover dirt through your garden."

She frowned. "You seem to have a touch of Male Answer Syndrome."

"What syndrome?"

"Don't worry, it's not—" She looked past me, and her face brightened. A man's voice from the doorway behind me said, "*There* you are!"

I turned. It was one of Andy's roommates, Dave Wick. Andy called him Wave. I kind of knew him, but we had never really talked. The familiarity in his voice and the way this woman perked up sparked a little jealousy in me. Matching his warm voice, she said, "Hi, Davy, I was hoping you'd find me. How are you doing?"

"Pretty good, though I could use a beer." Then he took a closer look. "Whoa, girl, we need to get you home!"

"I had a rough night, but I'm better now."

"Anything I can do?"

"Yeah, if you wouldn't mind grabbing me a beer too."

"Are you sure you should be drinking? You look like hell."

"It'll be my first one this afternoon. This week, in fact."

He turned to me. "Jim? As long as I'm up?"

I gave him my cup and said thanks.

"Back in a jiff."

I turned to her. "How do you know each other?"

"He's my brother."

"I didn't know Dave Wick had a sister."

She said, "Did you think I was his girlfriend or something?"

"An ex, maybe."

"Well, you can relax."

I said, "Does he know about Steve?"

"No, you're the first to hear my story."

"You didn't tell anyone at work?"

"At a grade school? No, I didn't tell anyone at work!"

"A grade school."

"All those innocent little ears."

When Dave returned with two full cups, he bent forward like a servant and handed them to us simultaneously. Then he straightened and said to her, "Congratulations. I'd given up on you."

"Stuff it, pal."

He chuckled and said, "Well, you kids have fun. I still need a beer."

After he left I said, "What was that all about?"

"Nothing. I'll tell you later."

But I knew. It was exactly the kind of thing a brother would say to his kid sister when he found her flirting with some guy. I sipped the foam off my beer.

She said, "He called you Jim."

"Sandusky."

"I just realized, Jim Sandusky, what kept me up last night. I couldn't get this image of Steve out of my head, frozen in that uncomfortable position. I didn't think of it at the time, but the way I crammed him into the freezer is how he's going to be in my memory forever. Because that's the way he went into the hole, you know? He just didn't look comfortable. I mean, it was dark, so I couldn't see very well, but he wasn't going to . . . you know, *adjust* himself from the way he came out of the freezer. I tossed and turned all night. There was a period between four and five this morning when I didn't know exactly what time it was, so I may have snoozed a little."

"You're holding up well."

"But I promised Dave I'd show. And you?"

"I know Andy from college." It seemed like days ago that I'd said the same thing to Suzy. I started to say something else to get past this thought, but the lights went out.

It was more than the lights—everything went out, including the music. The silence exaggerated the effect of losing the lights. There was a rise of confused party voices from the kitchen and patio. She and I looked at each other and waited. After a moment I heard Andy call for me from another floor. I called back, asking where he was.

"Basement!" It wasn't urgent; he simply wanted to be heard.

She said, "You're being paged." She seemed a little annoyed that I was being called away, but I felt an obligation to Andy.

I stood and said, "I still didn't get your name."

"Run along; see what he wants."

I apologized, then made my way downstairs. The high half windows let in a little daylight, and a shuddering yellow glow came from the far corner.

Andy said, "Follow the flashlight." I found him looking up at the breaker panel. He said, "Okay, so what did you say to Suzy?" His tone was friendly, but I could tell that this was why he had called me to the basement.

"What do you mean?"

"She just had an argument with some guy, dumped her beer into the toaster, and stomped out. She was supposed to be leaving with you."

"I didn't say anything to her. We were talking in the living room, she wandered off, and that other woman came back."

"That's Marla, Dave's sister. Anyway, the beer went into the toaster, and everything died." He moved his flashlight up the double row of panel switches. "There we go." One switch was tripped.

I said, "Did you unplug the toaster?"

"I did." He pushed the switch all the way off, then snapped it on. The basement lit up, followed by a rise of voices from the main floor above. The music came back to life. We headed back upstairs.

Andy said, "Sorry it fizzled with Suzy. She's a firecracker. A little hot, maybe, but if you catch her at the right time, you get the ride of your life. That's why I introduced you, by the way."

"She said it was her idea."

"Well, then, that's why I went along with it."

"Because I looked like I needed a good ride?"

With a pseudosolemn nod, he said, "Son, you have for some time now." Then he gave me a pat on the back. "To be honest, I wish I had thought to introduce you to Marla. That there's a keeper." He went back outside.

The living room was empty. I looked out the front window to verify the absence of the Fiat. It was gone, and I felt a little safer.

I went out to the garage to top off my beer. Three women were at the keg, but no Marla. I went around to the patio and found her at the barbecue, studying the offerings, most of which were in the dried-out stage between shriveled and burned. She seemed to be toying with the idea of reaching in with her fingers.

I said, "Careful, Marla. I'm not sure that still qualifies as food."

She glanced up and brightened. "You survived! Gee, you know about cats and electricity and everything."

"It was just a breaker." She looked at me for a second. I said, "At the panel."

"Well, I'm glad you didn't electrocute yourself and burn down the house." She turned back to the grill. "Andy told you my name."

"He did." I left off the part about her being a keeper. Instead I said, "You didn't finish your story."

"About Steve? Let's see . . . what's left? I suppose we still have my small-caliber neighbor who needs to hear the news. And there's a pile of dirt in my backyard, which by now probably has mountain goats climbing around on it. But you know what? I like the business about cats choosing to die in solitude, as if it's the only way they can go peacefully. It's got a good mysterious quality, which is perfect for Annie—the ancient and noble practice of cats passing to the next level. I think I'm also going to tell her that some people wait a long time before replacing a good cat, to honor the one they lost. What makes it perfect is that she's just the kind of person who would concern herself with that. She's so eager to believe whatever is the most inconveniencing."

Then she touched her forehead with the back of her wrist. "That was mean."

"It wasn't mean—it was catty."

"Oh, boy," she said. "Now I *really* need to get home."

"But I just got this fresh beer."

She gave an exaggerated sigh. "Some things we just have to deal with on our own."

"That's not fair," I said, setting the beer on the table. "I came all this way, and what do I get?"

She pinched me on the nose. "You get the girl."

Eventually, sure, but that afternoon all I got was to walk the girl out to her bicycle. Not even a kiss.

The next day I was a little hung over, and I spent the morning cleaning the kitchen. It's a tedious chore, so if I'm feeling kind of off anyway, the total cost isn't as great. I'm more likely to do chores when I have a cold, for example, so the healthier I am, the messier I am. Some people clean as a penance for the night before—Andy, for instance. I gave it a try in college, but the guilt thing never was compelling to me. It's an artificial condition, like setting the clock ten minutes ahead to keep from being ten minutes late. Anyway, I was at the sink, almost done with the dishes and entertaining myself with the memory of Marla lying on her back on the couch, when the phone rang. I answered, and she started right in: "I'm watching Annie right now, wandering around her yard as if it's an Easter-egg hunt, going, 'Steee-vie . . . Steee-vie . . .' in this tiny little voice."

"Has she seen the dirt pile?"

"I hope not. It looks like I buried Al Capone out there. They're probably studying satellite photos, trying to figure out if I'm hiding a missile silo in my backyard. I should have spread it around like you said."

"Just don't do anything obvious like put a cross on top of it."

"Still, I'd rather be somewhere else for a while."

"Like Norway or Australia?"

"No, like for the afternoon." I clutched, once again aware of my history of not responding well to this kind of opening. Then she said, "Like your place. I got your phone number from Andy, by the way."

"I'll bet that made his day."

"He even cackled. You'd think I was the one he was trying to hook you up with instead of that cookie Suzy."

"You know about that?"

"Yeah, he does it with Dave too. Andy the Dandy. He thinks he's being benevolent, introducing his pals to his conquests. Why do you suppose he never introduced you to me?"

"You make it sound so . . ."

"Vulgar? Sleazy? Insulting to everyone involved?"

I said, "I suppose he gave you my address."

"I didn't even have to ask. You know, he's going to take credit for this."

"Heck, let him."

After we hung up I brushed my teeth, then went through the apartment like a bachelor in a sitcom, filling a recycling container with socks and tennis balls and newspapers from the previous week. I slid it all to the back of my bedroom closet, feeling lucky to have gotten a jump on the kitchen before she called. By the time the doorbell rang I had a fresh pot of coffee started, the windows open, and early Van Morrison rolling out of the stereo speakers.

We found ourselves seated on the couch, as we had been the day before, except that now the air was charged with . . . well, *potential* is the only way I can think to describe it.

I said, "You and Dave seem to get along. The brother-sister thing."

"He looks out for me." She gave me a coy look.

I glanced toward the door as if Dave might break through.

"Will he want to kick my ass?"

"He's not a snoop, but at some point he'll want to know what's going on." Then she said, "For what I have in mind, he'll probably want to kick your ass."

That was when I got the girl.

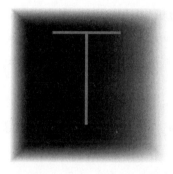he Monday following the attempted car theft was uneventful. Several times during work I started to call Sergeant Rainey to find out where things stood with the car thieves but couldn't bring myself to finish dialing. I imagined a number of courses our conversation might take, each one confirming his suspicion that I had taken the truck. This, together with the condition of the truck as I had left it, would surely turn him against me.

And I couldn't figure out a way to talk to Marla about Rainey's warning that one of them might come after me. He had seemed to think they would leave her out of it, which was a relief but also made me wonder what good could come from mentioning it at all.

A college professor had once told me, "Not to decide is to decide." He was cautioning me that some decisions we face are made whether we make them or not. But there was also an assurance that sometimes doing nothing can be a proper course of action. I decided to wait, to not talk to anyone about any of it and see which way things went. And I would react appropriately.

. . .

Tim called Tuesday morning. The Camry was ready. I asked if I could show up between one and two.

"I'm here all day."

I wanted to take one more look at the truck, and since I was about to give up the loaner car—my anonymity—I allowed an extra fifteen minutes on my way to Tim's shop. I circled out to the beltline and found the north entrance to the industrial area. From this direction the gravel roads were a little disorienting, but I soon found the familiar stretch. I drove by without slowing—the truck was gone. There were fresh gouges in the ditch where it had been lodged. The effect of the absence was almost physical, as if something had been removed from my chest.

I took a circuitous route to Tim's repair shop to shake the non-existent tail I kept imagining. The Camry was parked out front, and Tim was waiting for me at his desk, halfway through an apple. He nodded toward our car.

"They really did a number on it," he said. "I went and changed all the locks too, to make them work off the same key. And I had three copies made. Sorry I didn't call you about it, but I was able to use wrecking-yard parts, and the total wasn't that much more, so I went ahead." He showed me the sheet.

I said, "That's the total?"

"I can add to it until you're comfortable." We'd had this kind of exchange before. If a guidebook on local repair shops listed his, it would say he is an excellent mechanic and his prices are "extremely reasonable."

I wrote him a check for the amount, pulled a twenty from my

wallet and put it on top, and said I hoped he wouldn't take it the wrong way.

"How would I do that?"

"Just don't be insulted. It's a thank-you for being square with me. It's probably not enough, but I don't want to get into one of those things."

He said, "Neither do I."

We shook hands, and I left in the Camry.

On the drive back to the Deli I wondered what had happened to the truck. An abandoned vehicle—which this one obviously had been—might be reported the next day or it might sit for a month, I had no idea. It seemed doubtful that anyone would want it back except to sell it for parts or scrap. I decided that the cops had probably run the plates and either had it towed or compelled the owner to take it back, and there it would sit, inert against the curb, uglying up the neighborhood.

I couldn't ask Rainey about it because my *disposition* was that I didn't know enough to pose the question. I assumed that the truck was now at the address I had copied off the registration but decided not to risk driving past the house to verify something that mattered so little. I hoped that years later I might find the little square of paper behind my library card and not recall what it referred to.

By the time I got back to work, a lot of my bitterness had vanished. The Camry was running fine, and it hadn't cost all that much. I called Rainey and asked him to drop the charges.

"What brought this on?"

"I don't know. I just paid for the ignition repair, and it hardly hurt a bit."

"Well, good. This still might work out. We'll release them today, and who knows, maybe they'll feel a similar fading of grudges. By the way, we know a little more about them. Larry and Wade Hood. They seem to be close the way twins are close."

"This is important?"

"It's the grudge thing again. Larry is older. He calls the shots. Wade is the nasty one. It's like he's dealing with a chemical imbalance along with the abuse issues they both almost certainly have been dealing with since kidhood. Without Larry, Wade wouldn't last fifteen minutes before he did something to put himself in prison for a long time."

"So he's the one to watch out for."

"No, I think Larry is the one to watch out for. Wade is mean, but he's stupid. The thing about him is, he knows it, which is rare in a stupid man. He leaves the important decisions to Larry. If Larry says, 'Damn, I'm gonna eat me that baby,' Wade would say, 'Hey, I want some too.' So if Larry were to tell Wade to forget about that nice Mr. Sandusky on Juniper Street, that would be the end of it. But I'm not sure Larry would do this—especially after what happened to the truck later on. Someone, or a bunch of someones, beat the hell out of it with pipes and rocks. In fact, it's starting to look like my alien theory will hold up. That poor truck is so battered, it looks like it was dropped from outer space."

The next day I was working in the center of the island, checking my order list against a couple dozen cases that had been delivered that morning. It's relatively mindless work. On the sheet is the name of the winery, the kind of wine, and whether it's for a customer or the shelves. I locate the case, open it to see that the distributor or winery sent the correct bottles, and write the name of the customer on the box. Then I check the case off the list and close the flaps in rotation in the Escher stair sequence, each holding down a corner of the next. After accounting for all the cases, I stock what belongs on the shelves and put the empty boxes in back for recycling. If this sounds involved, it's not. If interrupted by a customer, or the phone, or the lunch rush, I won't lose my place. If left alone, an hour passes and I'm done.

Somewhere in the middle of this process I drifted into a kind of daze, reflecting on that strange night and what a mess it had become. It might have been better for us if the Hood brothers had gotten away with our car, just disappeared into the night forever . . . and then I noticed a man standing at the wall of wine, idly moving from bottle to bottle without really looking at any of them. His face in profile was vaguely familiar, as if I had seen it while leafing through the newspaper. Instead of going over to see if he needed help, I knelt and watched him through the gap between two stacks of wine cases.

He looked like the kind of guy who drank alone (though not wine—or certainly not the quality he was looking at now), and he also looked as if he got into a lot of fights. I could imagine him sitting at the end of a dark bar, thinking about the last fight he'd been in, or his next fight, maybe the one that had just walked in. Any reason he had for being here at the Deli had nothing to do with wine. When he turned to scan the room, his eyes passed over the island tables where I was hiding, and I had it: His photo had been among the throw-downs on Rainey's desk.

I set the checklist on the floor and used my razor knife to open a box of bottles destined for the shelves. I pretended to inspect the labels but was simply trying to keep my hands from shaking. Obviously there was no telling whether he was one of the extras they add to the stack of photos or one of the suspects. Since there were more extras, the odds were good that this guy was nontoxic. But when I factored in the likelihood that his being here now had something to do with the night of the attempted car theft, the odds changed drastically. If, as Rainey had said, Larry Hood had it in for me, I was probably looking at him right now.

I still had the shakes, but not as bad. I also had a creepy sense that he had been studying me peripherally the entire time, and I was in his danger zone.

I pulled a case from under one of the island tables. I had scrawled "Douglas/8" on the side of the box. It was a Malbec of which a regular named Bill Douglas wanted eight. I opened the box and removed the remaining four bottles, clinking them together to give the impression that I was working, not just hiding out. Then I peered between the stacked boxes under the table to monitor the man at the Wall of Wine.

He pushed the bottle he was pretending to consider back into its slot and looked around the Deli with the attitude of someone not seeking help from a wine steward but instead deciding what to do next. Then, without a glance in my direction, he left.

I stood and wandered toward the window that looks out on the parking lot, taking a casual swipe at random tables with the towel I carry through my apron string. I was trying to make my movement across the floor seem independent of his, as if I would have done the same thing if he hadn't just left. A car in the parking lot struggled to start; then its engine caught and revved. I stood at the edge of the window and carefully looked out. It was raining, and the Deli windows were slightly fogged. A white domestic sedan eased back from its parking space. I stood so that the wall hid me from the front half of the car. This angle exposed me to the rear end of . . . I could barely make out the letters . . . a Celebrity. There was a yellow oval Pennzoil decal in the passenger-side rear window, and the rear bumper sagged a few inches on the near side, even though there was no sign of it having been hit.

I used the phone at the sandwich counter to call Sergeant Rainey. As I was being transferred I went back into the storeroom for privacy. When he picked up, I could hear a hollow background sound of traffic.

I gave him my name and said, "Those throw-down photos you showed us—where do you get the extras, the guys who aren't the suspects?"

"Why?"

"They're cops, right? You throw in a bunch of plainclothes cops."

"Not just cops. They could be anybody."

"Really? Well, thanks."

"That's it?" he said. "No other questions?"

"No, I was just curious."

We hung up, and I went back over to the island, to my delivery lists. A moment later the phone rang. The woman on sandwich duty answered and held the receiver toward me.

It was Rainey. I listened as I carried the receiver back to the storeroom. He said, "You saw one of them, didn't you? One of the guys from the throw-downs came into your store." He was back to his cheap parlor trick of reading my mind. He said, "But you're not ready to talk this through." He was going too fast for me, and I couldn't come up with one of those neutral responses he seemed to appreciate.

He said, "Jim, you don't get to choose how it goes from here. If one of those—" he stopped himself. "Damn it, I *knew* something like this would happen. Look, here's what you do. Get a piece of paper. Right now, I mean. I'll wait."

I pulled an order pad from my apron and said, "Okay."

He said, "Take down these numbers. They're my cell phone and home phone." He gave me the numbers, and I read them back. He said, "If Larry Hood is stalking you, you may need to make a quick call. You may need to make it without being able to turn on the lights, like from the back of the closet at midnight or behind the chimney on your neighbor's roof. Put those numbers in your auto-dialer. If I'm not home Evelyn can tell you how to reach me. I'll tell her what's going on. I'll *apprise* her of the situation."

"I could memorize them."

"Don't even try. You wouldn't believe how hard it is to pull something out of your memory if you're not in the condition you were in when you put it in there."

"I don't understand."

"If the piano player thinks he'll be drinking when he performs a song, he should be drinking when he learns it."

"The piano player."

"The point is, you may need those numbers in a panic situation. If one of these guys is chasing you down the street, you're not going to be able to remember anything I tell you now—except that he's trying to kill you. And here's something else. If my numbers are in your autodialer, we're both committed to this situation. If something happens, we may be connected in a way we won't be able to deny ourselves out of. But that's okay. When things escalate, you have to try to keep up. So far you've done fine. But now you're in the stretch, and that's when the good guys tend to fall behind. Lose heart. They think that when the game is over, we all shake hands and go home happy."

I liked being called a good guy. I said, "What do you mean, I'm in the stretch?"

"He's stalking you. He's a predator, okay? That makes you the prey." He waited. "You're still not getting it, Jim. I can tell by the silence. He might be trying to figure out how to kill you, and you're wondering if he's a plainclothes cop. When you turn up dead, we'll know who did it, but you'll still be dead. Or maybe you don't know what 'dead' means."

"What am I supposed to do?"

"Go down to a morgue and look at some corpses. Study what isn't there—what isn't in a person's body—when he dies. *Appreciate the condition.*"

"No. I mean about him stalking me."

"Oh. Well, first you call the cops. Which you did, and that's good. But then you tell the truth. Which, face it, you're not scoring very well in that department. And finally, I need to hear some fear in your voice—at least some concern—before we're on the same page. Right now we're not even in the same book. You know those stories about women lifting cars off their children and wimpy guys tearing doors out of walls to escape burning buildings? That stuff really happens, but the people are on adrenaline. They aren't sitting there thinking, *I can always rip the door off its hinges.* I'm not sure you're capable of adrenaline."

"If I'm not capable of something, why are you riding me?"

"Because I think you can *get* capable. Right now it feels like you think everything is under control. It's like you're trying to make me yell and pound this phone against the desk. What I think I'll do, though, is tell your wife. I think I'll tell Marla what's going on, that this guy is still an issue."

"No, don't do that. She might not handle it very well."

"Good. That means she *listens.* I'll tell her, and she'll tell you, and *then* you'll listen."

"Is she in danger too?"

"No, this is about the truck. It's between you and Larry. I'm bringing her into it because that way I know you'll take it seriously."

"But why do we have to be adversaries?"

"Because you don't understand the game. Otherwise you wouldn't keep thinking we're on the same side. Even if you didn't steal the truck, you and I would not be on the same side. You and Marla aren't on the same side, and that's important too. She and I aren't on the same side, but we're close, which I'm sure you don't understand. One of these days you'll call me and say, 'You were right, Sergeant Rainey. I'm alone, and I'm scared!' I'll hear the whimper in your voice, and *that's* when I'll believe you got it."

"I'd like to say I understand."

"You might be starting to. It's not rocket science. But you aren't there yet." He hung up.

For the next hour I did nothing but think about what Rainey had said. Finally I came up with this lame little plan. Since it was based on deception, it began with a lie. I told John I had a scratchy throat and asked if I could borrow his car for a quick run up to the Safeway pharmacy. I wanted to kill a tickle in my throat before it developed into something. He handed me the keys and said, "Get some echinacea and some vitamin C. But don't sneeze on the steering wheel, please. The last thing I need is a cold."

"Thanks," I said. "The Camry is running crummy."

"From getting broken into?"

"The weather, more likely. Or bad gas."

He shook his head. "I've never known what that is."

I still had the scrap of paper with Larry Hood's address: Laredo

14/Condor 24. I said it twice to myself: "One-four, two-four, south-east Condor," memorizing by rhythm and rhyme, and put the scrap back in my wallet. In our town the even numbers are on the north and west sides of streets—depending on which two compass points the street runs between—and odd, obviously, on the south and east sides. I knew the neighborhood, a shabby little stretch of minimum-wage apartments and starter homes about thirty blocks from the Deli down Main, then east. When I reached the general area, I took Brant, the next street over from Condor, and tried to work out the house numbers from there. I didn't want to call attention to myself by slowing down in front of the actual house. On Brant I was trying to determine which was the backyard of the address in question, but the high fences along the sides and backs of the houses kept me from seeing through to the next property. It was all roofs and chimneys, not even a distinguishing tree.

I couldn't find a number on the first house on Brant, but the second one was 1421—very close to the number I was looking for. The next house was 1447, so the house I sought was almost certainly the second one in from 14th. I counted houses as I continued out to 15th, then idled around to Condor and started counting in reverse back down—but then I stopped because there on the gravel parking strip on the far side of the street was the white Celebrity. I pulled over beside a low chain-link fence on my right, a couple houses away. I wasn't ready. I walked myself through each step to be sure: The guy in the Deli, whose face I recognized from Rainey's photos, had been driving a car that was now parked at the address on the truck's registration papers.

Larry Hood knew where I worked. This was when I saw what Rainey had been driving at: A predator was tracking me. A predator against whom I had committed a serious offense was focused on me, had shown himself *as if wanting me to know he was there*. I was dealing with forces that were larger than me. Larger than my life.

I remained where I was, paralyzed by the feeling that if I were to continue forward Larry Hood would appear from nowhere and yank me out of my car. Or that the empty Celebrity would suddenly roar to life as if in a bad movie, lurch across the street, and smash into me in mechanical retribution for what I had done to the truck. Then I imagined Larry coming out of the house and walking toward my car. It felt as if my thinking it could make it happen. And the longer I sat there, the more likely it seemed. Now I imagined him coming toward me with a shotgun.

I locked my door and checked to see that the other doors were locked. If a face had appeared in any of the windows, my heart would have stopped. It was all I could do to keep from panicking as I shifted John's unfamiliar transmission into reverse and slowly eased back onto 15th again. I shifted into forward and headed away from Condor.

I tried to replay what had happened in the Deli. Somehow he had figured out where I worked. He already knew where I lived, which meant he could have followed me. In fact, he must have. He had followed me from home. He was tracking me like a big-game hunter and wasn't afraid to show himself. Did he want me to spook and run? Maybe he wanted a showdown. Or maybe he wanted me to fight, to make it more sporting, more fun for him.

Rainey wasn't talking about an understanding of the situation; he was talking about a feeling. I wanted to call him and tell him he was right, that I was afraid and needed his help. But then, unless I claimed to have followed Larry home, how could I explain knowing where to find the Celebrity? Such an inquiry would never be lost on the man. I had to keep this to myself. (It occurs to me now that Rainey's skills at his job were *impeding* his job; if he hadn't been so quick to see beneath the goings-on of daily life, I could have confided in him more.) My only real comfort was that this was between Laredo and me alone. Marla was out of it.

No, I had a second comfort too: Laredo still thought this was a one-way game. He didn't know I was tracking him too. For what it was worth, I knew his name, what he drove, and where he lived. And I knew that he knew the same about me, but he *didn't* know that I knew the same about him. I was starting to think like Rainey.

I could see why some ordinary citizens keep guns around.

It was a relief to make it back to the Deli without any misadventures. I handed John his keys and thanked him.

"Will you need a ride home tonight?"

"A ride?"

"Think your car will start?"

"Oh. Well, I don't know. I'll call my mechanic and see what he thinks." But I couldn't call Tim because he would insist on looking and then, of course, find nothing.

John said, "If you need me to, I'll stick around at quitting time while you get it going." He scanned the interior and said, "Better yet, we have things under control here. Why don't you leave early? That way you won't have to battle traffic."

I didn't want him to get suspicious, so a little later I went back into my office and looked up auto-supply businesses in the Yellow Pages. I called a place called Pistons. A guy answered and told me to hold. I didn't have a chance to reply. About four seconds later he was back.

He said, "Al," then waited.

I said, "Hello?"

He spelled it out. "This is Al. Can I help you?"

I said, "I have a question. What is bad gas?"

"When your farts burn your eyes." He paused for about one second, then said, "Okay, to start with, it's probably not bad gas. Especially this time of year. If it is, wait it out, run your tank about dry, and fill up with premium. From a different station, a different brand. But first try some gas-line antifreeze. In this weather you can get condensation in your tank, and your engine tries to burn it. Engines don't burn water. With a carb, they sputter, run funky. Injection, it'll probably just quit on you. So put this stuff in, it works immediately. I'm looking at a bottle of it right now, let's see, two thirty-nine."

"It works immediately?"

"Okay, not *immediately*, Einstein, but pretty goddamn quick. The alcohol in it bonds to the water in the tank, making it combustible. You get a tiny bit of steam but nothing noticeable. But the stuff has to work its way through the lines to the carb, or fuel-injection system, whichever."

"So if I did that in the morning—"

"You might be fine now. That's if condensation is the problem. Bad gas, like I say, this will help a little, but you'll have to wait it out. You won't know till your next fill-up. Anything else, you're probably looking at a tank-drain, tune-up, rebuild, or new car. In that order. You're hoping for condensation."

At three John and I walked out to the parking lot. I told him I had put in some gas-line antifreeze before work but didn't know how long it took.

John nodded as if I were explaining a metered valve on a spacesuit. I got in and put the key into the ignition, hoping on this drizzly day to have trouble starting my car. I rolled down the window. "Here we go."

John stepped back as if it might explode.

Not being part of the deceit, the engine started on the first try. It idled down to a soft purr, as smooth as it had ever run.

John said, "Gas-line antifreeze."

"I guess so."

"And you put it in when?"

"This morning. You can get it for two thirty-nine over at Pistons."

He shook his head. "Amazing. " He stood there for a moment, then said, "Now, go take care of that cold." It wasn't until I was almost home that I recalled lying to him about having a cold.

After dinner Marla and I were watching *The Hunt for Red October* when the phone rang. I got up, and Marla asked me if I wanted her to pause the movie. We had seen it three times before, so I said no and went into the other room to take the call.

"Hello?"

"Do you know who I am?" The voice was gruff and low, unfamiliar.

"No." I waited.

The voice said, "I know who you are." He let me think about this.

I said, "Are you one of the guys?"

"One of *what* guys?"

"The guys who tried to take our car." I didn't want him to know that I knew their names.

There was a long wait, and my heart started pounding. Then he said, "No, Jim, I'm not one of the car thieves." His voice was coming into focus—he was no longer trying to disguise it. "But what if I had been?"

"Sergeant Rainey?"

"Why haven't you gotten yourself caller ID? If your phone doesn't already have it, you can buy this little gizmo that stores something like twenty-five numbers. Simple precautions, Jim." Then he said, "I can't blame you for not thinking of it—I just thought of it myself. Well, to tell the truth, Evelyn thought of it. She asked me at dinner tonight if you had it. So how come *your* wife hasn't thought of it?"

From the background behind his voice I heard his wife say, "Oh, don't badger him."

Rainey's voice turned away from the phone: "Ev, he knows I'm kidding." Then he returned. "But you also get my point, don't you?"

"I do," I said. "I'll get caller ID."

After I went back to the living room, Marla asked who had called.

"Someone advertising caller ID for eight bucks a month."

"Do we really need to spend another eight bucks on the phone? For a *monitoring* device?"

he following afternoon I was invited
out to Stebbins Hill to sample their
new releases before I printed our next
newsletter. The winemaker, Paul, was a
friend, and Thursday afternoons were
best for him. It was Marla's night to
cook, so I left a message asking her to
fix something that would hold together
if I ran late. Since it was past two now, I said traffic would decide
when I got home.

It was nasty out, with an early-November rain and gusting wind,
but if I gave myself a little extra time, I could make the thirty-mile
drive to the vineyard without creating the kind of stress that changes
your palate—the balance of your ability to taste—by masking the
fruit of wine with acids.

I don't know if it was the traffic or the weather, but I was almost
to the freeway—after ten or fifteen minutes of stop-and-go—before
I saw the Celebrity in my rearview mirror. It was one of those medi-
ate/immediate situations; my heart rate changed before I realized
why. *Larry Hood is tailing me.* He must have been there all along, but

it was like something out of a cheap thriller, the way he suddenly appeared. I had checked behind me as a reflex because there are lots of rear-enders here even in dry weather, people trying too hard to make the light. I don't know if my eyes froze in the mirror, but after my initial realization that he was following me, I played it cool. The light turned green, and I drove on without doing anything out of the ordinary. There was no way to tell if he was simply following me or if he had a specific agenda. After Sergeant Rainey's warnings, I knew this was serious.

I made it through the yellow at the freeway on-ramp, and he ran the first part of the red. The merge onto the freeway put a car between us, but that car backed off, allowing Larry to surge forward and force his way in behind me again. He left his headlights off, and so did I. We were in heavy traffic and lousy weather, committed to our little game.

It was not a balance of him against me—I was finally making sense of this part of Rainey's warning. Larry was on the attack, and I was simply fleeing. If he made a mistake, I would get away; if I made a mistake, I might die. For the time being all I could do was deal with the limited visibility and slippery pavement. I told myself not to make any dangerous moves, not to instigate anything and just hope for the best, but then I slipped into a gap in the middle lane before I was aware I had seen it. The Celebrity rushed forward to fill the space I'd just vacated, then forced its way in behind me. A frustrated horn sounded behind him. We were going sixty.

It occurred to me that he had wanted a day like this to make his move, but for some reason this didn't bother me—even when I realized that, as Rainey pointed out, I couldn't just quit and walk away. I thought that if I had to deal with him at some point, sooner was better than later. Alone was also good.

I remained on my intended route, but the winery was no longer part of the plan. In fact, at this point I had no plan, no future. My entire existence was dedicated to acting and reacting, keeping my car in a certain lane, trying to avoid contact with other cars. The situation had turned me feral. We continued like this for five minutes, and the habits of defensive driving settled in as they never had before. I wasn't even hoping to lose him in traffic and ditch him at an exit. All I cared about was staying on the road.

I'm sure that at a deeper level this wasn't true. Somewhere inside me the same old Jim Sandusky I had always been was desperately trying to wish his way out of this mess. Deep down I was probably white-knuckled and panting, about to pass out from fear. Fortunately, that level and the level at which I was currently operating had no communication with each other. Perhaps the other Jim had *already* passed out from fear, allowing the feral one to take over.

I've had angry drivers behind me—guys I had cut off with a lane change who then dogged me for a certain distance, guys who wanted to go faster than me but couldn't get past because of traffic—usually at the first opening they roar on by and maybe flip me off, and that's the end of it. But Larry refused to pass. Perhaps he was trying to harass me into making a rash move and getting myself into trouble. I had a flutter of panic when I thought he might have done this before and was now hoping for a specific outcome. I considered hitting the brakes, but if I had, there would've been an instant pileup, cars on the slick pavement skidding and slamming into each other. This image got me looking toward the future again, trying to turn things to my advantage.

We were still in the middle lane. There was a home-remodeling truck just ahead in the fast lane, with a three-car gap behind it. I thought if I faked a lane change, Larry might commit first and I could slow down to block his return, then ease away from him toward the next exit on the right.

I signaled left. Larry didn't take the opening. I turned to see if there was still space. There was; the next car back was letting me in. Larry remained behind me. As I hesitated, not sure whether I should actually commit to the fast lane, he even dropped back a little. Instead of faking it I made the change, slewing a little in the process. I heard a horn and saw in the mirror that Larry had accelerated and forced his way in behind me again. There was one car length between the truck ahead and me. Larry was one length back.

I couldn't tell how much rain was falling because so much mist was perpetually being thrown into the air from tires rushing through the standing water on the freeway. My car was newer and safer and handled better than the Celebrity, but the Celebrity had more mass and power, which meant that if this cat-and-mouse game were to get physical, Larry would have another advantage. At one point, if he had forced me through the guardrail, I would have fallen a hundred feet to the train yard below. I noticed this without it registering emotionally. I wasn't scared; I was *concerned*. The truck ahead of me kicked up a gray veil I couldn't see through. On their fastest setting my wipers barely kept visibility at a safe level.

Well, not a *safe* level. There was nothing safe about what was going on.

I reminded myself that he wasn't trying to pass me and backed off a little, then a little more. I was now six car lengths behind the truck, holding my speed at fifty-five. My visibility improved. In the middle lane a car filled the space I had left. Larry Hood kept close behind me.

I eased a little left onto the shoulder, out of the spray from the truck's tires, and barely made out the shape of a vehicle stalled on the shoulder two hundred feet ahead. I swerved completely onto the shoulder as if suddenly deciding to pass the truck in front of me, as if I were using the shoulder to get around it. Larry followed. I accelerated, and he stayed with me. I was on the shoulder going sixty, then sixty-five, and the remodeling truck was four lengths ahead of me, then three, holding its pace in the fast lane. When I was almost to the stalled vehicle, which I now recognized as a Ryder van, I cranked the wheel and lurched back into the fast lane—and an instant later the impact of the Celebrity into the van was far more violent than I could have imagined. It was as if the collision had happened in my backseat.

The truck ahead of me slowed a little, but I had already backed off and was able to maintain a reasonable gap between us. After a moment I turned on my headlights, then willed myself to check each of my mirrors to see what I had left behind me. Traffic in all lanes had fallen well back, but I didn't see any slewing headlights, so I could at least hope there had been no further damage. I kept checking my mirrors, but now it was a show of confusion for the drivers around me, as if I thought something bad had happened but couldn't figure out what it might have been.

The woman in the middle lane kept looking in her mirror too—it was obvious that she had seen the wreck—but she didn't focus on me, only her mirror, so I maintained my show of surprise and concern, trying to match hers. Still, I had to get out of there; my presence was affording anyone around me—any of these potential witnesses to the collision—an opportunity to read my plates and work out a description of my vehicle.

I slowed, signaled right, and got over—traffic now being spread out and cautious—then signaled again and took the next exit. I made it safely off, turned right at the first stop, and angled away from the freeway. After wandering streets I didn't recognize for twenty blocks, I pulled into a shopping-center parking lot. No one had followed.

Which didn't mean I was in the clear, but at least I didn't have to explain anything to anyone for a while. If Sergeant Rainey had pulled up right then, I wouldn't have been able to come up with anything but the truth. I would have been on my knees in the rain, begging him to take my confession, including the part about stealing the truck and pounding on it.

The impact of the Celebrity into the van was still in my head: Nothing . . . nothing . . . *bang!* . . . then nothing. It replayed over and over.

I stopped on the perimeter of the lot, where no other cars were parked and shut off the engine. Then, without any transition that I can recall, I was gripping the steering wheel and rocking madly and yelling. If any citizens had seen me they would have stayed clear, but a cop would have cuffed me and run me in for being a nuisance to society and a danger to myself. I rocked and yelled until it was easier to stop than to continue, and when I finally calmed down, my face was wet. I don't know if it was tears or just sweat and drool. The windows were hopelessly steamed. The sound of the impact was still replaying in my head, but not at an insane rate.

I got out of the car and had no strength in my legs. I stood there trying to keep from collapsing. The rain had eased. I leaned against the car and waited for the next thing to happen.

Nothing did, and I gradually became physically capable again. I walked around the car, then walked to a light pole and back, then bounced a little on the balls of my feet like an old man starting his morning exercises. The cold weather helped. Finally I thought I might be able to manage driving. I got a clean towel from the trunk of the car and wiped my face, then wiped the fog off the insides of the windows. I started the engine and headed out.

After a couple blocks I started feeling better. The fact of the wreck was still there, still eating at me with a mix of horror and dread and something deeper, but the adrenaline—or whatever had caused me to rock and yell—had vanished. I felt changed. There was more texture to everything, like when you try on a friend's eyeglasses and are surprised to find that they help.

I had one more task to perform before heading home: I had to drive past the wreck. I wouldn't have felt it the day before, couldn't have seen how a person might feel obligated to drive past a wreck he'd caused. Today it was as obvious as the individual motes of dust on my rearview mirror. It was more than obvious; I didn't have a choice. It was my duty.

I toured the area until I found passage beneath the freeway and an on-ramp heading south toward home. I rejoined the flow of cars and moved into the far left lane to get the best view of the scene. The accident would have slowed traffic in both directions—well, not *accident* exactly. The incident.

It was a cliché to revisit the scene, and risky as well, but I owed it to myself as a citizen, and to the city—to the people whose job it was to clean up what I had caused—to view the aftermath. I don't know if penance was a part of it, but I felt something . . . perhaps a responsibility, having to do with appreciating what had happened, that might alleviate the imbalance between what I had caused and my distance from it.

"Responsibility!" Marla would have cried in disbelief. "In what world?"

In this one, Marla.

The rain started again, but driving wasn't too bad, and I began to wonder if I had imagined the whole event. But then we slowed to a crawl, and now I was dealing with a new dread that I was about to see other wrecks—perhaps even deaths—of innocent motorists. I tried not to think about that.

Traffic moved at a walking pace, our three-lane parade inching along in the drizzle as we approached the scene. With the freeway banking slightly to the left, the distant glittering lights of emergency vehicles reflected down the guardrail and off the windows of the on-coming cars. I signaled and was allowed to move to the middle lane, distancing myself from anyone at the scene who might glance over and recognize me in the flow of rubberneckers as we passed at this helpless pace. Also, if the cops had already arrived and one of them happened to be Sergeant Rainey, he would have more trouble spot-ting me one row of cars over from the guardrail separating the two directional flows of traffic.

An ambulance on the shoulder approached the scene, following the path I had taken such a short time ago. The van was just ahead now, and I could see the rear part of the Celebrity behind it. The ambulance stopped. A lot of cars had stopped, blocking the left and middle lanes— the drivers looking in their mirrors and talking on their cell phones— but there didn't seem to be any collateral damage. When I saw this, I started shaking again but was able to gain control by gripping the wheel as if it were what was shaking. I passed two state-trooper cars. Three uniformed officers in raincoats and hats with plastic covers were leaning to talk to different drivers, probably taking statements, getting versions of what had happened. I felt exposed, but at the same time I couldn't see how anyone would suspect that the vehicle respon-sible for the collision was at that moment inching along in one of the southbound lanes. Everyone seemed to be actively ignoring Larry's car, which for some reason convinced me that he was dead.

I looked, risking one snapshot glance, and then I was sure. The van's rear wheels were lifted off the pavement, and the whole vehicle was tilted toward me. The Celebrity had run beneath the far side at a slight angle away, as if Larry had veered at the last instant. No one could have ducked the tailgate structure of the van. The Celebrity was now shaped like a wedge, about three feet high, and its roof was pushed back and down, probably conforming to the seats—no, there would be some mutual conforming going on—with no airspace remaining. He had seen it coming. Poor Laredo, toxic no more.

When I looked forward again, I realized that the glance had given me the answer to a second question, one that had been rising to the surface of my awareness all along. A trooper had been reaching through the open window of the van as if to make sure the shifter was in "park." His routine manner told me the cab was empty; no one had been in it at the moment of impact.

I tried to focus on the fact that no one else had died. I don't know if I registered relief—I can't say I felt anything. The shakes meant something had trickled through—at least I registered this. I started to lower my window, then felt it would put me too close to the scene. I had reached my limit. Viewing the damage from behind a glass barrier was as close as I could get. I had satisfied my responsibility as best I could.

The windshield was fogging up again, so I wiped it with the towel, then turned the defrost fan to high. Traffic was beginning to pick up pace. I looked back through the drizzle to the wreck once more, still just fifty yards behind me. Larry's car, its engine steaming beneath the weight of the Ryder van, was a desolate sight. At this angle it looked like a lonely death, sad and forlorn, ending with a sigh. The van had a slogan printed across the rear door, easy to read even reversed as it was in my mirror: "We're there when you need us." I remember the phrase but nothing of the drive home.

I still wonder how I must have appeared. I probably drove the exact speed limit, coming to full stops at stop signs, and if someone had plowed into me—unless it snapped me out of it—I probably would have smiled and waved and tried to keep going. I believe that on that drive I was an imbecile in the original sense. Actually, I was probably pre-imbecilic.

The next thing I remember, I was in our driveway, seated behind the wheel with the engine running. My wallet was open on my lap. Marla was tapping on the window, asking why I had come home early, if anything was wrong. Her voice brought me back. I sat there looking at my wallet, trying to remember why I had it out. The only item having to do with anything would be the little slip of paper with Larry Hood's address. I started to look in the slot behind my library card, then recalled doing the same thing only a moment before. I leaned back with relief, now recalling that I had rolled the incriminating slip of paper into a pill and swallowed it.

"Jim?" Her small voice.

I lowered the window. "I saw a wreck on the freeway," I said, not caring if I was blowing my alibi. "It was pretty bad."

"Are you okay? What happened?"

"I was going to exchange some information," I said, folding my wallet and trying to shove it back into my pocket. It slipped out of my hand and ended up in the space between my seat and the transmission hump. While I dug it out, I had a sense that I hadn't responded to her question, that she wasn't concerned with why I had my wallet out, but I don't remember saying anything else.

It's strange that blowing my alibi had occurred to me at all. I was in shock because I had just caused a man to die violently, but part of me saw that by mentioning the wreck I was committed to being at the scene. I had either lost a dimension of character or gained one, but I was no longer immersed in the event. I had moved to an observational plane and was perhaps no longer capable of being immersed in *any* event.

I do know that survival mechanisms are complicated. Back in high school a girlfriend said she didn't want to go out with me anymore, and I literally couldn't hear her words. I saw her mouth move but didn't hear a sound. Or maybe I heard her words, but something in me couldn't handle them, didn't allow me to hear *what* she was saying. She had to say it three or four times before I received the information.

So now when I catch myself acting strangely, I assume it's a survival mechanism. I assume that for some reason I'm currently on overload, and my next step is to figure out why I'm overloaded. It's a little like being in a dream, realizing you're in a dream and wanting to wake up. It's an involved process, rising from the dream to being truly awake. Dealing with overload is like this except that rising from the condition can take years.

The only other thing I remember about that day is going inside to call Stebbins Hill and tell Paul I couldn't make it because of a wreck on the freeway.

He said, "I heard it on the radio. Some guy bought the farm. They're saying to use alternate routes, but where you were coming from, what choice did you have?"

I had a restless night. The sound of the impact was still fresh in my head. The only way I could keep it from sneaking up on me was to think about it, if that makes any sense. To concentrate on it. If I wasn't working through each step—from seeing the Hoods breaking into the Camry through the mad chase leading up to the collision—all my mind had to work on was the sound of the crash. It was good that I hadn't seen it as well. Lying beside Marla, I went over and over that same series of events and eventually found myself wondering about the degree to which I was responsible for Larry's death.

At first glance I *was* responsible; I had literally caused the wreck. But when I went a level deeper, I felt I should be in the clear. He had been following me by his choice, not mine. I hadn't forced him to do anything. If I'd had my way, none of it would have happened because it never could have gotten started. He wouldn't have been out there that first night, trying to steal our Camry—

Bam! The sound of the impact caught me by surprise. I must have flinched because Marla shifted away from me. After a moment we settled down, and in the quiet darkness I recalled Rainey's warning that it might go all the way. *Well, Sergeant Rainey, you were right. Except I was the can of Drano and Larry was the slice of bread.*

Are you sure he was trying to kill you?

Here it got a little sketchy. *Was* I sure? Was I *sure*? No matter how I inflected the question, I found that to ask it in the first place was to admit that the answer was no, I wasn't sure.

When I went back over the details of the chase, he *seemed* to have been trying to kill me. If so, setting up the collision may have been an appropriate response, but in the end I couldn't know what he was actually trying to do.

Nor could I prove anything. Without contact between our cars, there was no evidence that he had been the smallest threat to me or anyone else. I supposed that with a witness I could prove tailgating. (And here the district attorney turns to the jury: *Since when is tailgating a capital offense?*)

Wait—he had been stalking me. This much I did know.

I thought back to the Deli. Could I prove that he had come in? He had left fingerprints on some of the wine bottles.

This, however, established nothing beyond his presence in a place of business during its hours of operation. And how could I have known who he was? The only other time I had seen his face was when Rainey had had me look at the throw-downs on his desk. This didn't prove he was even a suspect in the attempted theft, just one face among many. Without incriminating myself, or committing myself to another tangled lie, there was no way to explain how I had confirmed his identity. I had found the Celebrity at the address on the papers I had taken from the truck.

The two lies I could tell were: first, that I actually *had* seen their faces that first night; second, that after recognizing him in the Deli from the police photos, I had followed him home in John's car. John's car so he wouldn't recognize me.

Bam! Another collision. This time I didn't flinch. I looked over, barely able to make out Marla's sleeping shape in the dark. You don't naturally share this kind of stuff with your wife, not when it's this new and strange. She would have been right to suggest that responsibility hadn't played any part in the actions of the day. And I would have been right that it had.

I wondered how severe the charges might be. I had willfully created a situation in which Larry had crashed into the stalled van. Second-degree murder? Manslaughter?

Okay, so prove I did it.

This was where it got interesting. At each step where I couldn't prove he had been trying to kill me, there was the same lack of evidence that I had caused the wreck or that I could have known who he was. Even an eyewitness might not be able to contradict me.

An eyewitness. Here was a troublesome notion. It was easy to imagine someone jotting down my plate number and reporting it to the police, and without any leaps of logic I could now see it on Sergeant Rainey's computer screen, highlighted, with that rise in music you get in the movies when the investigating officer is about to put it all together. Was it possible that he would look at my name with the oddly bemused expression he'd had when he'd questioned me about taking the truck?

No, Rainey wouldn't shrug off *whatever* this charge turned out to be. He wouldn't stand over a mangled body, give me an admiring nod, and say, "That was some darn quick thinking!"

But again, could he prove I had done it? Could even Sergeant Rainey prove it?

Back and forth. I had either survived a malicious attack or caused the death of a man who had merely damaged our Camry's ignition switch.

I felt the sound of the wreck sneaking up on me again. I was lying on my side, facing away from Marla. I opened my eyes and found myself looking out the window at the streetlighted maple on our parking strip. The sound receded. As long as my eyes were open it would leave me alone.

At some point I must have dropped off for a while, but when the first light of morning came, I was mulling the same questions, still making no headway.

Around two-thirty the following day, Sergeant Rainey came into the Deli and asked if I had a moment.

"Sure. Do you want to sit?"

"That won't be necessary." His look held me where I stood as he continued, "We have a funny little coincidence, something I wanted to pass along in person."

"Okay." I considered saying something about how he didn't seem like the kind of guy who believes in coincidence. He seemed to be waiting for me to say more, but I thought he was reading me, so I waited.

He said, "Yesterday there was a wreck just north of here on the freeway. You remember Larry Hood? One of the guys who tried to boost your Toyota?"

"Sure."

"Well, for some reason he tried to drive his car through the back of a moving van. His last week was a bad one."

"You mean he's—"

"He's as dead as a guy can get and still be recognizable."

"Yesterday?"

"Afternoon. A couple witnesses agree on a chase scene, with our friend Larry doing the chasing, both cars swerving in and out of traffic. Some pretty desperate driving for a mile or two. Evidently there were points of contact, which would leave scuffs and bumper kisses. Our recent Mr. Hood was an aggressive driver—uninsured, in fact, because companies kept dropping him. The man had anger management issues. Sleeping violence."

"So you're here because—"

He held up his hand to hush me. "I want you to look at this." With two fingers he extracted a folded sheet of paper from his shirt pocket and held it toward me. It was like taking part in a magic trick: I opened the throw-down photo of Larry Hood.

Rainey said, "Is that the man who came in here the day before yesterday? The man you called me about?"

I had no option but to tell the truth. "Yes." I folded the page and handed it back. "It's him." I waited for the handcuffs.

"Well, he's down for the count." He looked at me and said, "Jim, you can relax. I checked your car. It's why I dropped by—unofficially, by the way. But even if this *was* my case and I *had* found scuffs and bumper kisses, the worst I would ding you for is vehicular grab-ass. Let's just call it a happy accident."

 still couldn't sleep. For the next few nights almost any sound drew me back from what seemed like the brink of dozing off, and I lay there listening. The sound of the impact wasn't the problem anymore, having receded behind a general apprehension. I don't recall any particular thoughts that would have given me a sense of what was bugging me, but the surface noise was constant. When I heard a sound I couldn't identify, I studied it until I understood it. When a car idled into the neighborhood, I had to get up and go to the window. Maybe the car stopped and a neighbor got out, closed the door, and went inside, or it droned by and was gone. Either way the night would grow quiet again, leaving me at the window, looking out at nothing, thinking about nothing, my heart working half again harder than normal, pumping my restless blood.

Marla slept through most of it. She woke at times to ask what was wrong, but after a few nights of me acting as confused as she was, she seemed to get used to it and just slept. One night while I was at the window she rolled over in her sleep and flopped her arm across my side of the bed. I didn't want to disturb her, especially since I wasn't the least bit sleepy, so I pulled on a pair of jeans and a shirt and went downstairs to brew some tea.

I couldn't tell what was different in me that was keeping me awake. You would think that being exonerated by the cops would have the opposite effect, relax the tension, put me at ease.

I sat at the kitchen table and thought about work. Work was good. John was always looking for ways to improve the business without expanding. His latest idea was to host a regional wine festival in the fall, after the grape harvest but while the weather was still warm. The winery and vineyard owners he had approached seemed eager to participate. John was happiest (and easiest to work with) when he was involved in a large project like this.

Things with Marla were good too. She had survived a skirmish with a bad supervisor (whom she referred to as "Trouble in a Granny Dress") and been given the equivalent of a merit raise. The supervisor had transferred to another district, and Marla had been encouraged to fill the vacancy, but she'd withstood the effort, remaining in the classroom with her kids, where her heart was.

As I sat there I heard a clunk from upstairs, then the *thump-thump-thump* of Marla's heels as she went from the bed to the bathroom. I waited, heard the flush, then her heels again as she padded back to bed. There was no pause in the rhythm of her steps, no hesitation at the top of the stairs. She was fine with my absence.

Sleeplessness as an ongoing condition is doubly frustrating because it seems to cause itself; thinking about it can keep you awake. I wanted to be in the habit of getting tired at night, of going to bed and dropping off the way middle-aged people living relatively comfortable lives are supposed to sleep. Reading, usually the ultimate sleeping aid, was not an option now. My mind was too scattered to relax within the constraint of pages. Even a comic book would have moved too slowly to hold my interest. Television maybe, but the last thing I wanted to do was sit there in front of the glaring emptiness of late-night television.

After the house had been silent for what felt like a long time, I picked up my wallet and keys and slipped out the front door, locking it behind me. I got into the car with as little noise as possible, then let it coast backward in neutral down the slight decline to the intersection at 37th before I latched the door, started the engine, and turned on the lights.

I didn't have a plan except to find some nightlife that had to be happening somewhere. Back in high school I'd had an impulse to wander at night. I never responded to it, but around the age of fifteen I spent a number of restless nighttime hours at my bedroom window on the second floor of our family house, wondering where something might be happening, what that something might be, and how I might participate. My age and parents held me back, but one Saturday afternoon I did go so far as to climb out the window and hang from the sill by my fingers for a moment before dropping into Mom's flower bed below. It was a dry run for a time that never came. I got my driving privileges and then my stay-out-late privileges, and the impulse faded. I would have thought it had died, but maybe it had merely been dormant—maybe such things *always* go dormant rather than go away—and for some reason it had been roused to life again after all these years, now that I was nearing the age my parents had been back then. If I had satisfied the urge all those years ago, would I now be sneaking out of the house and heading downtown?

The streets that normally contained steady streams of traffic now had one or two rogue vehicles pacing themselves along the well-lit empty corridors past apartment complexes, closed businesses, and twenty-four-hour gas station–snack shops. It was a desolate world, offering not the slightest chance of an interesting event or conversation. I almost turned around, but not wanting to continue pacing at home, I drove on, crossing the river on the St. Stephen's bridge, entering the heart of downtown from the north, on Clark Avenue.

One curiosity was the number of young men on bicycles. I never would have imagined their existence, but they seemed to be everywhere. They were the age of the older skateboarders, with scruffy beards and streetwise eyes, and most of them had backpacks. I assumed they were involved in some level of theft, but I didn't really care. In fact, I was comfortable with the idea that a lot of what I was seeing had to do with illegal enterprises. There were also taxicabs and produce vans, and about every fifth car was a police car, but mostly it seemed to be calm, matter-of-fact, unsavory activity. I wanted to be within it without being a part of it, like standing in the surf as waves rush up and break around your ankles.

I hadn't expected to see so many women out at this hour on a weekday, but they were mostly hookers and exotic dancers and wouldn't have had any reason to be out now if these men weren't here. The streets in this part of town were one-ways, alternating in direction, with metered parking on both sides. The traffic lights operated in pointless precision to let the random vehicle through, and I wandered without effort or pattern.

At 10th and Washington I noticed some activity on the sidewalk across the street to my right. A few people in front of the second building down from the intersection were loitering outside an entrance, which had a dim red light rotating about once per second above a black door: It was an oasis of life. "Arlene's Fine Dining & Dancing" was painted in big white letters on the flat brick face of the building where there should have been a front window. It was a strip joint, and I doubted that the word *fine* could be applied to anything that had ever gone on inside, except perhaps what the owner paid for periodic health code violations.

I saw two open parking spaces directly across the street. Because 10th was a one-way street toward me, I would have to drive around the block. When the signal changed, I continued through the inter-section, then took a right down 11th and another right on Taylor. As I approached 10th again, one block below Arlene's, I noticed a theater at the corner closing for the night, men trickling into the lighted area beneath the marquee. They loitered for a moment on the shiny yel-low tile as they slowly regained their sense of purpose and headed off into the night. Above, in red block letters, a triple feature was listed: *Sheila Down Under, Members Welcome,* and *Lickety-Split.* At the lower right the fine print read, "Mature Audiences Only." I signaled for a right on 10th but had to wait for two male moviegoers to cross in front of me. Technically, I supposed, they were mature. I made my turn and saw that both parking spaces across the street were still open. I cut diagonally across the two empty lanes, nosed into the upper space, and shut off the engine. Then I locked my door and just sat there behind the wheel, watching out the passenger window.

There were two women in short skirts and heels and maybe eight men in jeans and bowling jacket–style windbreakers. Every one of them was smoking. A few men coming up from the theater joined them, digging into pockets for cigarettes. Others continued on. It was like viewing a fish tank in which different species intermingle but ignore each other. It occurred to me that my relationship with the night activities was similar to what the men going into Arlene's had with the exotic dancers—I was a nightlife voyeur. In a while I might go in and watch the guys watch the naked women. I grew drowsy instead.

．．．

I believe that at some point most couples have what might be called a crisis—an event or situation that tests the fabric of the relationship. Marla's and mine followed our effort to have a baby. She was pregnant for a while, then miscarried. We went in for the *removal* (technically it wasn't an abortion because Marla's body did the aborting), and after trying to get pregnant again, we had our crisis. The miscarriage itself wasn't a crisis because we were in it together, in love and pain together, and we remained emotionally close as we followed Dr. Reese's advice on how to conceive a second time. Marla kept a calendar, calculating her most fertile days and monitoring her temperature for her next ovulation. I saw to my side of things: no hot baths or tight clothing or orgasms for at least three days before Marla's fertility peak, optimizing conditions for my hearty little swimmers.

I can't say which of us wanted a kid more. During her pregnancy Marla wanted with her entire being to have a baby (even her *fingernails* softened in preparation), but she lacked my intensity. To draw a picture of her mood you might use warm pastels and apply them carefully. For mine you would use blue and purple and red crayons. You would press hard and color outside the lines. I ached to have this child.

My feelings toward fatherhood first surfaced about a week after Andy's party. Marla and I had been lying around in bed, talking about things in a long-term sense, and I asked how she felt about having kids. I was sure I wanted her to say something about kids not being part of her big picture, but I was wrong. She said, "I don't want to rule out the possibility," and I was surprised by a rush of relief.

On the evening of our first anniversary, toward the end of what was probably our nicest dinner out, Marla brought a shoeless foot up my lower leg and lodged it between my thighs. Her eyes glistened, and she said there was a distinct possibility that we could set something in motion tonight if we . . . well, you know.

I said, "Wow." I was stalling, of course.

"Yes," she said. "The Big Decision."

I said, "Are we ready?" I felt ready, but we hadn't really talked about it in terms of calendars, of fitting a child into the pattern of our lives.

She said, "I am." After the slightest pause, and still with tenderness, she said, "But it's okay if you aren't, especially the way I ambushed you with it just now. We'll have other opportunities." She moved her foot around, causing some stirrings in me that were potentially embarrassing in a public place. She said, "We're still young."

I reached beneath the table and rubbed her calf, enjoying the gritty weave of her pantyhose. "No," I said, "I'm here. I'm with you all the way."

"Sure, fella. You just want to get lucky." I could feel the couple at the next table look over, but I didn't care. I pressed my groin into her foot and clamped my thighs on her lower leg.

I said, "I'll meet you under the table."

She laughed, extracting her foot. "Finish your dinner, or no dessert."

At home we snuggled into bed in a comfortable tangle of arms and legs, and I moved my hand onto her belly, feeling the warmth we hoped would soon become incubational. Part of the thrill for me, even on that first night of trying, was a new dimension to the meaning of my life, a validation I couldn't have foreseen. To put it simply, the woman I loved without reservation wanted to have and raise a child with me. I felt a strange new sense of purpose, as if I were standing on the planet for the first time. I mattered in a way I had never mattered before.

Our first effort didn't take, but three cycles later she tested positive, and I wept with an unfamiliar fondness—a sentimental love for her and for our child to be. She said, "You old softie. Is this how you want your son to see you?"

We had been aware of his existence for one minute and Marla had already pronounced him male. I said, "Brian."

She said, "Brian Cole Sandusky."

There was a sharp tap on my window. I jerked awake. It took me a moment to remember how I had come to be in the car. A uniformed cop was peering at me, shining a light around the interior. He made tiny circles with his finger, and I lowered the window.

He said, "Drink too much?"

"None." He studied me and gave a sniff of inquiry, perhaps hoping to catch a whiff of alcohol or pot smoke.

"Do you know where you are?"

I pointed at the traffic signal. "That's Washington. We're on 10th."

He said, "You live in the city?"

I gave him my address.

He said, "So what's the deal?"

"I couldn't sleep, so I just drove around. I was sitting here thinking, and I guess I dozed off."

"Yeah, you were pretty zonked." He looked at me steadily for a long moment, then said, "It's four in the morning. Monday going on Tuesday."

"That part I know. I've been out for about an hour."

"Out of the house?"

"Asleep. I left the house at about two thirty."

"Well, you should get on back. Where did you say you live?"

He was checking my story. I recited the address. He patted my door and stepped back, giving me the official okay, the universal let's-move-along gesture. It's how alien space-traffic controllers give the go-ahead to ships leaving on another routine visit to Earth to cut circles into cornfields. The way Saint Peter ushers souls through the Gate. I started the engine, thanked the cop, and headed for home.

I slipped into the house like a thief. Things were just as I'd left them. I regretted having fallen asleep in front of Arlene's because I felt even more awake now than when I had left, and I wanted to go back to bed.

Still, I gave it a try. I went on up to the bedroom, slipped out of my clothes and under the covers. Marla adjusted a little toward me, a habit of making contact.

In a sleepy voice she said, "You have icicle-butt."

"Sorry."

She made another small sound and shifted to give me more room. It may have been my prowling around the city at all hours or my relief at her acceptance of having me back in bed (however cold my butt might be), but I dropped off and slept the sleep of the dead.

I awoke to Marla pushing on my shoulder.

"Hey, sleepyhead. Are you going to work today?"

"What time is it?"

"Ten. I'm covered at school until noon. Should I be worried about you?"

"You're kidding. It's ten?"

"No, I'm not kidding. I've shaken you awake three times already. Which is what happens when you wander around like a zombie in the middle of the night."

I didn't say anything. I couldn't tell whether she meant wander around the house or the city. Silence can be the most suspicious response to some situations, so I said, "People need less sleep when they get older."

"I think that refers to a *lot* older."

"The phrase is purposely nonspecific."

"But I don't think this is that."

"Are you mad at me?"

"No, sweetie, I just want you to face it, whatever is keeping you awake."

At the Deli I had trouble concentrating. I kept finding myself staring at something—a box of wine, my shoes, the clock—without a sense of why. It was like waking up from a deep sleep every half hour. The last two times I looked around to see if anyone was watching and found John looking back. Finally he came over and asked how I was doing.

"Had a bad night. Not much sleep."

"You're welcome to use the couch in my office."

"No, I'm like this when I lie down too. Can't sleep, can't wake up."

"Well, stick to simple projects today. Don't operate heavy machinery."

"Like cars?"

"And don't bait me. I want you home early, but yes, drive carefully."

Marla looked up from a paperback at the dining table and took a fork out of her mouth. Before her was a bowl that had held something with red sauce. "Hey, it's only six thirty. Are you okay?"

"I'm fine. I need to do some work here. I'll be on the computer."

"Do you want me to heat some of this spaghetti for you?"

"I ate before I came home. But thanks."

At this time we had an older iMac, which John had let me take home after yet another computer upgrade at the Deli. We kept it in the office and used it for e-mail and letters and our digital photo album.

I left the door open because all I meant to conceal from her were my thoughts. I couldn't get Larry Hood out of my mind. Not what I had done to him but what he had done, and then my reaction. The distinction was beginning to gel, and with it I was getting a fix on where I stood with myself.

He had initiated everything. He was dead as a direct result of action I had taken, but all I had done was react to situations he'd created, starting with when he and his brother had tried to take our Camry. It was true that I had aggravated things by taking the truck, but I had done to him precisely what he had been trying to do to me. In fact, it was twice that I had met the man in his world, on his terms, and beaten him.

Something about this bothered me.

For one thing, his world was an ugly place to be. To out-thieve a guy, then out-joust him on the freeway and cause his death, shouldn't be points of pride. But I did feel some level of satisfaction, and this satisfaction bothered me. I was relieved to have beaten him, even amazed to have survived, but I sensed something lurking beneath these feelings.

I thought back to the moment before the collision. I had seen the stalled van and immediately—in the philosophical sense, before processing any information—had swerved onto the shoulder ... here I paused, recalling a calm that had washed over me. In seeing the van I had seen a solution to the most difficult problem I had ever faced.

Had this brought about the calm? It might also have been caused by shock. Accelerating toward what could easily have been my own death, I might have been on overload even before his car hit the van.

I took our thesaurus from the shelf above the computer and looked up *calm*. No help. I tried to recall the phrase that had disturbed me, something about beating him at his own game twice. I had proven myself to be the better man. *Better* sent me to *transcendent* and *eclipsing*. I liked *eclipsing*. I had eclipsed him. The total eclipse of Larry Hood.

I had seen *superiority* among the listings under *better*, and in a way I had felt superior, so I looked it up. *Abnormality* gave me a start because of its weird accuracy—I certainly didn't feel normal any more—but it was a dead end. I flipped back to *superiority*, and just above it was *superior*, and then *arrogant*. I felt a small quake of fear as I sensed where this might lead. And before I could look up anything else, the word I had been dreading leaped from a dark place in my heart: *contempt*. I had felt contempt for Larry Hood as I had led him into the Ryder van.

I was still at the desk when Marla poked her head into the room.

"It's so quiet in here. What kind of work are you doing?"

I turned in my chair and raised the thesaurus. "Now I'm just thinking."

"I'm good with words. What are you stuck on?"

The truth felt safe here, so I said, "*Contempt* is as close as I got so far."

She flinched. "Don't write about contempt."

"Okay, then I'll write about puppies. Which means I won't need this." I set the thesaurus on the desk and turned on the computer. She remained in the doorway, so I opened a new file and titled it "PUPPIES" in capitals large enough for her to see.

She said, "You win. You have my permission to write about contempt. Anyway, I'm off to bed." She didn't ask when I would be along, and I didn't reply to the unasked question. She came over to the desk for a kiss and headed on up.

After renaming the file "Contempt," I just sat there. I couldn't get past that single word.

A little after midnight I heard the sound of a car idling down Juniper toward our house. It was just a soft whir rising from nothing to a murmur as it came closer. The engine held steady for a moment, then died. I waited for a door to open, for someone to get out and shut the door, but there was no other sound. I imagined the driver just sitting there.

But no one just sits there. I thought it might be Shelly Ferguson, the sixteen-year-old daughter of Stacks and Poor Bruce (which was what we called her husband after Stacks got the boob job), only now being driven home from a date, and they were leaning across the space between the front seats, locked in one last kiss . . . no, it was too late for that on a Tuesday. She would be running across the yard toward the house, already in trouble.

I listened for any clue as to what was going on out there, and as I listened I realized that if someone—a car thief, perhaps—was being careful about getting out of his car, the sound of him carefully opening the car door might not carry inside to me. I couldn't let go of my certainty that a car had come up the street and stopped before passing our house and that the driver was still out there, just sitting. It occurred to me that if I got up to check from our staircase landing, I might see the exact same thing I had seen that first night, some guy or guys breaking into our Camry.

I think I actually *hoped* something sinister was developing out there and I could walk through it again—only this time do the right thing by making the phone call—and by doing so exonerate myself from my previous errors and misadventures and thereby break the cycle of my sleeplessness. I recall specifically deciding to handle the next attempted theft with a call to the cops. I moved from our office to the staircase landing and stood back from the window so I couldn't be seen looking out.

Parked across the street was a car I didn't recognize. In the long space between the Fergusons' Subaru and a VW camper parked well behind it sat a small, older foreign car from the '80s, badly in need of a wash. From this angle, and with the streetlights on the far side, the windows were opaque. They may have been tinted except that owners with tinted glass never let their cars get this dirty. I couldn't guess what color it was, except for the front quarter panel on the driver's side, which looked primer gray. I kept still, just stood there watching.

After a moment, almost like a trick of vision, a faint movement of smoke drifted up from the top of the driver's-side window, which must have been open an inch or two. The smoke dissipated, and after a short while another trace of smoke emerged. The driver really was just sitting there.

After another few minutes the car door opened slightly and a hand reached down to the street and set an aluminum can on the pavement, then withdrew. The door thumped shut, and I could barely hear an empty rattle of the can rolling into the darkness beneath the car.

I tried to remember if this car had been around before. All it takes is one teenager on the block to give rise to all sorts of nocturnal activity beyond the influence of parents, however vigilant they try to be. We keep our bird-watching binoculars in a drawer in the kitchen. Just as I left the window, an engine started. I continued down the stairs, but by the time I reached the front door, the car was gone.

There was a slight haze of blue exhaust hovering in the empty parking space. After a moment it was gone too.

I went up to bed to crawl in beside Marla and lie there, staring at the ceiling in the dark.

During Marla's pregnancy I had some pastel to my mood too. There were times when I would find myself reflecting on how the genetic combination of the two of us might develop. I would shake myself out of gazing at the dining table and realize that I had been imagining our young man seated there, drawing a picture or putting together a jigsaw puzzle. I had been imagining him learning how his unique set of tools applied to the world at large. Marla would look up from her book with a glance that asked what I was thinking. I would tell her, and she would say she found herself thinking about him like that too. But after she miscarried it was too painful to talk about. And still later, when her reproductive system had healed from the removal and we were trying again, neither of us raised the issue of our hopes at all. I don't know if this was her or us or just me. More and more I felt it was me, and she was simply following my lead. Which made me wonder if men are more naturally inclined to shoulder this kind of weight. Perhaps our genetic wiring compels us to deal with sources of stress on our own, allowing women—the ones who must carry the child—to maintain a positive focus and keep good feelings flowing through the amniotic environment that the fetus inhabits for those critical nine months.

For obvious reasons I'm sketchier about Marla's feelings. Periodically, during the unforgettable span of only thirty-eight days that we were aware of our child, I would find her sitting in our easy chair, staring into the middle distance, lost in a reverie I'd never witnessed before. You've seen it in paintings by the old masters, the same tilt to a figure's head, the angelic countenance as the woman (or cherub or saint) gazes upon nothing. But real people have real lives, and this alone will add lines of care or humor or frustration to the most innocent expression, whereas the faces in the paintings offer no evidence of baggage of the past or concern for the future. This is what I thought defined the images as art: They seemed unconstrained by the laws of the physical world. Now I was seeing it in a real person. Like the figures on canvas, Marla simply glowed. (Perhaps the old masters had hired pregnant models to sit for their depictions of holy people.) I felt there must be more to it than just chemical responses to electrical firings. I did know that when a woman is pregnant, her hormonal activity can change radically, and that hormones can put people in strange and wonderful emotional places; so yes, hormones might have explained everything I saw in her. But I had the distinct impression that there was something else going on, something that called to mind a bone-deep shift in her reasons for being.

The following night I didn't try to kid myself. My restlessness rose as the sun went down. After dinner we read a little and watched the news; then Marla said she was heading up to bed. I told her I would be along in a while.

"You aren't tired?"

"Nope."

"People need sleep more than food. It's a fact."

"Thanks, but I'm not hungry."

"Remember how you were this morning? What did you do, sleep all day?"

"Not a wink."

"Well, whatever it is, I think you need help."

"You mean like a glass of whiskey?"

"I mean if you were a dog you owned, you would have taken him to the vet by now."

"And the vet would have charged me fifty bucks and told me to keep an eye on him."

She gave me that look of hers, amusement with a hint of exasperation at the finish. But she also gave me a kiss and said, "Well, then, I'm going to keep an eye on you."

I said, "That'll be fifty bucks."

She said good-night and went up to bed. I found an unsolved Sunday *Times* crossword in the newspaper stack waiting for recycling and worked on it until the house grew quiet again. I imagined the eye she had promised to keep on me slowly closing . . . now completely closed . . . and I slipped out the front door to the Camry. I had been parking it facing the other way, making it easier to coast down the slight slope through the intersection before I started the engine.

I cruised down Mill Boulevard toward a more dubious part of town. Mill slants between two neighborhoods, meeting both gridded areas at a forty-five-degree angle. The resulting triangular blocks have stripper bars and car-parts stores and small motels offering rooms by the hour. Generally the area is foot turf for hookers and shabby night people of the drug world, and if you follow the boulevard far enough down toward the river, that's all it is. There are fewer streetlights here than over by Arlene's, and these people have a colder surface. This might be the difference between legal and illegal vice. Citizens there, denizens here.

The unofficial public attitude was that putting pressure on crime here would simply force it into nicer neighborhoods. The police, the mayor, even the press seemed to consider the area a contained burn and left it alone. Without innocent bystanders even crimes of violence can be written off as victimless because they're doing it to themselves.

Tonight everything seemed to be happening indoors, or in cars that were parked and idling with their lights out, the occupants turning to study me as I approached. Their eyes were either furtive or challenging—trying to read me, I suppose, to determine my position in the nocturnal food chain. *Do I eat you, or do you eat me?* Keeping my eyes forward, I tried to seem casual and innocent, not worth a second thought. Neither predator nor prey.

A slouched figure leaning against the side of a closed business watched me idle past. A skateboard leaned in an identical slant beside him, like a son imitating his father's posture. He looked to be in his early twenties, with the oversized army jacket, languid quarter-moon face, and feral eyes of an urban stray. From the safety of my car I held his eyes with mine.

He raised his chin; I raised mine in reply. In my mirror I watched him watch me for a time; then he turned to watch for the next car. I couldn't tell whether his head movement had been to acknowledge my presence or indicate something beyond my comprehension. Perhaps he had access to items or activities that might be of interest to the more experienced night motorist. I was curious enough to consider circling around and asking him for directions, just to see where the exchange would lead, but this would get me more involved than I wanted to be. I had to be okay with not knowing.

I continued on, still looking for whatever the area had to offer a voyeur of inner-city nightlife. The entertainment I sought was not my own. I wanted to see how other people passed their late-night hours, but existence in this hard corridor seemed to be survival-level only. There wasn't a feeling that violence was about to erupt—no risky get-rich schemes being played out—but there must have been an established hierarchy in which someone like me wouldn't figure. I couldn't help wondering whether the average denizen chose to live like this, was forced to do so by bad luck, or had emotional needs that couldn't be satisfied by any other means. Would anyone *choose* to be here?

The question applied to me too; I had to either participate or leave. The dashboard clock read two thirty-two.

I turned onto the next arterial that would take me across the river to the other side of town. After some exploratory grid-street driving I found myself on a familiar route, cruising up Washington toward the small aquarium of life outside Arlene's. The light at 10th stayed green, so I kept going up to 11th and around the block like last time.

A parking space across from the porn theater was open, so I pulled in but left the engine running while I thought about whether or not the comings and goings here would be as diverting as those outside Arlene's. The tiled area beneath the marquee was lit, though all interior lighting was off; closed for the night. To the right of the box office stood an old weathered hooker in a black skirt, black leggings, and a sky-blue puffy down coat. She took me in with a single glance, then looked down at the tiles, seeming unaware of anything other than her own general weariness. I wondered what an hour would cost. Bargain-basement sex, discount coupons, a going-out-of-business sale.

I turned off the engine and set the brake. When I looked toward the theater again, I saw that another woman had appeared near the curb at the corner, standing as if expecting her ride to arrive at any time. She wore a parchment-colored dress that reached below her knees and matched her low-heeled shoes. Her gloves matched her purse. She might have been the wife of a judge, someone who moved with a habit of dignity, someone who belonged somewhere else. Everything about her separated her from the rest of the night, especially the old hooker behind her, the one who years earlier had lost any trace of allure.

A transient in a military green raincoat with a half-filled black cloth sack over his shoulder like a dark-side Santa Claus slouched through the lighted space between the two women. He fired off a remark (an offensive one, I imagined—I heard the tone but not the words) toward the elegant one, and she turned her head away, almost theatrically averting herself from his presence. When she turned back, she looked straight at me. I looked up the street, but only for a moment. When I looked back, she was still looking at me. Finally she glanced down 10th, then stepped into the street and crossed in front of my car—this was her only act that was out of character—crossing the street up from the crosswalk with the "wait" sign still lit. She stopped at my door and lightly tapped on the window with a gloved finger. I lowered it four inches.

"Can you give me a ride?" Her voice was like a sip of whiskey with a hint of honey stirred in.

"I'm sorry. I can't go anywhere for a while."

She blinked. "Are you waiting for someone?"

"Yes," I said, hoping she would drop it and leave me alone. I felt that if she pressed it, I would weaken and take her wherever she needed to go. I also felt that I might be developing a habit of getting into situations my instincts warned me against. Actually, I was already there, having started by sneaking out of the house that first night and driving off in someone else's truck—but so far no one else was involved. My life had enough upheaval already. I certainly didn't want to end up in another predicament I couldn't explain to Marla.

She said, "Your wife?"

I had to put an end to this. I said, "I can't help you."

She gave me a weak smile and said thanks anyway. I raised the window, and she went back to where she had been. She wasn't stiff in any way. Her dress fit perfectly—the material caught the streetlights with a shimmer—but she managed to walk in a manner that minimized the action. My focus was on her shoulders and the small of her back, and I was relieved that she had let me turn her away so easily. She stepped up on the curb and stood in the same place as if now certain her ride wouldn't show. I no longer existed in her world. A few men and women of a more obvious type moved up and down the sidewalk around her, but they didn't exist to her any more than I did now. Finally she pulled down the sleeve of her glove to look at her watch, then turned away and walked up the block into the darkness. The weathered hooker ignored her. I didn't know what to make of it. I almost got out of the car to call out that I would give her that ride, but resisted and finally pushed her from my thoughts.

I wasn't sleepy at all. I leaned back against the door and tried to relax. Cars passed intermittently, some holding to the speed limit, others slowing before accelerating again. Up the street I could see that Arlene's was doing moderate business. *In the room the women come and go, talking of Michelangelo.* The loose association came to my tired mind from a lit class at college, the ebb and flow of people, mostly men. There was a bit of a chill in the car, which would also help to keep me awake.

She wasn't wearing a coat. The realization came to me from nowhere. The woman in the parchment dress should have been wearing a coat. I turned the thought every way I could, but it just got more surreal.

A movement over by the theater caught my eye. The weathered hooker was crossing the street toward me, following the path of the first woman. I turned in my seat to keep facing her as she passed in front of my car. I also reached to lock my door. She came around and with her middle knuckle knocked on my window, which I opened the same four inches.

"You're killing it." She sounded like she was chewing a wad of gum, with a contrived kind of sassy, nasal quality to her voice.

"Sorry?"

"You're killing the action. Guys see you and keep driving. I lost three possibles in the last fifteen minutes."

"Do they think I'm a cop or something?"

"I don't." She sighed and rolled her eyes. "But some people might."

"I have a right to be here, though. I mean, it's legal, isn't it?"

"Not really," she said, looking up the street as if she might beckon a cop over to support her in the matter, but she was just asking me to move on. I couldn't get rid of the impression that she was working at a little wad of gum with her molars. Her makeup broke about even, masking some of her erosions, highlighting others. I couldn't imagine what it would take for me to seek comfort from her.

She pointed up the street toward Arlene's. "See that red light? You could park there and we wouldn't have this conflict. Just two hundred feet up the street and I'm happy." After a pause she said, "So what's it going to be?"

I felt certain that I was more legal than she was—I was merely loitering while she was soliciting sex—but I also thought this might end up a pot-and-kettle argument. More important, the last thing I wanted was to bug someone, no matter who they were. This was her world, not mine. My backing off would be the lesser concession. And if a cop actually did appear, I thought he might indeed side with her.

"Okay, no problem." I started my car. "Hey, I have a question."

"I suppose."

"What's the story on that woman who came over here a little while ago? She was wearing the dinner dress—"

"I know the one." She gave a hard chuckle. "Monique. Not your type."

"Monique."

"Don't get your hopes up. 'Bill' is what the cops know him by."

"Wait. That was a guy?"

"Like I said, not your type."

"Wow, I guess not." Then I said, "Seems like a dangerous game."

"Oh, he's tougher than he looks. A lot tougher." She looked up the street again. "Anyway, are you going to help me out here?"

"Sure. Sorry."

As if justifying the cliché of her nasal voice, she took a pack of gum from her coat pocket and pulled out a stick. She pointed at me with it and said, "I'm sorry too, but I'm guessing you have a wife to go home to, and some of these guys don't. And with you sitting here I can't help them out."

I was glad she said this. It made me think she was actually a nice person stuck in a lousy job. There are times at the Deli when we have to ask homeless people to move out from beneath our awning because they're bad for business. I hate running them off, but there are other places for them to take shelter from the weather. On the other hand, the homeless are just pausing in their life of urban foraging, while I was disturbing the very action I had hoped to observe. Among undesirable elements, I was the undesirable element, sent home first by a cop and now by a whore. Neither the referees nor the players want spectators on the field.

Crossing the St. Stephen's bridge back to the east side, I wondered what would have happened if I had agreed to give Monique (aka Bill) a ride. Probably nothing more than an aborted exchange and a U-turn back to the same street corner. I had either passed or failed a test, and I couldn't tell which.

The bone-deep shift in my own reasons for being came when I saw our son's heartbeat on the ultrasound screen—the black-and-white, *self-renewing* motion—distinct from the movement of Dr. Reese's wand and from Marla's adjustments to the intrusion. This tiny seed of life, independent of our parental life forces, had taken hold and begun to grow into our little man. Seeing his pulse altered my sense of wonder. The mysteries of the universe began to move in on me, to where they were almost within reach. Think of how an ancient, dusty grain can be taken from an Egyptian tomb five thousand years after being placed there and how, after being immersed in wet soil, it will grow into living wheat. *Existence!* There is such a strong life force in things, it seems that given the slightest chance, they must flourish. That heartbeat was the presence of life in my own child, and with it the wonder of existence had become personal, as if the finger of God had reached down and touched my life by offering us a son.

So how could it be that in the middle of a dark night Marla woke me with a wail, hurried across the hall to the toilet, and sat there bleeding as if her period had sneaked up on her—as if a pregnant woman could be *having* a period? At the time I didn't know she was bleeding, of course, but I could tell from her cry what had happened.

I turned on the bedside lamp and phoned the hospital. The desk nurse said she would advise Dr. Reese, and he—or someone—would see us as soon as we arrived. She told me to drive carefully and avoid unnecessary risks, and she hung up. I could see Marla's hands on the other side of the open bathroom door, gripping her knees as she sobbed brokenly. When she came back to bed, she curled into me, and I put my arms around her.

"Oh, Jim, I lost him!" In her quietest voice, "I think I lost him."

I hugged her and said, "I know, I know," and we lay there in each other's arms, lost and helpless in a way even now I can't think how to describe.

I did know we had lost him, but only in an abstract sense. It hadn't really hit me yet, which I now think was good because otherwise I might not have been able to manage the drive to the hospital. I told her they were ready for us but continued to hold her.

"In a minute." She wasn't doing very well. Neither was I.

So the finger of God had touched our lives again, this time extinguishing our son. I lay there holding Marla, tormented by questions, none of which had any chance of being answered because none pressed for an understanding of what had actually happened, the difficult details. I had no interest in the science behind the failure: what life-sustaining requirement had been denied him; that this particular combination of our genetic structures wasn't viable; or that Marla's body had sensed a problem and made the hard decision for us, spontaneously aborting the false start.

We do that, you know. Dr. Reese told us later that humans are at the top of the list of creatures that spontaneously abort fetuses. We emotionally hold life more dearly than our bodies do.

Well, yes. That's where surgery comes from. Surgery is us telling evolution that we'll take it from here.

Then I thought: *No, surgery is simply our effort to correct what our bodies can't.*

I found myself one step removed and wondered whether we'd developed surgeries as a matter of course, the way we developed the upright walk. Which in turn made me ask whether ethical choices really are *choices*. Sometimes morality feels like something we're born with, such as hair or fingers—or perhaps more like an organ—and we either embrace what the secretion inclines us to do or train ourselves to control or resist it, the way marksmen quiet their hearts to steady their aim. This thinking seems fuzzy and broken to me now, but it's exactly how it came to me.

It seemed then that, like bile and hormones and even our thoughts, moral actions are directed by something physiological. When we behave badly, our morality gland squirts a fluid into our bloodstream and we feel crummy. At some point in our history we started calling it *guilt*. Someday two Belgians will synthesize the secretion and be awarded the Nobel Prize. And later we will have debates concerning the ethics of injecting a guilt serum into repeat felons such as Larry Hood.

It was a heavy hour before they got us into the ultrasound room.

Any hope we might have been harboring faded when the screen gave us no heartbeat—no possibility of a heartbeat—only a grainy stillness. For me this was the worst, this stillness, made no less *lifeless* by movements of the wand as it almost frantically sought what it had so easily found there one short month before. Dr. Reese said, "Well." Just that single flat word. Hearing it and seeing the absence of movement on the screen was when it really hit me: Our boy was gone.

he morning after talking to the hooker I had trouble getting out of bed. Marla pulled me to my feet, but bringing me to consciousness was another issue entirely. I had to sit to get dressed. My balance was off, and I couldn't hold a thought. Even focusing my eyes was a problem. I ambulated down to the kitchen, slumped into a chair, and picked at a piece of toast until she came around to my side of the table and pulled on my hair to tilt my head back. Never in my life had I felt so tired.

She peered into my face and told me I looked like a dead man who hadn't fallen over yet.

"I can't seem to get my motor going this morning."

"If you get stopped on your way to work, they'll throw you in the drunk tank."

Still being held by my hair, I said, "I'd pass the Breathalyzer test. They would have to let me go."

"No, they'd throw you in the tank and send the Breathalyzer out for repairs. No one can look like you do now and not be drunk out of his gourd." She released my hair, and my head dropped forward until I was staring down at my plate again. A piece of toast rested there. It had been picked at.

I said, "Or hers."

"What?"

"You said, 'his,' but it's not just guys. Women can be drunk out of their gourds too."

The room rang with silence.

I said, "You know what this house needs? A pet. We should get a dog."

More silence, proving my point about a pet. I almost said so but instead said I'd take a shower.

Marla said, "Now you're moving in the right direction. No dogs. What this house needs is for you to live in the present, deal with your current condition. Take the damn shower. I'm late for work. See you this evening."

At the Deli John wouldn't let me even take off my coat. "The only reason I'm not calling the paramedics is that you managed to get here. But I have to send you home."

"I know. Bad for business."

He didn't say anything.

I said, "I can't sleep at night. At least until three or four anyway. What if I tell Marla not to wake me up tomorrow and see how late I can sleep?"

"Now, there's an idea. You're no good to me like this. Or to yourself. Sounds like your circadian rhythm is off."

"Sure. That's probably it." I had no idea what he was talking about.

"Your daily biological clock. It can get disturbed, and now you're on a twenty-five-hour clock, as if you're moving west one time zone every day. Perpetual jet lag. Has anything big happened recently? You don't have to answer, of course, but it might be a good question to ask yourself."

I thought for a moment. "Wouldn't that be east?"

"No, it's west. You drag the day out by following the sun. If you go east, you hurry toward the coming day, shortening the one you're in. But that's not the point. The point is, you might not be a twenty-four-hour person anymore. You might've had a phase shift."

"Phase shift."

"The guy who told me about it is an athlete. You know how they get—the body is a temple. Guys like you and me, our bodies are more like washing machines or boat motors. With athletes every little nuance changes their performance, and they have to figure out how to compensate. You're an ordinary guy, so you might have to deal with bad days now and then as those extra hours per day start to pile up. Every certain number of days your clock will jump from late to early because you can't follow it around the cycle. After a while you'll look like you do now if you're on a twenty-five-hour clock."

"Around the cycle?"

"Okay, then, through the time zones. See, right there—usually you follow me. Usually you track what I'm saying."

"Usually you make sense."

But it wasn't his fault. How could he know I was no longer ordinary? Finally he told me to sleep through tomorrow morning. I almost pointed out the circular pattern to the conversation, but I lost the thread and had to let it go.

John pointed at me. "Hold on. I have something for you." He went to his office and returned with a book. He was leafing through the pages, and by the time he got back to me he had found what he was looking for. He handed me the open book and said, "Read those first two lines." It was a book of poems by an Islamic mystic named Rumi. The lines were:

What was said to the rose that made it open
Was said to me here in my chest.

Before I could respond John said, "Ever read this guy? Some surprising stuff in there. Hang on to it for a while. It's good night reading."

When I got back to the house, I flopped out on the couch. I opened the book of poems but couldn't read a single word. I lay there hoping sleep would overtake me. But if I did doze off, I would be up all night for sure. Then I thought, *That's like being on the verge of starvation and worrying that a snack might spoil your appetite for dinner.* I held the closed book on my chest and closed my eyes.

How could our son's heartbeat be extinguished so easily? So randomly? Even now, when I asked the question, I didn't want an answer. It was really a question of fairness. Why did it have to be our baby? Why did it happen to us? And if it was indeed fair for this to happen, why couldn't life have been *un*fair this once by letting us have our boy?

The caprices of existence seemed capable of a ruthlessness I hadn't felt before, and it occurred to me that ruthlessness can backfire. When God killed our son, he reduced himself from a spiritual entity with an interest in our welfare to a series of random events. When God killed our son, he killed himself.

I was never a fervent believer. I quit going to church when my parents let me quit—as a freshman in high school—and I never returned the way some did, the way my parents probably hoped I would. Even back then I felt that if there actually were a God, we humans wouldn't be any more able to figure out the smallest nuance of his strange plan than a dog would be. Which paralleled my feelings about the zodiac, or palm reading, or throwing bones to peer into the future: Even if an alignment of physical objects has an effect on the paths of our lives, I can't see how anyone would know how to interpret it.

If someone were to ask me what I believed, my honest response would be: I don't think about it.

Do I refuse to think about it?

I don't think about that either. It's uninteresting. Notions concerning a Larger Purpose to our existence are no more compelling to me than are the personal lives of movie stars.

Is this the absence of religion?

Maybe. I certainly don't want to witness another miracle. I don't need the hand of God reaching down to meddle with my life again. I don't play the lottery, so any adjustment to the random events that make up my relatively happy life would most likely have a negative effect. His almighty finger is cold and bony, and although I don't believe it carries evil, it certainly can be cruel. I think the loss of our son erased my religion.

It's probably more telling than I can appreciate, but what helped me get through the difficult night of our miscarriage was a remark made to me by an elderly woman in the waiting room while Marla was in surgery. This woman was sitting across from me, reading a magazine. She looked up with a sad smile and said, "It happens."

Those were the words I needed to hear. They may have been the only words I *could* hear. They were as comforting as a hug, and, as they sank in, something in me relaxed. Either I let go of an emotion that had been crippling me or a tension faded on its own. I suspect that we as a species don't want our individual sufferings to be unique.

I hope I thanked her, but I don't think I did. I may have nodded. I know I didn't consider the sense of her words at the time, or what she had seen in me that prompted her to offer them. I don't believe she had overheard anything between Marla and me, or between the staff and us. Sometimes I think that the only way humanity can tolerate itself is by exercising its ability to empathize. Empathy is one way humanity renews its membership with itself.

Which makes me wonder now, with the benefit of distance and perspective, if what I felt from the elderly woman's words was a communal comfort, a sense that we might not be alone in this world, that even strangers can share, and thereby ease, grief.

I awoke on the couch feeling somewhat refreshed. I was still holding the book John had lent me. It had been written in the thirteenth century, translated recently. I was disappointed to find that most of Rumi's writing was about God. I would rather have read about daily existence. I didn't get far enough to learn what kind of god his god was, but I did find a great deal of joy in his phrases, joy that did not speak to me. But the line John had pointed out resonated in a way that none of the other writing did.

> *What was said to the rose that made it open*
> *Was said to me here in my chest.*

What a gem! The translator must have felt a similar opening in his chest when he realized what Rumi had been trying to get across on paper eight hundred years earlier. The life of his words.

I set the book aside and went into the kitchen for something to eat. It wasn't quite two in the afternoon, and there was nothing I wanted to do but go up to the Deli and put in at least half a day. I see now that part of this was me wanting to be with people, that being by myself allowed those percolations I hadn't been able to work into words to rise to the surface and remind me they were still there. It was as if they weren't speaking to me, really, but instead to my other unresolved issues, becoming a part of them, an accepted member of the fold that would haunt me for the rest of my life.

Marla was a bit distant that evening, which I thought had to do with my being distant to her. It might have eased my burden to tell her some of what had gone on recently, but it would have doubled my burden if she were to take it wrong.

Sure enough, that night I slept fitfully, with dreams that woke me with sudden sounds: doors slamming, falls from a long way up, thrown objects striking walls—all recalling to me in perfect replication the sound of Larry Hood's car slamming into the Ryder van. None of the dreamed sounds were sparked by real sounds. The night was silent. I jerked awake several times and probably twitched in my sleep too. At one point Marla got up and went down the hall to the guest room to sleep, the way she did on those rare nights that I snored. It helped a little, knowing my restlessness was no longer disturbing her, but the dreams kept coming.

Then I was awakened by a gunshot.

Before I knew it I was sitting up with the phone in my hand, ready to dial 911. I paused, listening for a car to drive away or for one of the neighbors to come outside to investigate. The world remained still. My ears were numb from the shot. Our digital clock radio read two eleven A.M. I waited, holding the phone, replaying the sound in my memory. It had been bigger than the collision, and different enough for me to separate it from any other sound I had heard or imagined recently—but what bothered me more was that it had come without any dream-story the way the others had.

Why wasn't Marla awake? She should have been calling to me from the guest room. How could anyone sleep through such a noise? Was she huddled in terror, afraid to make a sound? Could the shot have come from inside the house? From her *room*? My heart sank, yet I felt strangely composed as I got up and started toward the guest room in the dark, trying to listen through the ringing in my ears. The only sound now was the slight creaking of the floor. The guest room door was ajar. No lights were on in the house, but the streetlights from the next block over shone across the adjoining backyards, giving some illumination to the room. I approached the bed and knelt beside her.

Her breathing was steady, but she was in fact breathing rather than lying in a pool of blood. (I hadn't really believed she had been shot, but I could make sense of it, that she might have been. And disbelief is often our first reaction to disaster.) With the deepest relief I saw that she wasn't hurt. Whatever else was going on didn't matter as long as she was okay. I watched her softly breathe for a time, then backed out of the room and quietly pulled the door closed.

I was still convinced that the explosion was more than a dreamed sound, so I got dressed and went downstairs. Evidently I would have preferred to stumble upon an armed intruder rather than let him roam the house unchallenged. I certainly wouldn't be able to get any more sleep until I was convinced that Marla and I were alone.

The front door was locked and dead-bolted, undisturbed. I worked my way from room to room, turning on lights and looking for broken glass or anything out of place. All the windows on the first floor were closed and locked. The back door was dead-bolted as well. The house was secure. I ended up sitting at the kitchen table, listening to the night. Eventually I convinced myself that the shot had been so loud and close that it must have come from inside my head.

I turned out all the lights and started back upstairs. On the landing I looked out the window the way I had that first night when I'd seen Larry and Wade Hood breaking into our car. With the lights off I could see out the window without reflections. Up and down the street everything was peaceful, gently bathed in streetlights and the glow of a partial moon coming in at an angle from behind the house. That foreign car with the gray front quarter panel wasn't here now. I thought I should walk around our property, just to take a look.

I never used to kid myself about what I was doing. For example, before this whole thing began I never would have found myself out by the curb at almost two thirty in the morning, checking on something I had probably imagined, and then find that I had brought my wallet and car keys. I never would have looked up at our bedroom window and thought that with Marla out of earshot at the back of the house I could start the car where it sat without waking her. I was making decisions behind my own back, as if I were both the strict parent and the naughty boy, trying to put one over on myself.

I had no desire for another run-in with the old hooker, and I'd seen most of the rest of downtown, so I stayed on Cleveland, east of the river and south of Mill, cruising at exactly the speed limit. In our town the cops can pull you over for this, especially during the small hours of the morning. I guess it's considered suspicious behavior to act according to the letter of the law. I wasn't trolling for cops specifically, but I was definitely trolling for something—*anything*, actually—

and wouldn't have cared about being pulled over. I would pass the Breathalyzer test. I was ready to take any test they wanted to throw at me. Being pulled over would have helped me feel a part of society again.

I was in a familiar neighborhood, one I hadn't seen in a long time. There would be an all-night grocery just up the street. A soda pop sounded good, something cold and fizzy, with lime in it. I parked in front of the store. Although the painted sign beside the door still said, "Open 24 hours," it was obvious that the place was closed. There was a pop machine out front beside an ice freezer, but I had wanted the experience of going in past the counter, where an older fellow seated at the cash register would be trying to stay awake on a slow night by watching TV with the sound turned down. He would nod hello without saying anything and with a quick appraisal decide I was harmless. I would select my bottle from the cooler—a Squirt or Quench, if those were still around—and return to the counter, avoiding an exchange of pleasantries with the merchant (who would be 99 percent wanting to be alone again and 1 percent relieved that I wasn't there to rob him). He would hand me my change and drop the receipt into the wastebasket, completing the late-night encounter between two urban strangers. I sat in the car thinking that I hadn't really wanted a pop at all. I'd wanted to relive that experience.

Marla and I used to live four blocks over from this store, on Agate Street behind the grade school. That first summer we would walk down here in the evening for ice cream. Sometimes we would get two sweet rolls to set out by the toaster oven for breakfast the next day. I had forgotten this period, which had been short, and a blur besides, because we'd been lost in the early days of love.

Marla had seen the open-house ad in the Saturday-morning paper. She told me to put on my shoes because it started in ten minutes and it was a ten-minute drive. We found the address and parked in front of the small bungalow. It was part of an area that was on the rise, though it still had more than its share of rental houses. Before we went in Marla stopped and said, "This is it." The yard was a flat expanse of sunburned grass surrounded by a four-foot-high chain-link fence.

I said, "I'm looking at a desert. There's nothing here."

"Exactly. A blank slate. We can do whatever we want."

The interior was neat and cozy, with some built-ins and a fireplace. The kitchen had good space and light and looked out over a backyard that had a maple toward the back fence but otherwise was another blank slate. There were quite a few other interested people, but we didn't mind. Marla said that as a couple we were too cute to be turned down.

We lived there our first year together—our honeymoon year—which was in fact closer to fifteen months before we married and had a real honeymoon. During her free time Marla dug beds into both the front and back yards. The landlords, barely older than we were, said they would pay for any plants and trees we put in as long as we cleared it with them first.

There must be seminars in which landlords are advised to deduct the cost of shrubs and trees from the rent if their renters are willing to work in the yard. Every week Marla called with new ideas, and she kept getting the go-ahead. I helped with some of the heavier labor, but for the most part she simply made decisions and went to work on her own. She seemed to be turning the rental into the place she wanted to live for the rest of her life. (In fact, it was more like a practice pad, but I didn't see this then.)

In the front yard she dug beds along both side fences and plugged them with three carloads of plants. A narrow concrete path ran from the sidewalk to the porch, dividing the front lawn into equal squares. She had me dig a hole in the center of each, shoveling the dirt onto a blue tarp. Meanwhile, she took the pickup I owned at the time over to the nursery and returned with two pear trees, which I waltzed across the yard, shook out of their buckets and rolled into the holes. The next weekend she planted some kind of climbing vine—honeysuckle, I think—along the front fence to reduce the chain-link barracks look. That's how it went for the first couple months, and soon the yard was how she wanted it. How *we* wanted it, I should say; it was beautiful. It was this yard that made me want to find a house to buy. I wanted to own the work we put into a place.

Over the years I had forgotten the house number. The street name was easy because we had always referred to it as the Agate House, but the numbered cross streets weren't registering. I idled down Agate for three blocks before I found the familiar run of houses, ours second from the end. I sat in my car in the middle of the street with the engine idling. It was three in the morning.

They had painted it since we'd left, gone from a light-gray body and dark-gray trim to a soft yellow body and walnut-brown trim. Supporting the porch roof were two large boxed pillars, the left one bearing the four address numbers in red glaze on white ceramic tile. This and the scalloped shingles covering the pillars were what set this house off from its neighbors. I could imagine the crazy month almost a hundred years earlier when this entire row of houses had gone in, the constant syncopated industry of hammers and saws. Each was distinct from the others simply by variations in the porch pillars.

Marla's pear trees were twenty feet tall now, and the shrubs around the foundation were full and neatly trimmed. She had done a good job of shaping our first nest. We had been innocent here, just starting to learn who we were as a couple and what path in life we would take together. I couldn't recall any of the decisions that had led us from the people we'd been in this house to who we were now, but in the years since living here we had come a long way. In some senses we were very much the same people, and in other senses we were horizons beyond those younger selves. It was no surprise to me, then, to find myself stopped in front of the first house in which we had lived together. It was like looking back toward the path I needed to find again after my momentum had carried me through this strange detour.

The attempted theft had pulled me off course, gotten me behaving in unfamiliar ways. I was caught between my world and the world of the Hood brothers, and I wondered what it would be like to be them, to steal cars on a regular basis. The technical aspects—disabling the keyed cylinder or sorting through the color-coded ignition wires—were beyond me. And I also lacked the internal structure—the emotional and ethical twists that allow guys to steal cars without being crippled by guilt. But I wondered what a guy would feel when he was, as Rainey put it, committed to the act.

The car parked beside me was a fairly late import, well kept, worth thousands of dollars. The neighborhood had improved since we had lived here. What would be the first step? Probably trying the door to see if it was locked. It's a common enough practice in the quieter neighborhoods for people to leave their cars unlocked. I looked up and down the block on both sides of the street. Every porch had its light on, but not one window was lit. I got out of the Camry and went around to try the door of the parked car. It opened with a click. No alarm, just the silent glow of the dome light.

I sat in the driver's seat and gripped the wheel. I was beginning see how some guys took to this kind of enterprise—so much value just sitting there at the curb, almost daring the thieving brothers, or the backpack bicyclists, to hop in and go. It didn't make the idea of stealing cars any more tempting to me, but it made sense that guys did it. I remained in the seat and closed the door, and the light went out.

I leaned back and wondered how much you could get for a stolen car. As with anything without a fixed price, you probably waited for the other person to name a number, then you named a different number, and the two of you worked toward each other. But where would you take the car to begin the process? How would you even begin to find out? And I couldn't drive away in both cars—what would I do with the Camry? Maybe park it up the street and figure out a way to come back for it a couple days later. As I sat in this stranger's car, thinking through all these things, I grew more relaxed than I would have thought possible.

One thing Marla's short pregnancy gave us, as she moved through her days with her angelic countenance, was a tension-free relationship. She no longer cared about the mess in the kitchen, politics at even the local level, whether to take paper or plastic. And because she didn't care about these things, they bothered me less too. I'm not saying I miss it, but for that short time we had a seamlessly warm and close existence.

I myself may have been the only aspect that didn't allow it to be perfect. I was aware of how good things were, which was part of the problem. Marla was immersed in the moment—she was *being* it—while I was at least one level removed from the experience by noticing it. This removal alone disqualifies the relationship from having been perfect.

But Marla was truly happy. She had the pregnant-woman glow

but had it in a way that makes me think few people know what this common phrase really refers to.

Guys don't tend to reach that level of reverie. I'm not sure we even have access to it. You hear about monks or the really high-level karate guys reaching a plane, sure. I can't speak for them. Maybe they get there, and maybe they're experiencing something else entirely. But I'm talking about ordinary guys—guys who punch a clock, get caught in traffic, shop for birthday gifts, live in the world.

It's not that we're cheated of it, but maybe. Or maybe we haven't figured out how to achieve it—how to even *want* to achieve it. I don't think men in general are hardwired to crave reverie. Some, perhaps, and I'm sure not all women have Marla's ability to fall into a state of peace, whether they're pregnant or at any other time. But I think most men are different from most women in that, to be content with their place in the world, they have to be doing, whereas women are being. Guys go out and find a place, build it up and defend it, and women inhabit the place. I'm not talking about pregnant, barefoot women in the kitchen. What I'm getting at here is the same hardwiring we had ten thousand years ago, when our species survived by acting as a community in the wasteland, when the average person had no chance of providing for his or her needs alone. When I refer to happiness, I mean having a deep itch scratched, a primal urge satisfied.

There was one time when I was just out of high school that I accidentally relaxed into something approaching what I saw on Marla's face—the euphoric glow. I was alone in the house, stretched out on the couch, listening to Pink Floyd, of all things. I wasn't dozing, but almost, and suddenly this feeling washed over me: I didn't want to be anywhere else, be any*one* else, didn't want anything else to be happening. I wasn't lonely, wasn't hungry, didn't have to pee or phone a friend, didn't care about the past, the future—I had no concerns, no anxieties, no emotion in any sense. It lasted five seconds at most, and it was heaven, a state of true peace. If I hadn't experienced that, I may have thought Marla had the countenance of a fool when she was carrying our lost son, but it now confirmed my feeling that she had the bearing of a holy person, a saint. All of her questions had been answered. It was as if she'd had a visitation, and now she was complete.

Later I was told that I had been at the edge of falling asleep on the couch, that this euphoric experience at the edge of sleep is fairly common. What brought me out of it was a fear that I might be dying, which I was told is also common.

The reverie was wonderful, for as long as it lasted, but I like hunger. I like the needing and the anticipation and even the confusion of daily life. I like to work crosswords, not to solve them but to be in the act of solving them. Tension before it is satisfied. Closure may satisfy tension, but it doesn't satisfy me. When I complete a puzzle, I get the feeling of closure, but it's not as strong as my disappointment in no longer having that particular puzzle to work on. The only real satisfaction comes when I'm about two-thirds of the way into a tough one and see that I'm likely to finish. I don't think I would do well in what (as I understand it) Christians call heaven. It sounds more like permanent retirement, like just hanging out the way that kid with the skateboard was hanging out. Imagine yourself on a sunny afternoon, leaning against a perfectly white building on a clean street, waiting for something to happen but knowing nothing will, ever again. Hanging out isn't living. It's what we do between the times we live our lives. And above anything, I like living. We've all heard death described as "going to one's reward." This is meaningless to me. Being alive is my reward. Death comes next, nothing more. Death is either the next thing or the last thing, but it's not an improved condition, and certainly not a goal. If it turns out that there actually is a God who meddles with our lives, I'll probably spend a good deal of eternity pissed off that he didn't let me live longer before calling me "home" to heaven.

I think we get a lot of work done in our lives because of a primal dissatisfaction, but to feel fulfillment, that's a good thing too. I don't envy Marla for having been immersed for so long, in contrast to my brief dip. In fact, I think I can truthfully say that I would want everyone on the planet to feel it before me—I would happily (in the superficial sense) see all people attain Nirvana, and when the last person succumbed, perhaps I would allow myself to succumb as well because there wouldn't be anyone else to share living with. But this won't happen, obviously, and I'm satisfied applying my mild discontent as leverage against life to accomplish a few small things before I die. What I live for is the tension between knowing what I need and satisfying that need. It's tension that makes my life seem rich. Usually satisfying a tension means I'm not aiming high enough.

Come to think of it, I just touched on a negative side to true happiness. It's something like complacency, an assumption that all will be well soon. You can't monitor anything when you're at true peace, which means you would be beyond managing a relationship. I would have to give up Marla to feel such peace, and I would rather live in hell—

I've come full circle. My definition of heaven is hell. I would rather live in hell than be without Marla. Or rather, heaven without Marla would be hell.

I awoke falling toward the street. At first it was like a dream, but my palms on the cold pavement told me it was real and woke me to the moment. I saw a pair of black, polished shoes and the dark, smooth material of pant cuffs—someone was standing over me. I had dozed off, probably leaning against the door of his car, which he had just now yanked open.

He said, "What do you think you're doing?"

"Wait." I groped for the steering wheel to pull myself back into a sitting position. When I got there, I let go of the wheel because it wasn't mine. I was afraid to look anywhere but at the speedometer. "I fell asleep."

"You don't just fall asleep in someone else's car." He was working himself up, starting to yell. "Is this about drugs? Am I going to find a needle in there?"

"No, not drugs."

"Get out of my car!" He didn't seem to realize that he was standing in my way. "Do you want me to call the cops?"

"No, please. I—"

"I said, do you *want* me to call the *cops*?"

"No, really, I don't." It was well past daybreak. He was probably heading to work when he found me here, snoring away.

He said, "You have a count of two. One . . ."

I started to step out, and he gave me room. He could have decked me, but I didn't care. He wasn't all that big, and in his white shirt and tie coordinating with his charcoal slacks and shiny black shoes, he didn't seem like the kind of guy who would turn loose here. No matter what he did, I decided not to fight back. I slowly sidestepped so that we weren't nose to nose. He pointed at the Camry, but he was still glaring at me.

"And you blocked yourself in!"

"What?"

"You couldn't have stolen it anyway—you blocked yourself in!"

"I wasn't trying to steal it."

"Then what were you trying to do? This isn't a park bench! It's not a bus station or a halfway house—what were you trying to do?" He was still yelling, but I started to sense that it was because he was afraid . . . or perhaps not afraid but on unfamiliar turf and not wanting to give me a chance to escalate. I saw an opening to knock him aside and run for my car, but I was determined to take my lumps. It was like the need to view the wreck of the Celebrity. I had created a debt of some sort, and if I didn't repay it now, I might pay for it for the rest of my life.

But how could I respond to this guy in any way that made sense and alleviate the tension between us? No truth, no lie, however short or long, would satisfy his question. "I don't know what I was doing, but I wasn't trying to steal your car."

"Maybe you were trading. Is *that* one stolen? Are you laundering *cars*?"

"No, it's mine." Now all he had to do was ask me to prove it, and he would have the papers to the Camry, giving him the same information I'd had on Larry Hood. The parallels were clear, and probably not accidental. I believe we create such parallels subconsciously.

I said, "Look, I used to live here. Marla and me, we lived here for our first year. She planted all these . . . everything you see in your yard, my wife planted."

"What does that have to do with you getting into my car?"

I wanted to talk about the house, and our past, but had to pull myself away. I said, "It was unlocked."

He glared at me.

I said, "I don't know why. I don't know what else to say. I'm tired, but I can't sleep. I was driving around; I used to live here; your car was unlocked; I woke up behind the wheel. I don't know anything else. Do whatever you want."

He said, "Okay, okay, but look, you scared my wife, which *really* pisses me off. She's pregnant and doesn't need to look out the bathroom window and see someone stealing our car. Whether you were or weren't doesn't matter; it's what she saw. You're lucky I didn't let her call the cops." He looked back toward his house, held the look for a moment, then gave an "it's under control" wave. I fought the urge to look toward the window; it was a private exchange, and I had squandered my right to intrude.

He turned back. "What would you think if you looked out the window and saw someone in your car?"

"I know," I said. "I'm sorry. I'm messed up right now."

He said, "That I believe. You obviously need some kind of help. Start with some sleep."

I gave a halfhearted chuckle. He tensed a little.

"'Sleep,'" I said. "I don't know what that word means anymore."

"You were sawing logs when I found you just now."

"Another mystery. The only way I get any sleep is behind the wheel of some car. And I guess it doesn't have to be mine."

"Well, the experiment is over. Take your problems somewhere else. You don't live here anymore."

When I pulled up in front of our house, I saw Marla in the bedroom window. I tried to prepare myself for whatever she was about to throw at me and went upstairs to make it easier for her. She was fully dressed, seated at the edge of the bed, waiting for me. I had no choice but to remain standing. It was going to be bad.

"Where have you been?" It was a demand, not a question, and she didn't let me reply. "You overslept, didn't you? Wherever you were, *whom*ever you were with, you overslept and got home too late to lie about it."

"There isn't anyone else. Last night, I couldn't get to sleep—"

"You couldn't wait to get out of here, you mean. You sneaked into the guest room to make sure I was asleep, and then you sneaked out of the house and drove off. Where did you go? Where do you *usually* go?"

"Usually?"

"Stacks said you're doing this every night. Is she wrong?"

"Stacks? What does she—"

"She's seen you. She said it's almost every night."

"Why didn't you say something before?"

"Oh, no—don't you *dare* try to switch the blame to me! Last night was the first I knew about it, but even if it hadn't been, it would *never* be my responsibility to bring this up first. I came out and watched you drive away, and she came out and told me, and that's what really steams my clams. I don't know what's she's up to over there—drinking gin and surfing porn, I imagine—but she stood there and said," here Marla went into her ditzy-blond bit, "'That's quite a habit he's got himself into. I hope it's not some floozy, but with men you can never tell. Especially at *his* age!' You're lucky she didn't see you steal the truck that night."

"No floozies. I've being driving around is all."

"No, that isn't all! Sneaking out on me is a lie—you're lying just by doing it! And you're telling another lie by pretending you don't know the first is a lie. That's two lies before you've even opened your mouth. You're hiding some strange truth in a storm of lies and truths and half lies and three-quarter truths, and it's up to me to sort through it all, and I don't have the energy."

"I think I can explain—"

"Explain? Every night you sneaked out, you had a chance to explain. You could've decided to stay and talk to your wife about why you felt this need, this *compulsion* . . ." I started to respond, but she jumped back in. "*And* I'm giving you a chance now. So explain. Please, Jim, I'd like to hear it. Why are you sneaking out on me?"

"What woke me last night was a gunshot—now I'm thinking I dreamed it—but I went down to the guest room to see if you heard it too. I was quiet because I didn't want to wake you up. Which obviously didn't work. Then I checked the windows downstairs and took a walk around the outside of the house . . . look, there is no one else. And I'm not *looking* for anyone else either." As if it were a list, I said, "I thought I heard a gunshot, I couldn't sleep, I went for a drive, and yes, I fell asleep—but it was . . . the car was parked, and I was alone."

"You just pulled over and fell asleep."

"Yes."

"You're keeping something from me."

I could tell her about the parked car I'd crawled into, but this would prompt more questions, some of which I wouldn't be able to answer. I had developed a secret life with secret forces that were beyond my understanding, let alone my ability to explain. She sat there watching me until she finally said, "Forget it. I've already made up my mind, and I don't want you to change it." She paused but held up a hand to say she wasn't through. "I called Dave last night after you left. I thought there was a chance he knew something that I didn't, my husband and my brother out shooting pool and drinking beer. He called back about an hour ago to see how I was, and the phone just about sent me through the roof. I thought it might be the cops, the coroner—all night my mind was filled with suspicions and doubts that I wasn't aware of, and the phone turned them loose. You don't want to know what's in my head right now."

This was when I saw that I shouldn't try to win this fight. I didn't know why, but however it turned out, I needed to let her do what she felt she needed to do. I didn't want anything artificial to come out of this. No false intentions, no lies, no manipulations.

"I know I've been odd. Ever since that accident I've been sleeping poorly. I keep dreaming about the impact, and for some reason driving around is the only thing that gets me tired enough to sleep."

"I don't believe you."

"I know. That's okay."

"I mean, yes, I believe you about that part. That's the easy part because it doesn't matter. But you're still keeping something from me, and you're telling me the truth about this in order to avoid telling me what's really going on. Hiding a larger truth behind a lesser one is a lie too. If it's not another woman, what's the big deal? Aren't I going to find out about it anyway? I mean, if we're a couple, won't I find out? And if I don't, isn't that worse? For us, I mean. I'm thinking about us."

I felt the slightest relief. If she believed me about not seeing another woman, it left me a couple ways to—

"See?" she said. "Right there you're trying to figure out what to say. There was a time you would answer no matter how peculiar or complicated it was." She studied me.

I let her. I looked away, out the window to the street beyond, where our Camry sat, where this whole thing had started. I had made a mistake in judgment, and it just kept going, rolling into a larger and larger ball, and I was in the middle of it, tumbling out of control. I still wasn't sure if I had caused it or reacted poorly to it, or if it had simply happened. But now a man was dead, and Marla was furious with me—it felt like she was leaving forever. I decided that if she asked me specifically, or if she guessed any part of what was going on, I would explain it all, try to unravel it in such a way that it would make sense to both of us, however long it took. I started to weigh what might happen if I were to say the wreck on the freeway wasn't an accident, but she said, "I'm going to give you a chance to think about it. I'm going over to Dave's house. You can figure out how to tell me what's going on or learn how to live alone. Like you're doing now anyway."

"Dave's?"

"I'm not about to move back to Alabama over this."

Alabama. At least she had retained something of her sense of humor. Her folks lived two hours north in a rural, Republican town where the people drove either very old or very new domestic trucks with flags and flag decals and the men wore baseball hats with feed-store logos. She referred to this town as the state of Alabama.

She said, "This is not a separation, Jim, except separating me from the phone. When those two thieves tried to steal our car, you left me alone and went out and did some things that still don't make sense. And now you're doing it again, going out again, and all I'm left with is that damn phone. I want to be clear about this: I'm not leaving town. I'm certainly not leaving my job—those are my *kids*! I'm not even leaving you. But if you're going to roam the streets in the middle of the night, I don't want to know about it. If you end up in jail and they give you that one phone call, I don't want to have to answer and then go down to bail you out. Or to the morgue and have them show me your body. And me see your chicken moles and say, 'Yup, that's him.'" She was crying now. "'That's my husband. How did he die?'"

I have four moles on my right shoulder. She'd once said they form a perfect one-inch square, except it leans. I had laughed and said, "You can't have the words *perfect square* followed by the word *except*. A chicken is a perfect square except." And she'd said, "My point exactly. Look at the constellations, the one called Leo Minor. Three stars. It's a triangle. If three points can be a lion, four can be a chicken. You have chicken moles."

That's how we used to argue. That's as bad as it got.

She said, "Are you listening to me? This is not a kid's game. You can't just go off into the night without letting the person you're living with know what's going on." She sniffled and wiped her eyes with the heel of her hand. "It's a rule, Jim. You have to learn the rules. And then you have to follow them."

"I know."

"I'm not so sure." She collected herself. "Anyway, Dave agreed. I'll stay with him, and he'll answer the phone. He'll talk to the cops, or the coroner, and he'll talk to you. I don't know if he'll have a beer with you, but if so maybe you can get drunk and spill your secrets. Maybe you can word it in such a way that he'll understand it, and he can translate it for me. I didn't think I'd *ever* be glad we lost Brian. Congratulations."

That one went into my heart like a knife. I sat on the bed and waited for her to finish me off. I heard a car pull up. Marla said, "Get some sleep, get some therapy, but get this figured out!" She got down on one knee and studied my face for a moment. "See, right now I can't tell if you know I'm even here." She brought her face within ten inches of mine and spoke as if I were still a long way in there behind my eyes (which I was, a tiny figure at the far end of a dark corridor). She said, "Figure this out. Do you hear me? Find someone you can talk to—I think you need that. But not Stacks. If you let that woman—"

"Don't worry. She's got nothing I want."

She remained face-to-face with me and said, "Are you pretending you have control over *any* of this?"

When Dave knocked on the door, Marla said to me, "You stay here." She went downstairs, and I fell back on the bed and listened as they put her things into his car and drove away. Then I got tired, the way I used to in high school when my hormonal wars were at their height, when on weekends I slept fourteen hours at a stretch. I grew four inches that year. I had always looked back on that period as my final incubation, but here I was again, tucking back into myself, preparing for some new emergence.

As I lay there on the bed I felt her presence fade. She was doing what she had to do, and it was the right thing. And letting her go was the right thing for me to do, which I was sure she felt, which in turn must have fed her desire to leave. I couldn't even try to appreciate how distant I had become, I was so deeply woven into my cocoon.

 don't remember the weekend, the hollow days. I thought about Marla constantly, but I didn't worry about her, if that makes sense. Perhaps the only downside to her situation was a longer bike ride to and from work and a longer walk to a bus stop on rainy days, either of which she would happily endure if the person she was living with stayed home at night, behaved predictably, didn't try to hide anything. And, as she pointed out, she wouldn't be waiting for the phone to ring during the small hours, when the news couldn't be good.

I did miss her in the general sense. I missed our life together, the kiss each morning to bring in a new day, a kiss last thing at night, and all the little things between those two priceless kisses. But when I thought about this, I saw how impossible it would be to just go back and restart that life. What I had to do now was deal with the mess I was in, and hope—no, not hope but actually *trust*—that she, and our life together, would be waiting for me. It was difficult to focus on the mess, but I knew if I didn't, the mess would begin to focus on me.

I thought about the difference between hope and trust. Hope is when you focus on the thing: *I hope it won't rain.* This is what you think as you stand at the window and study a darkening sky. Trust is when you focus on something else and let time and circumstances take care of the thing: *I trust it won't rain.* This is what you think as you go out to work in the garden instead of standing at the window staring at the sky.

The worst part about her leaving was the empty house. Single people should have pets just to keep the echoes down. On the other hand, the empty house allowed me to stretch out in a way that I hadn't been able to for a while. I still had the hardest time getting to sleep, but I didn't drive around every night out of restlessness; I could now pace at home. To do so, though, I had to either turn on the radio or rent movies. I tried commercial TV but ended up skipping from channel to channel like a stone over the surface of those insipid shows. Recorded music, even jazz and classical, was impossible. I needed sound from somewhere other than my own brain, but I also needed it to be unfamiliar. There's a clinical term for this, I believe, when a person needs to constantly process new material to keep his head from exploding. Foreign films were the best because they didn't have patterns I could detect. They had to be dubbed, however, because I didn't have patience for subtitles. Dubbing removed a lot of the emotion from the voices—a lot of the *quality*—but it did leave the story intact, which was what I wanted, a story other than my own to think about. If a person can be obsessed with maintaining an absence of focus, this may be the best way to describe my state of mind.

At the Deli on Monday John asked about the book of poems he had lent me, and I said I had cracked it now and then but hadn't been able to immerse myself. He told me to hang on to it and said he thought I seemed better. He knew Marla had moved out, and, being naturally supportive, he tended toward a positive slant on things. He trusted that I wasn't the bad guy, and I think he trusted that Marla wasn't either, and this alone went a long way toward making life at the Deli generally tolerable. It seemed to have been months earlier that Larry Hood had come in to let me know it wasn't over with him.

Just seeing Marla in her pregnant reverie should have made me happy. And I suppose it did, but it was a qualified happiness. With it came a sense that if I were to leave, she wouldn't notice my absence with anything more than a vague curiosity. It wasn't overwhelming, this feeling of being left out—in fact, it was still part of my pastel mood— but it was there. Her emotional priorities had changed. The kids she taught were still wonderful, but they weren't hers, and weren't part of her reverie either. They were now simply part of the maintenance side of her life, along with eating and sleeping and paying bills and shopping for dinner. And me.

Don't get me wrong; there was warmth between us. We still snuggled, still worked the Sunday *Times* crossword puzzle together on the couch after breakfast, still talked through the spectrum of domestic conversations without bickering the way some couples do when they have come to take each other for granted. She never made me feel unwelcome, but then again, she never made the garlic press feel unwelcome either. It would be right there in its drawer whenever she needed it.

At times I felt that if I hadn't been trying to make the relationship work, it would have disintegrated like an ancient book turning to dust, all that information and emotion and effort lost forever, and we would have found ourselves standing there turning into total strangers, confused as to how to walk away from each other.

She would deny it, of course, and she would be right. Obviously I was a huge part of her world. She wouldn't have tried to start a family with just anyone, or by herself, and if I had suddenly disappeared, she would have been devastated. It was simply that now, perhaps from genetic necessity, all of her arrows were pointing inward. And to participate, I had to turn my arrows toward her.

One evening a few days after Marla moved out, I was lying on the couch when the phone rang, dragging me out of whatever internal stare-down I was having with the bleak landscapes of limbo. The handset was on the coffee table, within reach. It rang again, and I looked at it, thinking there was no one I wanted to talk to. Even if I had found the energy to get caller ID, as Rainey had suggested, I wouldn't have had the energy to get up now and go look at the little gizmo. I would have preferred slipping back into my trance, but instead I worked through a mental list of who might be on the other end. Marla occurred to me first, not because she was the most likely to be calling but because she was the most important person in my life. I still hadn't figured out how I might explain my behavior to her, and I didn't think she should be back in the house until my pacing had settled, until I knew how to talk to her about Larry Hood. Rainey was on the list because I couldn't imagine any news from him being good. It occurred to me that it might be the other Hood brother, Wade—Rainey's warning had penetrated at least this far—but with his warning had come the assertion that Wade wasn't very bright, so it didn't make sense that he would use the phone as a means of stalking me. The fourth ring came before I could think of anyone else, and the answering machine always kicked in on the fifth, so I picked up—I guess it's what you do when you're trying to be in control but not clear on what you're trying to be in control of.

"Jim?" It was Marla's brother. It took me a second to realize I was okay with this. In fact, I was relieved; he could act as our intermediary.

I said, "Dave. What's up?"

"The real question is, what's up with you?" His tone was sharp, not the tone of an intermediary.

I said, "What do you mean?"

"The midnight prowling. Marla says you sneak out of the house at night, and one night you came home after breakfast. You got something on the side?"

"No, I'm just driving. I can't seem to—"

"That's what she said you'd say. It doesn't mean anything."

"I know. But most of it is so—"

"You're sleeping better, I bet."

"Not really." Actually, I was, to some degree, but didn't want to admit it.

"Where do you go?"

"Different places. Mostly I just park and sit—" He started to say something, but I cut him off. "Dave, please. Don't attack me like this."

"I'm not attacking. You should see me when I'm attacking."

"You aren't giving me a chance to answer. I'm not hiding anything from you, and I'm not lying, but you're not letting . . ."

He wasn't listening to me but instead to a voice in the background. Then he said, "I don't know why she's defending you, but she says I'm attacking. So let's try again." He waited, and I waited, and then he said, "Okay?"

"She's listening?"

"She asked if I minded, and I said why not."

"I suppose she told you about the two guys who tried to steal our car."

"Yeah, and you stole their truck instead. Great move, by the way. I can't believe you wrecked it."

"Great move?" I couldn't tell whether this was a compliment or sarcasm.

"It's the only part I understand. You see the opening, and now you're in the truck, hitting the gas with the bad guys behind you, and now the cops are coming—it's getting all gnarly—it's perfect! Then piling it into a ditch makes total sense. I would've been jumping on the hood, howling my head off. She disagrees with me, by the way—she's shaking her head right now, thinks I'm a galoot. But trust me, man, it's brilliant." Then he said, "Hold on."

I waited, hearing Marla's voice in the background.

Then he said, "I guess we belong in the zoo together."

I said, "Can you get a little privacy? There's more, and I don't want her cutting in or distracting you from it. You can tell her later."

"Okay, sure." I heard him put his hand over the mouthpiece, which muffled the next thing he said, and her reply. Then I heard a distant clunk of a door closing.

He said, "She's gone."

"Is she mad?"

"No, I think she expected it. Go ahead."

"I suppose she told you about the wreck too."

"Yeah, you wrecked the truck. I just said that."

"No, the wreck on the freeway."

"She didn't say anything about a freeway."

"There was a wreck on the freeway. I was right there, fifteen feet away. This car ran into a stalled van at full speed, and the driver died.

Like I said, I was right there, and I keep replaying the sound of the crash. I hear it when I start to go to sleep, and then I'm wide awake again."

"I don't get it. What's the big deal?"

"But you're still with me?"

"I think so."

"Okay. So the owner of the truck? The one I took and wrecked?"

"What about it?"

"Him, not the truck. I'm talking about the guy."

"Got it. What about the owner of the truck?"

"He's the same guy in the wreck on the freeway."

"The guy who died."

"Same guy."

He said, "Wait. The guy who tried to steal your car—and you drove off in his truck—*that's* the guy who died in a wreck on the freeway?"

"And I was right there."

After a silence he said, "You lost me again."

"I'm not telling it very well."

He said, "First, how do you know it was the same guy?"

"A cop told me. The cop who was here when they broke into our car—"

"The same cop too?"

"Not exactly. He wasn't at the wreck. He knew about it and wanted to inform me that the guy was dead. This cop is one of the good ones, by the way. Rainey. He's trying to help me through whatever mess I'm in."

"Sure." He still sounded puzzled, as if he thought he had all the pieces but couldn't quite fit them together. He said, "I can see how a guy might lose sleep over that."

"There's more."

"Great. My head is already full."

"When the wreck happened, I knew who it was."

"Right. This cop Rainey told you."

"He did. But it was more of a verification. I already knew."

"You recognized him?"

"Yes." This was a version of the truth—I didn't want to go into the complications of getting the address from the truck's registration papers, finding the Celebrity at the address on the papers, the driver of the Celebrity coming into the Deli . . . it was almost too much for me to hold at one time, let alone explain to someone else.

"I saw him in the rearview mirror just before the freeway on-ramp."

"I think I'm with you. I think I'm there."

"I played it cool, acted normal, but when we got into freeway traffic, I hit the gas and tried to lose him. He kept on my tail, and for a while there it felt like he was trying to run me off the road. At one point I got onto the shoulder and started to pass this one truck, and there was a van on the shoulder."

Dave was silent.

I said, "I swerved, and he didn't."

"Boom."

"That's the sound that's keeping me up at night."

"Wow."

I didn't say anything.

"Give me a minute here."

"Sure." I waited.

Finally he said, "And Marla doesn't know any of this."

"Nope."

"And you don't want her to know?"

"What I don't want is for her to think I intentionally killed someone."

"She wouldn't."

"I'm not so sure."

"No, I'm saying it's a fact: You didn't kill him. He did it to himself. Were there any witnesses? Do the cops know? You mentioned this guy Rainey."

"I'm clean with the cops. Rainey has no idea that I was at the scene."

"There you go. Slam dunk."

"Look. Just because I got away with it doesn't mean I didn't do it."

"He was chasing you. Or maybe you haven't told me the whole story?"

"No, that's pretty much it. He was chasing, I was trying to get away, there wasn't any contact between the cars, I missed the van and he didn't."

"See, I think you're in the clear."

"I still can't sleep. Don't forget, that's what we're really talking about, the fact that I can't sleep. It's why Marla is at your place and I'm driving around at night."

"Okay, I can see why you're losing sleep. And why you haven't told her. Which gets me back to what she said when she left the room just now. She wants you to tell her everything. In writing."

"Why? Did she hire a lawyer?"

"No, she just wants you to be . . . *lucid* was the word she used. She said you haven't been lucid these past few days. She's not in a hurry, but let's face it, she can't stay here forever."

"Loud and clear."

"So should I tell her any of this now? I mean, if she asks. I don't want to lie to her, but I will if you need me to."

"No, that's okay. It looks like she's going to hear it anyway."

When I did any late-night wandering, I headed out around midnight or one and didn't get home until five, having picked up a couple hours of sleep while parked. Mostly I would sit in front of Arlene's with the car doors locked and work on a crossword puzzle until I was drowsy enough to doze. The same cop who'd woken me that first night tapped on my window to talk once more, but then—I guess trusting that I wasn't up to anything illegal—just let me be. I began to feel invisible in a good way, but I think what really happened was that I had become an accepted presence, sitting in the Camry and observing as if I were a private eye on a case having nothing to do with anyone who happened to notice me. Whatever these people thought about me was fine as long as they didn't take it personally. If it kept them from bothering me, they could assume I was some poor bastard of an ex-husband keeping tabs on his stripper ex-wife. (In fact, had one of these people confronted me, I would have said, "My wife is in there right now with this loser.") The lower I was in their esteem, the more likely it was that they would think I was one of them.

To park I would circle the block as I had the first time, going through the intersection up from Arlene's, taking a right at the next block, then down and around past the theater before turning up 10th and crossing to the far side. I took this route because of the old hooker, who always bent and waved as I drove by. It was a big, friendly wave rather than one that beckoned, making me think she noticed every vehicle and had a backstory on all the drivers. *Blue-truck cowboy: always looks like he'll stop but never does.* A little later: *Acura girl: bar wait-*

ress just off work, looks me over, not judgmental. Then I drive by: *Camry guy: waves back, parks across from Arlene's now that I drove him off. What's his real story? Doesn't leave the car, can't stay away.* Except she wouldn't wonder what my real story was. Why would she unless she thought it might intersect with her own?

One evening—actually, it was about three in the morning—when I was looking back down the street toward the theater, I saw a car stop in front of her, idling in the No Parking stretch with its lights on. She stepped forward, the passenger door opened for her, and she ducked in. The car moved up the street toward me, and as they passed she put her arm behind the guy's headrest, waving to me with her fingers before burying them in his hair, with him looking straight ahead as he drove through the intersection and me waving back. I felt a connection, however small, a mutual reference. This hooker was my attachment to the planet now, the only person in the after-hours world who let me know I was alive.

After the bars had expelled their last customers—after the doors were locked and the CLOSED signs appeared in the bottom near corner of curtained windows—the last-call survivors found their cars or bikes and, with the strange care habitual drunks take at this hour, made their various ways out of the area. After these people were gone a different kind of people emerged. This was a tougher sort, less bound by rules, further removed from the structured world. I don't think many of them had a place to go home to. They left me alone, as the other sort did, but if I was awake around then I always re-checked to see that my doors were locked.

In our town the hinge between one day and the next is from three thirty to four thirty in the morning. Weekends might be different, but on weekdays, if it's before three thirty in the morning, you are still up from the night before. After four thirty you got up early for the coming day. Cars that aren't tracking quite as they should at four thirty have drivers who need more coffee, not less alcohol. This isn't a major insight; it's the kind of thing that comes to you when you consistently can't sleep through the hinge hours. It's the kind of insight that at the time seems to hold a major truth, and you write it on a scrap of paper, but it pales in the light of the following day. And throwing away the scrap of paper doesn't always rid you of the insight.

If I dozed through daybreak, commerce would begin around me, with diesel roars and the hiss of air brakes as deliveries were made to storefronts and service entrances of daylight businesses and the bowling jackets and baseball hats gave way to suits. I would turn in my seat to face front again, start the engine, and head home.

I didn't feel numb at the time, but I was. Sure, I was moving about, putting in my hours at work, going through the motions that define a conscious being, but there wasn't any volition in it. I had been in this automatic state since the incident with Larry Hood, and maybe even earlier.

A few months after we started trying to get pregnant again, Marla's period was late and she said it felt like the other time. I could see a guarded hope in her face that she might sustain this one, but two or three days later—even before we could get in to see Dr. Reese—her period came. It was thicker than usual. *Viscous* was the word she used.

I asked if she was okay.

"Oh, sure." She stood there for a moment, then said, "Well, shoot," as if she had overcooked the rice.

The next Saturday afternoon she was up in the bedroom for a little while, and I thought she might want me to join her for some lovemaking outside the fertility schedule. It was what she used to do on weekends before we were trying to get pregnant, go on up to bed, usually with a book, and when I came looking for her—often not sure what she was up to—the twinkle in her eye would say it all. This, I always thought, was our best sex, and the rest of the day would have a special warmth and coziness, whatever else we did.

When I went up, I found her sitting on the bed with her note-book and monthly charts and fertility thermometer. She didn't even look up. She said, "I can't do this anymore."

"You mentioned adoption a while back."

Her reply made it sound as if she'd thought it out and didn't want to walk me through the process: "No, I think I'm done. Let's call it a day."

That evening, as she was rinsing dishes, I came up from behind and slipped my arms around her middle and nuzzled her ear. Her only response was to stop working. She didn't tense up; she just stood there. I said it was okay, that I was fine with her decision. She nodded and set the pot she was working on in the sink. I leaned around to check for tears. Her face was dry. I wanted to say something else—anything to get her to talk to me—but I couldn't find the words. I was losing a part of her, and even as it receded I had no idea how to retrieve it, or even look for it.

We went to bed. I leaned over for our good-night kiss, which she held slightly longer than usual. When I pulled away, I looked at her, trying to understand what was going on—and trying to let her know I was just trying to understand. She made an effort to smile, which didn't help; she had always been pretty good about raising issues that were bugging her. The fact that she didn't say anything made me afraid to ask what was wrong. I gave her a second kiss and a soft "Good-night," then rolled away the way I usually did to sleep. She turned toward me and hugged me from behind for a while, and, in the quiet of the night, with her breath brushing the back of my neck, she said, "Please don't leave me, Jim. Promise you won't leave."

These were the hardest words I had ever heard. The odd thing was, I couldn't respond right away, and I couldn't bring myself to request the same of her. What do you say when you think your wife is preparing to leave you, and she doesn't even know it? It took an enormous effort to tell her not to worry, that I never would. When she stopped hugging me and slowly dropped off to sleep, it felt as if she would never hug me again.

Why didn't I ask what was wrong? I've thought long hours about this.

Imagine looking out your kitchen window and noticing that there aren't any birds in the garden. You realize it's been quite a while since you last saw birds there, and without them the entire yard seems dead. You're standing there with a sense of failure and loss when your wife enters the kitchen, and now you're worried that by pointing out the lack of birds you might impart to her the despair you're feeling. If she believes the birds will never come back, she might have no reason to continue working on the garden, to continue living in the house. Isn't it natural to keep it to yourself and figure out on your own how to get the birds back? If nothing else, not asking what's wrong might buy you a little time.

Stacks Ferguson came over once. This was in the evening, when most people were having dinner. I had eaten at the Deli and was waiting for the Japanese movie titled *Eat Drink Man Woman* to come on at eight, and there was her tap at the door. I opened it.

"Karen."

I didn't invite her in, but she came in anyway. She went to the middle of the living room and turned with her near arm raised to smooth back her hair, offering a view of her torso in profile. Then she turned to me.

"Jim, I'm being stalked. I don't know how else to say it. Someone is parking in front of our house on weeknights. It's usually late, and he just sits there. It's creepy to have a sex maniac probably watching me with binoculars. We have binoculars too, but I can't see into his car. It's a trashy little Mazda with tinted windows. Have you noticed it?"

"No, but I'll keep an eye out."

"And you know what a wimp Bruce is. He wouldn't lift a finger, even if I told him about it. Which is why I haven't. Knowing him, he would call the cops and then just sit back and let them do the dirty work."

"No cops?"

"Oh, Jim, you are so cute! The last thing we need is patrols cruising through here like it's a ghetto or something. Remember how it was when your car got broken into? I felt like I was on one of those reality crime shows where the TV audience sits at home making fun of people who are trying to keep from getting arrested."

I didn't know what to say to this, so I just waited for the next remark to drop from her brain like a fig and roll out of her mouth. She said, "At least he isn't stalking Marla, because I haven't seen her around."

"No, she's over at her brother's."

"I feel *awful* about that! I can't help but think I'm to blame."

"Thanks, Karen, but it wasn't you, I'm sure."

"She shouldn't have left. A wife shouldn't leave. It looks bad."

I wanted to be clear about Marla being blameless. I said, "No, actually, it was a good idea. The way I've been acting recently—pacing when I'm not at work, driving around at night—I was making us both crazy."

She looked confused for a second. "Well, I certainly have to admire you for being so honest. You said driving? Where do you go?"

"I just drive. I see a lot of the city." I almost missed an opportunity here and quickly added, "It's not someone else. I don't have it in me to cheat on her." I was hoping she would comprehend what I was really telling her and just go back across the street. I said, "I'm as faithful as an old hound."

"That's what I told her! I said, 'Jim wouldn't have an affair!' I hope she believed me."

"I think she did." I tried to steer her toward the door, and she let me.

"Well, I certainly hope so. And Jim," she turned and touched my chest with her finger, "you are *not* an old hound."

"Really, Karen, we'll manage."

I got her going again and had her almost to the threshold when she turned once more. I saw the contrivance of the move, but at the same time I had to admire it; she really did convince me that I was rid of her—and even when I saw it coming, she timed it perfectly and I stepped right into that rebuilt chest of hers.

"Well, excuse me, Jim! Darn these things!" She laughed and looked down, inviting me to look too (which I did), then got serious. "I want you to know, if you ever need someone to talk to about anything—or just share one of those wonderful wines you're probably always bringing home from work—I can . . . well, I have a good sympathetic ear. I would be happy to talk to you about anything at all."

"Thanks, Karen, I'll keep it in mind. But I'm sure we'll be fine."

As she headed back across Juniper I considered asking her to send that daughter of hers over with a sympathetic ear. Shelly's emerging sexuality was almost certainly what had sparked this woman's identity crisis in the first place. Marla had seen it coming, and we'd both been amazed at how accurate her prediction had been—that Karen would channel Shelly's libido and go a little crazy. The first item on the list had been to get those tired breasts refurbished. The competition was painful, how Karen flounced about in front of her daughter's boyfriends—with their own sexual urges exploding right then—followed by an act of outrage at Shelly's accusations. It was a competition neither could win.

On Monday evening I decided to go through the motions of an ordinary guy spending an ordinary evening alone. I thought it might be my first step toward returning to normal. I had the idea of getting started on a written explanation of my recent behavior for Marla. I might not get anything on paper, or even in pixels, but it wouldn't hurt to start thinking about it.

I fixed myself dinner rather than eat at the Deli before I got off work, because you can kill a good amount of time in the kitchen, even if it's just some fried chicken thighs, diced potatoes, and gravy made of what's left in the skillet. Brown dinner. I ate in front of the TV, watching the last half of *Casablanca*, the way an ordinary guy might.

I wished I had half the character of Bogart's character. But character isn't something you just go out and get. Actually, you go *in* to get it—you go deep. And the way you start is by doing the right thing, which I couldn't seem to do. I thought Rainey might have something to say, perhaps that along with adrenaline, you don't just *decide* to have character. I wondered what he would say to the idea of acting as if you had character—could this *instill* character? I was considering this notion when I heard a car idling down Juniper Street. It stopped, and the engine died. I waited for a door to open and close, but the night was silent. I looked out the front window, but other than the reflection of our living room in the glass, all I could see was the lighted living room of the Ferguson house. I went upstairs without turning on any lights. From our bedroom window, through the slats in the blinds, I saw the Mazda with the primer-gray fender, again parked on the far side of the street. No way was this guy stalking Stacks.

I took some clothes from a rocking chair in the corner and set them on the dresser, then situated the chair as far as I could from the window while still being able to sit in it and view the parked car. For a while nothing happened. Then I saw some smoke escape through the top of the driver's window, just as before.

What if I'm looking at Larry Hood's brother? I tried to develop this notion, to work it into a course of action. If that really was Wade, he could go nonboring on me, and I would be helpless. If that was Wade, he was waiting for something to tell him it was time. But time for what? These thoughts came in low tones, almost as casual observations. What would Bogart do here? Then I thought, *He would follow the script.* The real question was: What would Bogart's *character* do? Then I went a level deeper: Obviously Bogart's character would follow the script too, which would have him confront the figure in the car and live long enough to deal with the information. The main character in a Bogart movie doesn't die midway, and, more important, he behaves as if he knows this. Which is mistaken for toughness. The randomness of real life doesn't come through in the old movies. Noble action comes through, but you're always aware that a script is being followed. I had no script here, no clear course of action. I wanted to go out and talk to this guy, but I also wanted it to be someone other than Wade Hood.

I *hoped* it was just some kid who was out tooling around, pausing here to smoke a few cigarettes and drink some of his dad's beers. Or some other kid—male or female—waiting for one of the neighbor kids to sneak out of the house and hop in, as they had arranged between classes at school. Three kids on our block might have set up such a rendezvous. But then, for all I knew, this was one of Rainey's men, or Rainey himself, keeping an eye on me. Except Rainey didn't smoke.

But it might be Wade, and if so, he is stalking you! I sat there and tried to assume that it was Wade. The smoke continued to slide through the gap in the window, and after twenty minutes the door opened and a hand rolled an empty can beneath the car.

I tried to imagine what he was thinking. I did this not by reasoning through it but by sitting in the dark bedroom and watching him. I thought he might not be thinking anything, just staring at our house the way some people stare at a waterfall, or a fire through the woodstove door. The way I had been staring at my life recently.

I recalled sitting in John's car and looking at Larry Hood's Celebrity, parked at the address on the truck papers. *If that is Wade Hood out there, he's waiting to kill you.* But it was no good. The words were coming to me in Rainey's voice instead of my own. I repeated them over and over but couldn't make them sound real.

I jerked awake to the sound of an engine starting and almost fell out of the rocker. I watched the car roll away. A slight blue haze of smoke in the empty space remained, and six aluminum cans rested near the curb. It was four in the morning on Tuesday.

fter work that evening I sat at home and listened for the Mazda. After a couple of hours during which nothing happened, I realized there was a tension in the waiting, another in the watching, and neither were tensions that would do me any good. It was like waiting for a briefcase to explode. It doesn't matter if there's a bomb in it, or just a stack of papers from the office; at some point you just want to get it over with—the tension seems worse than the explosion might be. If the Mazda guy did show again, I was afraid I really would go out and confront him, which, from this safe remove, seemed just plain stupid.

Instead I locked the house and drove down to Arlene's, taking my usual route around the block past the theater. The old hooker pointed as if to acknowledge that I was unusually early. I waved the way I always did, then parked across from Arlene's on 10th, in the first space after the intersection with Washington. I locked my door and sat so that my back was against the door and my feet were on the passenger seat. The slowly turning red light was out the rear passenger window, and the theater was out the back, a couple of hundred feet down the street. I saw the old hooker come out to the sidewalk for a moment, as if to verify that I was settled in, then stroll back under the marquee and out of sight.

The usual number of pedestrians moved up and down the sidewalks. Maybe they were the same individuals I had seen the other nights; I couldn't say. They were faceless to me, remote particles of a general fog of humanity drifting the streets. I remember thinking that perhaps even in winter these people held to their routines, that this level of society might be just as patterned as any. And I wondered if my noticing meant I was prejudiced in a way I hadn't been aware of before. It was an elitist inquiry, wondering in what different ways these night people resembled normal people. But even the homeless have patterns, as I knew from dealing with them in front of the Deli, urging them to move on down the sidewalk so they wouldn't keep our more timid customers from entering. Off they would go, with their shopping carts and their black plastic bags of belongings. They usually came from the same direction and around the same time of day, so yes, they kept to a schedule of sorts. I wanted to be above such musings, above wondering what separated me from them, them from regular people, regular people from me.

Then I took a mental step back and mused on the musings one has when one's life is off course, when one is headed down what seems like a one-way, dead-end street, when one is slowly becoming one of the night people.

Suddenly a man's face peered through the windshield, asking what time it was, his voice muffled by the glass.

He had a tight black stocking cap covering even his eyebrows and ears. His eyes were small and darting, but somehow they never left mine, and his hands were also in constant motion. As a kid he probably had people always asking if he had to go to the bathroom. His whole body seemed to be anticipating something violent, a blow from behind perhaps. His intensity implied that he would beat the tar out of the next person who asked if he had to go to the bathroom.

I lowered my window a crack. He came around to the door and squatted until he was at eye level. He asked again for the time. Our voices had to arc to clear the slightly opened window. I looked at my watch and said, "About ten thirty." As I looked up again, I verified that my door was locked.

He glanced past me without pointing. "You ever go in?"

"To Arlene's? No."

"They got some nice ladies."

"I can imagine."

"But you're staying out here. Just sitting in your car."

"For now."

"Kind of faggoty, isn't it?"

I didn't say anything, hoping this would compel him to leave.

He said, "What if I buy you a beer?" His hands opened and closed.

"Thanks, but the last thing I need is a beer."

"Coffee?"

"Actually, coffee is the last thing I need. Then beer."

"Seems like you just don't want anything I have to offer."

"No, I just don't want anything period. Except to sit here."

He frowned. "What if I gave you a hundred bucks to get out of the car?"

"Thanks, but I think I'm just going to sit." I adjusted the rearview mirror, as if it needed it.

He said, "For now."

Again I didn't reply.

"Are you telling me to fuck off?"

"No, nothing like that." I tried to shrug casually. "I'm just tired. Nothing sounds good."

He thought for a moment, then said, "What's the point?"

"Of what?" I looked straight ahead, relieved that the window was between us. The keys were in the ignition. Doors locked.

He said, "Staying out here. Just sitting in your car."

"I'm thinking. Trying to figure out some stuff."

"Sort of like confession, isn't it?"

I shrugged again, trying not to appear confused, but it was a weirdly penetrating question. I got queasy, as if I'd eaten some bad food. *Sort of like confession.* Given the entire exchange, how could this remark be the one that seemed threatening? He put a hand on the car door and pushed himself upright. Without watching, I could feel him looking down at me through the cracked-open window.

When I risked looking back, he said, "Drive safe." Then he winked like a used-car salesman and headed back down the block. I watched him in my side mirror. He stopped, looked back up the sidewalk, then opened a car door and got in. I turned to look through the passenger-door mirror. Headlights came on, and a little foreign beater pulled out and headed up the street, leaving a familiar haze of blue smoke. It was the Mazda I had seen parked in front of our house, now being driven by the guy who had just asked me about confession. In the better lighting here I could see that the car had an unbelievably bad paint job, with overspray on all of the chrome and glass, including the headlights—no part of the vehicle caught light. Then I realized that this was intentional; it was all about stealth. As he passed my car this guy reached out his open window and pointed as if his hand were a pistol, his thumb the hammer. Without a ghost of a smile, he pulled the imaginary trigger, and the mimed hammer fell. He ran the red light at the intersection and continued up 10th at a steady pace until he was gone.

I got out of my car and looked up the street, trying to figure out what had just happened. This was the guy who had been staking me out. I was down here in part because I was trying to avoid him, yet here he was anyway.

We weren't in any kind of holding pattern. A holding pattern is stable, except for perhaps a decay factor. This was more of a pressurization. He and I were like a paper cup filled with vinegar beside a paper cup filled with baking soda, both in a sealed jar: Nothing seemed to be happening, but it was not a stable condition. Part of what confused me was whether I should be hoping this guy was in fact Wade Hood or some new element in my night world, my strange new life. I tried to recall whether I had seen his face among those in the throw-downs but got nothing. Which didn't mean the face hadn't been there. No one had been wearing a stocking cap in the photos, and his agitation could never be captured by a camera.

Standing at the intersection, I glanced around to see if anyone was watching. Down the block, at the edge of the lighted tiles beneath the theater marquee, the old hooker was looking back. Without really thinking about what I was doing, I crossed the street and walked down the sidewalk toward her. She stood there and watched me approach.

She was shorter than I had judged from my car, but she had a large presence, a reminder that I was in her world, subject to her rules.

She said, "You never get out of your car—what brings you down the block now? Not my good looks." This remark shamed me because right then I was thinking that, under the fluorescent lighting, she looked even worse than I remembered. The way she looked back at me made me think she was reading my mind.

I said, "I might have a favor to ask."

"Ask away." She looked up and down the street and back to me.

I said, "You can say no or tell me you don't want to help, but please don't blow it out of proportion."

"The meter's running, honey. Don't make it look like you're trying to get a twofer here."

"What I might need is . . ." I didn't know how to finish.

She said, "Drugs? A set of golf clubs? Just come out with it. You're not a cop, I'm not a cop. We're just having a chat. A nice little curbside chat."

"I think I'm looking for a gun."

"Come on, honey, a gun? You're not the type." Then she shrugged. "So, who knows, that may work in your favor. Okay, you want a gun. Where else have you looked?"

"This is it."

"You thought of me first? How sweet."

"I know it's hard to believe—"

"No, that part's easy. Looking across the street at a broken old shoe like me is the closest you've been to the underworld. It's like staring at the door of Arlene's up there. It's where a guy like you enters. And you haven't been able to manage even a peek inside, so maybe this is your limit. Maybe talking to me is your limit. That places you, honey."

I put up my hands. "Okay, I get it. This was a mistake."

"No, don't. I shouldn't make fun of you. You're in a jam. Let's get back to the gun. Are you sure it's where you want to go? What about something safer, like cops or lawyers or, hell, even a priest?"

"I've talked to the cops. They can't help me. And lawyers and priests don't handle this sort of thing."

She laughed. "That's right. They come later." Then she said, "What sort of thing?"

"Actually, the reason I thought of you is that no one knows I've been here. This is outside the pattern of my life."

"News flash, honey—this *is* the pattern of your life. You're my new best friend."

"No, I mean until recently. The *known* pattern of my life. Which means it won't be traced from you to me. The gun, I mean. Or from me back to you."

"Sure. But what sort of thing?"

"These two guys tried to steal our car. My wife called the cops, and they caught them, put them in jail. They're brothers, and one of them—"

"Two black guys?"

"What? No, I mean from the same family. Two white guys. And a few days later one of them died in a car wreck, and the other one has been . . ." Even as I described it, I couldn't believe how sketchy it all sounded. "Well, he's showing up here and there, letting me know he's around. The cop who arrested them said this guy gets a little psycho. A little dangerous."

"Got it. The cops can't do anything unless he does something first, and whatever he does will have hair on it. And little puppy-dog you thinks a gun is going to help."

"I don't know what else to do."

"What does *she* think about all of this?"

"My wife? She doesn't know."

"Hold the *phone*, honey! What if he's at your place right now? What if he's opening the front door and she thinks it's you?"

"She's not there. She moved in with her brother a while ago. And this guy doesn't know where her brother lives."

"Ah. And there she stays until this is all over. That's good." She looked past me to the street and waved at a car cruising past. "Okay, so what kind of gun are we talking about?"

"Something reliable. It doesn't have to hold a lot of bullets. I need to hide it, but I want to be able to stop this guy if I have to."

"Okay, one cop gun, hold the relish."

"Maybe so. I don't know about guns."

"Me neither, but I might know a guy who might know a guy. I'm introducing you is all. Providing a connection for a friend in need."

"Well, thank you."

She looked at me for a moment. "I may have something tomorrow or the next day. Some information, that is. If you drive by and I have something, I'll give you a friendly wave like you just saw me give that Chrysler there. Like I usually give you. It won't do either one of us any good to have you keep coming over to talk to me. It'll look like we can't agree on a price."

"I'm not sure when I can be back."

"Whenever. Have cash on you, as much as you're willing to spend. But don't bring a bunch of little stuff. His amount won't end in a ninety-five. It'll be a nice round figure." She slapped her bony hip. "Like mine used to be."

Before work on Wednesday I drove over to our bank to withdraw five hundred dollars. Just inside the door a customer-service person said hello and gestured toward the only feature in the room, a chrome post holding a sign: "Please Wait Here." Suspended from the ceiling was a monitor with my face on the screen looking up. Being paranoid doesn't mean you're not being watched.

A teller called me forward and at my request counted out a stack of twenties. She packed them into an envelope and asked if there was anything else. Suddenly five hundred didn't seem like enough. The hooker had said to bring as much as I was willing to spend. I tried to remember any movie in which someone had bought a black-market gun. But I was afraid to call attention to myself by asking the teller to count out another stack of twenties. If five hundred turned out to be too little, I would have to come up with another plan. Back in the car I put the fat envelope in the glove box and took a long moment to study myself in the mirror. Every direction available to me now was a bad one.

Brian Cole would have been six at this time, tackling first grade, marching home with his little friends, then breaking off from the group and counting aloud the steps up to our house for his afternoon snack . . . when these images come to me I tighten up inside. After all these years it still feels fresh. If I have a glass of wine when I think about what we missed, and will continue to miss, I wallow in it.

Perhaps if we had adopted, if we now had some other little guy marching through the house, I wouldn't get maudlin and sentimental over our loss. I think this too, when I'm having even a single glass of wine. And I still get maudlin and sentimental. In short, I weep.

There are lots of reasons to have kids. When Marla and I decided to make our effort, it was because we loved each other and wanted to have a focus for, and a progression of, that love in our lives, for the rest of our lives. But I also believe that having a child because you accidentally got pregnant and didn't want an abortion—this can be fine too, depending on the atmosphere you provide for the child. Marla herself had been such an accident, and she'd turned out to be the most stable and happy person I've ever known. I think most reasons to have kids are good because they lead to loving households, which is what a kid really needs. On the other hand, no reason to have children is good enough to raise them in a cold or mean environment.

We had never talked it through, so all I have are impressions of why we didn't adopt. On my side of the question, I never came around to feeling right about the idea. I didn't want a replacement child, and I didn't want a diversion child to shield me from the pain of losing Brian. And because I overthink everything, I didn't want to raise a child who would sense any of this backstory and eventually come to feel that he or she was a replacement or diversion child . . . but it's all murky, this tangle of feelings and memories, and it gets worse when I dwell on it as I have here, even without wine. As always, when I work through this stuff, I realize that Marla's feelings may have been somewhere else entirely. She'd said she wanted to call it a day on the whole business, but there may have been more to her feelings than being wrung out. At that time I felt that we were fairly well aligned, but that doesn't mean we were. Losing Brian broke our hearts, and no heart breaks cleanly.

Stacks told Marla that we had jinxed ourselves by naming him before he was born. They were at a neighborhood meeting to organize a holiday food drive when she volunteered this brilliant insight. I don't go to those affairs, so I learned this after Marla got home and I asked how the meeting had gone.

I said, "That woman needs a slap."

Marla said, "Believe me, I was this close."

After we went up to bed and the lights were out—which was when we had our best conversations—I told her I shouldn't have said that about the slap.

She said, "Not to worry. I meant it when I said I was this close. That woman's mission in life is to make people want to slap her. She thinks that chest gives her a certain license."

"You have to admit, she does have the chest."

"Once they've been worked on, they're cans. The woman's got a set of cans."

"Well, thanks; now they're not even fun to think about." I rolled away in a pretend funk. She tucked in behind me, snaked her arms through mine, and hugged me, making sure I felt her small, perfect breasts pressing into my back.

We knew we hadn't jinxed anything by naming Brian Cole, but we also saw that it had set us up for a larger disappointment; it had given him more substance than he would otherwise have had. In fact, naming him had given him the most substance he would ever attain in life. On the other hand, it was such a sincere name, and came to us so spontaneously, that I don't see how we could have resisted.

Supposedly names impart qualities to the named. During that dark period after losing him, I looked up the two names *Brian* and *Cole* to see if they had special meaning. I guess I was hoping for something along the lines of "sensitive" or "shy," but no. Evidently Brian means "strong one," and Cole means "warrior."

"Strong warrior." What a joke. He couldn't survive the only event that everyone on the planet survived *by definition*: birth. He didn't *apply* himself (as I imagine the birth angel writing in the "comments" space of his report card). He didn't take the assignment of getting born seriously enough, didn't try hard enough when it really mattered, and so he was held back, wasn't allowed to graduate into the world.

All I remember of work was that I couldn't stop thinking about the gun, about how strange it was to be thinking about buying a gun. Marla wouldn't even have discussed it; a gun is never the solution. By definition, if you're thinking about guns, you're looking at the problem wrong.

Generally I would agree, but I don't have time to look at other options.

You're being stubborn.

He's the one who is stubborn, stalking me, showing himself the way he did, miming shooting me. I can't count on the same luck I had with Larry.

But you've closed your mind to other options.

Not if I'm still talking to you.

But she was right; I wasn't getting anywhere with this thinking. I tried to reason with myself, using Rainey's point of view, but I couldn't come up with anything beyond his warnings at the station that first night. I could imagine him saying a gun was only an escalation, but he also might say a gun was the only way I could protect myself in this particular situation. He would ask if I was sure it was Wade, to which I would have to say no but add that, given what he'd said in front of Arlene's and the fact that he was driving the same car that was parking outside our house at night, I was pretty sure.

But—and this is what really matters—are you sure he's out to kill you?

Of course not. But I want to be ready for him if he tries.

You have to be sure.

And while I'm figuring out how to be sure, he might kill me. As you said, the cops might know whom to pick up for the murder, but I would still be dead.

That's what I remember of work on Wednesday. When John walked me to the door, I had no idea what he was seeing in me, nor do I recall what I said. Given the way he nodded as he locked the door behind me, it must have been appropriate.

At home I was afraid to turn on the lights. I went through the house, pulling all the curtains and shades, but still left the lights out. Our kitchen, which faces the back yard, doesn't have curtains or shades, so anyone who happened to be prowling around in the yard could look right in.

It was about eight o'clock when I thought about Rainey again. I still had his number, and he had said to call at any time, and he was the only person I wanted to talk to, but I didn't know why I wanted to talk to him. I certainly couldn't tell him I was thinking about buying a gun, and I couldn't tell him Marla had left me because the way he picked up on things—especially if he got the timing right—might lead to the incident on the freeway . . . but the more I thought about it, the more I wanted to talk to Rainey. I may have simply wanted to hear in his voice that he still thought I was one of the good guys. He was a touchstone to my former life, my previous self.

Could I call him and keep it casual, just pass the time of day? I didn't know, but I dialed his home number.

A woman's voice answered, "Rainey residence."

"Is your husband there? Sergeant Rainey? I don't know his first name."

"Who is this, please?"

"Jim Sandusky."

"I'm sorry, who?"

"Jim Sandusky. I'm just a guy who—"

"Jim . . . oh, *that* Jim! I'm so dense. I'll get him."

"No hurry."

"No? Are you sure? Well, that's a relief! I'm Evelyn, by the way."

"Hi, Evelyn."

"Okay, I'll get him."

After a moment Rainey's voice said, "Hi, Jim. Ev tells me it's not urgent."

"Is this an okay time to call?"

"Anytime is okay, urgent or not. I've been wondering how you are."

I reminded myself to keep it casual. Casual was my *disposition*. "I wanted to thank you for helping me out, back when our car was broken into. For the advice."

"Just doing my job. Well, not really, but it had some twists that kept me interested."

His use of the past tense helped.

I said, "I didn't have any real reason to call except to say thanks."

"I'm glad it worked out. Everything else okay?"

I had a conflicted feeling that he was both offering a confidential ear and warning me that I probably shouldn't use it. I went with probably shouldn't use it. As I made this decision, I felt myself slip into a stream of inevitability, and the surface was already over my head.

I said, "Actually, things are about back to normal."

As soon as I hung up I went upstairs in the dark and looked out every window that provided a view to Juniper Street. There was no Mazda in sight.

I went out to the Camry and, taking a circuitous route and keeping an eye in my mirrors for the Mazda, headed down to the theater below Arlene's. I drove up 10th, keeping in the right-hand lane. As I approached the theater the old hooker leaned forward and gave me her friendly wave. I started to pull over to the curb, but she frowned and circled her hand behind her, which I took to mean she wanted me to give her a minute. I drove slowly up the street past Arlene's, then around the block and down to the corner of Porn Theater and 10th. When I got back, she was on a cell phone. She raised her free hand like a traffic cop, telling me to stop the car right there in the street. A moment later she put the phone in her coat pocket and came up to the passenger side. I reached over and unlocked the door. She opened it.

"I was just talking to your man. You're still interested?"

I nodded.

"Do you have two fifty?"

"All I have is twenties."

She said, "Doesn't come out even. Two sixty, then. Thirteen twenties. That'll take care of the bullets."

"Bullets?"

"I thought about it, honey. You're trying to hide your tracks. Buying bullets leaves tracks."

I didn't say anything.

She looked at me. "Why the long face? You're always so serious!"

"I'm trying to keep up."

She nodded. "I can see that."

I said, "How does it work? Do I give the money to you?"

"No, hold on to it. We don't want anyone to think you're cutting a sex deal here. *Especially* one for two sixty."

"Sorry. You can't know how weird this is for me."

"Honey, guys are constantly telling me how this or that is weird for them. What you do now is drive up one block past where you usually park, and pull over there, and just sit. Have the money ready and your window down. This guy will drop by in a little while and tell you what to do. Whatever you do, don't look back and give me a big thumbs-up. Don't get creative. Just sit there like you're afraid to do anything except follow instructions. There might be another guy watching. Don't worry about him, and don't look for him."

"Two sixty doesn't seem like much."

"I asked him to do you a favor."

"But why? We don't even know each other."

"You remind me of my son." She chuckled to herself. "No, I don't know why." She got serious. "But if this doesn't help, honey, I'm done with it."

"Sure."

"Okay, now go park your car the next block up from Arlene's. I really do hope it helps. Nice guys like you shouldn't be involved in this sort of thing. I'm Sally, by the way. Old Sal. Your man might ask."

I drove up the block and parked on the left side of the street. I pulled out the roll of bills, counted thirteen twenties into a stack, and put the rest back into the glove box. I counted the stack again, folded it twice to where it was about the size of a Tic Tac box, and held it in my left hand.

After fifteen minutes, in my passenger-door mirror I saw a guy cross the street behind me. It was then that I remembered to have my window down. The guy stopped, then withdrew into the doorway of a closed shop about thirty feet back and stood there with his hands in his pockets. He seemed unconcerned by anything and didn't once look in my direction. In fact, now that I think about it, he looked everywhere except toward me. I left the window down, playing the part of someone who was afraid to do anything except follow instructions.

A few minutes later, in my mirror I saw another guy cross the street and come up the sidewalk. When he was about even with the first guy, he called up the street, "Hey, do you know the city?"

I half turned, but not enough to see him. I faced forward again, trying to let him know that I didn't want to be able to identify him. He came up to my door and squatted so that his face was level with mine, not caring whether I could identify him or not. I inhaled slowly, half expecting to smell the cliché of whiskey, instead smelling the cliché of cigarettes.

He said, "I think we have a mutual friend."

I said, "Sally."

"If you have some paper for me, hold it out. I'll take it, then you point up the sidewalk like you're giving me directions. Don't make a big deal of it, just reach and touch the windshield with your finger."

His gloved hand appeared as I held out the folded bills. He took them and put them in his pocket as part of the same gesture. I pointed ahead as he had told me to and felt him look up the sidewalk, then back at me.

"Okay, put your hand down. Wait until I'm gone before you open your door. I put it in the gutter."

I nodded, but I didn't have a sense that he had dropped anything in the gutter. He stood and headed up the sidewalk. As I waited for him to turn the corner, I thought that at worst there would be no gun and I would be out the two sixty. It would also mean I had lost the old hooker as a resource. But then, according to her, I had lost her anyway. So it would be just the two sixty and back to square one. I made my peace with it. He turned the corner.

I opened my door, groped around in the gutter, and felt a heavy lump tightly wrapped in taped paper. It was heavier than I thought a pistol should be, but it definitely hadn't been there when I'd parked, so I had to trust that it was what I had paid for. I slid it beneath my seat and closed my door.

In my mirror I could see the other man still standing in the doorway. I tried to memorize his unconcerned demeanor and made a mental note to practice what I was seeing so that later, when I was carrying a gun, as I felt sure this guy was, I would be ready to switch from seeming relaxed to pulling a pistol, if things suddenly took a bad turn.

· · ·

At home I took our dish-washing gloves from the pan beneath the kitchen sink, then carried the brown paper package upstairs to our bedroom, where no one outside the house could see what I was doing. I put on the gloves, stripped away the packing tape that held the package together, and found myself looking at a revolver in a ziplock bag. It had "38 S.&W. special" stamped on its short barrel. I removed the gun from the bag and held it up to see if it was indeed loaded. I could see the brass rims of six cartridges.

I opened the cylinder to remove the bullets, then closed it again. I pulled on the trigger, but it wouldn't move. There was a little lever against the frame of the gun, which I clicked into a new position with my thumb. When I pulled the trigger again, the hammer rose backward and kept coming until it snapped forward with a good, solid click. Even the bullets were heavier than I expected. I held each to my ear and shook it. The powder granules inside made a soft, metallic rhythm. I put the bullets back into their holes in the cylinder, swung it shut, and returned the gun to the plastic bag. I put the bag beneath Marla's pillow, then went back downstairs to wash the dish-washing gloves and return them to the pan beneath the sink.

Finally I went back upstairs to lie down. Perchance to sleep. If only I could keep from dreaming.

I have a puzzling sense that my own effort to have a child was a mild form of salvation. Throughout our pregnancy I felt I was being saved by the promise of his arrival, and afterward I never lost this feeling by having lost him, so I don't understand the nuances. Perhaps we males develop a measure of guilt when we sexually mature and carry it until we have a kid, and even having tried to have children is enough to exonerate us from the relative irresponsibility of bachelorhood.

On Marla's side of the aftermath, I think that in the catacombs of her heart where she keeps her dark feelings, she felt that I had failed her because I had done nothing—could do nothing—to save our son. Maybe she blamed the universe, all of creation outside herself, and since I was a part of this universe—was its nearest representative—I took the hit. Who knows, maybe she blamed herself. Or felt no blame at all. Maybe I blamed myself for not having been able to do something to prevent this awful turn of events and saw in her crushed silence a reflection of my own accusations.

Anyway, we tried to have a child, we failed, and a part of us went dormant. But we got through it, got through the hard times, and eventually our look to the future shifted back to including just the two of us, though that phrase had replaced its feeling of intimacy with an element of disappointment.

One evening we went out with friends to dinner. We listened as they talked about the problems that come with raising a child. Even how difficult it was sometimes to find a good babysitter. The husband said, "It's the best and worst decision you will make in life."

His wife said, "Sweetie, not the worst."

He paused. "No, of course not. But you know what I mean."

"Oh, I do indeed."

While this was going on, Marla reached beneath the table and found my hand and squeezed. I looked over and saw tears in her eyes. But she smiled softly, and I knew we would be okay.

hursday morning the sky was overcast, the pavement wet. It had rained during the night without waking me. I looked at my nightstand clock and worked through some unfamiliar arithmetic; I had slept eleven hours without interruption for the first time since my teens, and it had been dreamless. I felt more a part of things in knowing that they could happen without my awareness, without my permission or instigation. Somehow this made me feel more in control, and control seemed more important than anything.

I took my first cup of coffee into the office, sat down at our computer, and, without pausing to think about what I wanted to say, wrote out a draft of the events leading up to Marla's departure. Basically I tried to explain my participation in a vehicular fatality on the freeway. It turned out to be a little under four pages, more of an outline, really, but it felt complete. I saved it as a document titled "The Incident" and shut off the computer.

When I looked at the clock, I almost fell out of my chair. I was late for work. I had spent four hours on those four pages, and it had felt more like twenty minutes. And it also felt like twenty pages.

I called the Deli and told John I was on my way.

"Take the day off if you need the sleep."

"No, I'll be right in. I was writing, lost track of time."

"Are you taking classes?"

"No, it's personal stuff."

When I got there, I asked if he had a minute. John always has a minute. We went into his office, and I asked if I could leave early that evening.

"Not a problem. You could have asked over the phone."

"I want to work a regular day but leave around dark."

"Is there anything you want to talk about?"

I told him about being one car away from a high-speed collision on the freeway. A guy had been killed.

"I remember. That was the day you were going out to Stebbins Hill."

"It's why I didn't make it. And why I started losing sleep."

"I believe we talked about phase shifts."

"Right. I still don't think it was phase shifts. Every time I started to doze off, no matter what time of night, I would hear the one vehicle slamming into the other, and it was like a gunshot. It got into my dreams. Last night was the first night in two weeks that I slept right on through."

"Do you know why?"

"Maybe. I think I might be past it, but I wanted you to know. It's been hard on Marla too."

"I hope she's okay. I really like her."

"I think she is. She's still over at her brother's place."

"I understand. I went through something similar. It takes time."

"What happened?"

"We don't need to go into mine either. It was military. Vietnam. It might've been different because there really was a gunshot—but in the end we're talking about the same thing. Just give it some time, have a little patience with yourself, and you'll be fine. Sometimes it's just a decision, sometimes a different angle of looking at things. Sometimes just breathing. If this was what you were working on this morning, you're on the right track. Healing is more important than being here on time. Where are you on that Rumi book?"

"I've been skipping around. I'm not much of a poetry guy."

"But you got a sense of it?"

"He seems to be telling me to calm down, which doesn't really help."

John said, "Think about what he had to go through to get some of those thoughts on the page."

"Isn't poetry the toughest form of writing? I read that somewhere, but it seems true."

"No, what I mean is, you don't get born into a loving home and an easy life and just start writing that stuff. It looks like wonder and joy, but that's where he got to, not where he came from. That poor bastard must have dug himself out of a basement."

That evening I kept being drawn to the bedroom window to see if the Mazda was back. In a way I did feel calmer, but I hated being cooped up, unable to go out and drive around. Having a choice would have made the wait easier. What I needed was an activity, a diversion. The draft of the written explanation to Marla was still in the computer. I thought I might go over it, change a few things if they needed it, and get it in the mail.

I couldn't get through the first page. It was as if a high school kid had reworked my four-hour effort into a poorly worded list of excuses and denials. Usually I save rough drafts in separate files so I can scavenge phrases and maybe some structure, but this was so bad that I dragged the whole document to the trash icon, then selected "Empty Trash" so I wouldn't be tempted to waste any more time on it. Not one pixel survived.

After opening a new document I centered the cursor and typed, "The Wreck." This seemed more honest than "The Incident." When I got going on the body of the piece, it flowed easily, the whole adventure taking on a kind of inevitable quality in which I felt almost helpless in my participation. I was well into it when the phone rang.

It was a little after ten, a little into the window of time when bad news becomes the most likely reason for the phone to ring. Caller ID would have been good, but the only time I ever thought about getting it was at night when the phone rang, after the phone company had gone home for the night. I decided to let the answering machine take the call but then weakened before it could. Marla's brother Dave was at the other end, unfriendly from the first.

"What's the deal, Jim?"

"What do you mean?"

"Don't give me that. I told you she wants to know what's going on, and she wants it in writing. You've had plenty of time."

"I was working on it just now."

"Yeah? Read me some."

I glanced over at the blank screen. "It's not the easiest thing to write. Have you said anything to her?"

"Not my job, man." His tone cut off any chance for me to respond. He said, "Look, she's going crazy here. If she keeps it up, she'll

kill herself. If I don't kill her first. Everyone needs you two back together. Which starts with an explanation from you. In writing."

"Can I talk to you?"

"Isn't that what we're doing?"

"No, I mean in person."

"Oh." He paused, and I thought he might be looking at his watch.
"Okay, I'll be there in a few minutes."

"Wait. Not here."

"Why not?"

"I'll explain." Then I said, "Don't bring Marla. I'll explain that too."

"I wasn't thinking of bringing her."

I said, "I'm serious. It has to be you and me alone."

"This is like a bad movie. Are we going to meet in the old abandoned warehouse at midnight?"

"Just about." I gave him directions to the vacant lot in the industrial area where I had hidden the envelope. He asked if it was easy to
find, and I tried to picture it in the dead of night. Finally I told him
to drive slowly and look for a blackberry vine across the road where
he should stop. When he saw that, or anything unusual, he should
stop and listen for my voice.

From our house I took the first right off Juniper and drove up 40th past
Fred Jackson's garage, away from where I would eventually be going, to
see if the Mazda was behind me. The street in my mirror remained dark.
I crossed Fulton on an obscure outlet and drove into the industrial area
the back way, which took me past the ditch where I had wrecked the
truck. The gouges in the dirt were still there, though no longer fresh
because of the rain we'd had since the truck had been towed.

I eased into the vacant lot, backed up tight against the brambles to one side so that my car couldn't be seen from the entry, and killed the engine and lights. When I opened the door, the dome light came on, and so did a buzzer. I pulled the keys, which stopped the buzzer. I switched off the dome light, got out of the car, and clicked the door shut. Because of the heavy overcast, hardly any light from outside the lot made its way in.

It was cold and still. The fog of my breathing held for a time before floating off. I worked my way to the entrance of the lot and carefully extracted six feet of vine from the blackberry brambles. It was like pulling barbed wire, difficult to avoid the thorns while still holding firmly enough to get it free of the snarl. I used a rock to separate the end from the rest of the length, pounding it to a pulp against the packed gravel. As I laid the vine across the road I heard a car approach from the direction I had come. It seemed too early to be Dave, so I retreated behind the wall of overgrowth. Only when the car droned on by did I realize that its headlights were off. I wished I had risked taking a look. All I could tell by the sound was that it was a small car. As I listened it rounded the next curve, and the night grew quiet again.

The gravel road was illuminated somewhat by area lights placed here and there in the broad, undeveloped industrial park. It was probably city code, but it seemed to me that the owners wanted to show potential buyers that electricity ran to all sectors.

A strange tension comes from not being sure what is about to happen. About every thirty seconds you cycle through a series of questions: *Was that Dave who just drove by? If so, why did he have his lights out? Will he come back? If not him, who? Wade* was my first thought, Wade in his stealthmobile. The other, however remote possibility was Sergeant Rainey, or a detective he had put on my tail. Or just a wandering citizen, or Rainey's imaginary youngsters looking for another abandoned vehicle to pound on. *Could anyone have followed me without my knowing it?* I thought I had been careful, but it hadn't occurred to me that he (or anyone) might be driving without headlights. *Would I have spotted such a car?* I had seen too many detective movies to not want a cigarette.

Five minutes later, from the direction in which the car had gone, headlights slewed around the curve and into alignment with the road. This car approached more slowly, and its engine sounded different. I made my way back toward the Camry and stood beside the driver's door, ready to hop in. Headlights pierced the thick brambles, but I felt well hidden. The car nosed up to the opening of the lot and stopped in the road. My heart quickened. The engine quit; the lights died. A door opened.

Dave's voice: "Hey, Jim?"

I moved toward him. "I'm here."

He said, "This is pretty bizarre, man."

"Did you have trouble finding it?"

"No, I drove straight here. Where's your car?"

"Backed up against the brush in there. Someone drove by a minute ago, and I thought it might've been you."

"I saw him too. Driving without lights. He slowed up when I passed him, but I could tell it wasn't you, so I kept going."

A train's horn sounded in the background, then the rumble of a big diesel engine.

He looked around. "So why here? Why not some all-night diner?"

"I thought it would be safer here, but now I'm wondering."

"Safer? From what?"

"I tried to keep from being followed, but I was watching for headlights."

"Why would someone be following you?"

"That's what I want to explain. And now I'm thinking we might not have much time."

"Then let's hear it."

"Remember those two guys who tried to steal the Camry?"

"Marla won't let me forget. She's like a broken record."

"That cop Rainey told me they're brothers. Larry and Wade."

"From the same family?"

"According to Rainey they are."

"And one of them died in the wreck you told me about."

"That was Larry. And since then someone has been following me, staking out the house."

"That's not just someone, Jim. That's the brother. You think that was him just now?"

"Maybe. I didn't see the car when it went by, but if it was a Mazda . . ."

"Okay, this is getting a little creepy."

"Was it a Mazda?"

"I don't know. I'm just saying it's creepy."

"What's important is you're safe. And Marla is safe with you. That's part of what I wanted to tell you. The other side of it. If you stay away from me—"

He put up a hand to stop me and looked up the road.

I heard the same sound. The car with its lights out idled around the curve, moving slowly toward us. I stepped back into the shadows of the overgrowth while Dave remained near the entry of the lot.

I said, "Okay, remember, this might be him. Don't mess with this guy. Fake like you're peeing or something, then get out of here."

"The last thing I'm going to do is pull out my cock."

"I said fake it. He's watching you. Stop talking to me. Tell him you're from out of town. Make up a name."

"Jim, I play sports. I can handle confrontation."

I wanted to get into the Camry, but I also wanted to hear the exchange and be close by if Dave said the wrong thing. It seemed stupid to own a gun and not have it with me at a time like this. Only when it was too late did I think of feeling around for a couple rocks, the oldest of weapons. The rock I had used to sever the blackberry vine would have been perfect. Okay, the pistol would have been closer to perfect.

The approaching car came to a stop behind Dave's car. Over the idling engine a voice said, "Broke down?" It was the same voice that had asked me about confession. And the same tone.

I heard Dave say, "I got turned around. I pulled off the main road to take a piss, and now I can't find my way out. I thought the river was over there, but now I'm not so sure. Three beers don't usually do this to me."

The engine died, and in the silence the guy said, "The river is there, Fulton up there. What's your name?"

"How come I can't hear the traffic? If Fulton is up that way?"

"Did you pass another car back there, or was it just me?

After a hesitation Dave said, "Yeah, a little ahead of you."

The guy said, "Interesting."

Dave said, "Look, man, I'm late. If that's Fulton, that's where I'm going. My wife's going to kill me as it is." He opened his car door. "By the way, your lights are out."

"No kidding."

"Yup." I could hear Dave get into his car. At the same time I could hear the other guy get out of his and say, "You forgot to take your piss."

Dave said, "No, I didn't. Watch where you step."

"Hey!" the guy called out in a sharp voice. "Do you know a cunt named Marla Sandusky?"

To his credit Dave called back, "Sorry." He shut his door, started the engine, and drove away at a casual speed. I was alone, behind the loosely woven screen of brush, with this guy just ten feet away. The mist of my breath curled and dissipated. The silence was deeper than any I had experienced.

I heard the guy mutter, "Too bad. I'm going to use a soup can to cut biscuits out of her face." Then came the metallic snap of what sounded like a large folding knife being flicked open. He said, "So where did you go, Camry boy? We have some bones to pick, you and me."

A few seconds later something sparked as it fell through the vines between us, then lay in the duff, glowing. His cigarette. I was helpless to do anything but hold as still as I could and hope he would just let it smolder. After a moment his car door clunked shut. Then nothing. I waited in the near dark and watched the glowing tobacco ember. This lasted long enough for me to wonder if he was staring through the brush, seeing either a glint of light reflecting off the Camry or a patch of color from my clothing. I didn't dare move even to see if I was catching any light.

Simultaneously the glowing end of the cigarette exploded and a gunshot filled the night. A piece of something hard struck my thigh—it wasn't the bullet, I was certain—and smaller stuff peppered my clothes and face. I jumped but managed to stifle the urge to run. I stood there and concentrated on regaining the use of my ears. Their ringing gave me a sense of claustrophobia, as if my survival depended solely on being able to hear whatever sound he made next. Which, in a way, I suppose it might have. I stood there, deaf, trying not to wince, dreading another shot. I could only hope that it too would miss me.

The next thing I heard was the hollow clatter of an empty aluminum can hitting the gravel, then the snap-hiss of another being opened. He started the engine and pulled out slowly, continuing in the direction Dave had gone, but still at a crawl. When the sound of his car grew smaller, I stepped around to the lot entrance and peered down the road. His lights never came on.

Rainey was wrong. This guy's meanness might have made him stupid, but he was no idiot. He was a hunter, and he was tracking me, and he was good at it. And the bones he wanted to pick weren't conversational.

I checked my thigh and found no wound, no mark on my jeans.

Something made me want to take the empty beer can with me, removing the evidence of his having been here—of *any* of us having been here—but I thought better of it because I would also have had to find whatever was left of the cigarette butt in the brush and use a branch or something to erase his footprints in the dirt shoulder of the road, and his tire tracks. The more I erased him, the more I would be establishing my own presence. And what could I do about my own footprints and tire tracks? It was mostly gravel here, but you always leave tracks.

I waited until I could no longer hear the Mazda, then went back and got into the Camry and headed in the other direction. I left my own lights off until I had looped all the way around to Fulton, and traffic, and civilization.

A few blocks from home I wondered whether Wade would return to his stakeout on Juniper. Perhaps he already had. I parked one block up from our house and one block behind, then walked until I could see the back of our house through the neighbors' side yard. I slipped up their driveway, past their detached garage and toward the fence we shared. I regretted having to step through their back garden, but I had no choice. The fence itself was no obstacle, just a four-foot-tall border mark. I got our spare key from beneath the side-burner lid on our barbecue and let myself in through the back door. I took the time to replace the key, not knowing when I might need it again, then went in and dead-bolted the door.

I went upstairs and peered out onto the street but didn't see the Mazda. Before I turned on any lights I went through the entire house and dropped the blinds of each window.

The phone startled me. I regretted having turned on the lights. This time I let it go until the machine kicked in. After our outgoing message, Dave said, "Hey, it's me. I hope you make it home, man. Marla's in bed, so I can talk, but—look, that doesn't matter. Call anyway, I don't care what time it is—"

I picked up and said, "Hello."

Dave said, "You made it! Are you okay?"

"I'm fine."

He said, "I just drove away."

"I know. You did the right thing."

"He *named* her! You don't just drive away!"

"You do with this guy. We have to keep our heads. This is real. He doesn't know Marla's maiden name, which means he doesn't know who you are. If you stay away, you're both safe. That's what you have to do. You have to stay away."

"He might've have seen my license plate. He could trace me with that."

"One, he isn't that smart. Two, he would have no reason to. I'm the one he's interested in."

"Man, this is very bad. It has to end."

"Can Marla hear you?"

"Okay, I'll talk lower." After a pause he said, "You're right. This is real."

I didn't reply.

He said, "You were right about everything."

"If I was right about everything, I wouldn't be in this mess."

"Are you kidding? Anyway, I'm getting a gun. I know a guy—"

"No, Dave, don't."

"Are you asking me or telling me?"

"Look, do you see yourself actually shooting this guy? The fact that he's following me doesn't give you the right to kill him. It doesn't give *me* the right to kill him. Does that make sense? I need you to stay out of it and keep Marla safe. Please."

"I just realized he knows what I look like. We were face-to-face."

"So don't let him see you again. He doesn't know you and I have anything to do with each other—and even if he did, he wouldn't know how to find you. He stuck around after you took off. He just stood there and had a smoke and talked to himself. And he didn't say anything about you. He didn't even think about following you. You and Marla are safe. That's what's important."

After a moment he said, "No wonder you can't sleep."

"Yeah, well, don't worry about it. Or go ahead and worry if you want, but stay away. This is between that guy and me."

"'That guy and I.'"

I knew he needed to win something here, but I said, "I'm pretty sure it's 'that guy and me.'"

"You know what? Fuck you, Jim. Does that make any sense? Fuck you!"

"Dave, please. A couple days is all I ask. This is Thursday. Give me till Monday."

"I have some vacation time coming. I'm going to take a week off; I'm going to find that guy and shoot him. Think of it as an anniversary present. By Monday he'll be dead and Marla can move back home."

He hung up.

I didn't yell into the dead receiver the way they do in the movies, but I wanted to. Instead I hung up, trying to suppress the feeling that a clock had just started ticking. A clock without much time on it.

I went up to bed and lay there in the dark. After a while I realized that I was now relieved of wondering whether or not I had been awakened that other night by a real gunshot. I knew now that I had imagined it because the quality had been so different from the sound of the shot Wade had fired less than an hour ago. With this thought, something deep within me settled, as if I had been perpetually asking myself about that dreamed shot. I went to sleep vaguely thinking that growing old is a process of accumulating such questions, most of which go unanswered, and they weigh on you without your being aware of the weight, let alone where it is coming from. The burden of these unsettled issues would be greater than the pull of gravity.

Marriages fail over far less than the loss of an expected child. Relationships of all kinds can spontaneously abort without anyone seeing it coming. Given the stress some couples endure, it's amazing that so many hold together. The forces working on your heart come from surprising directions.

Say, for example, that shortly after miscarrying a woman finds herself periodically drawn to the guest room closet doorway, where she stands and stares at a collection of infant artifacts donated by friends whose children are now toddlers. With each item she constructs a ghost history, such as the brightly colored plastic car seat that will never carry her little boy to the store and the pair of tiny sheepskin booties she has been spared the frustrations of pulling over his bicycling feet as he lies on his back, resisting the morning ritual of getting dressed. She stands there at the open door, transfixed by the physical reminders of her loss.

Her husband—his own loss augmented by seeing his wife immersed in a suffering he can't soothe—is late for work one morning because he removes the car seat and the brown paper bag with the booties and other baby things and drives it all over to the Goodwill donations drop-off on Lincoln, a couple of blocks from the Franklin Heights Deli.

He knows she has noticed—at some point she *has* to notice—but she doesn't refer to it, and he never finds the right time to raise the issue because there can be no right time. It had been a mistake to hang on to those baby things, but it had also been a mistake to get rid of them. He had missed the point—those things had been all that remained of their child—but there was no way to correct it now. When he saw her in the doorway he imagined the collection of baby things as a mausoleum, but now he realizes it was a shrine. He imagines himself initiating the exchange: "I donated that stuff to Goodwill."

"I know."

"I thought—"

"It doesn't matter."

"I thought it was hurting you to have them around."

"How dare you make that judgment!"

She wouldn't say this, nor would she snap at him. He amends her reply to: "I wish you had talked to me first. They were important to me."

"I know. They were to me too." This is so true it would start to break him, and he would lack the energy to say, "I couldn't stand to see you in the doorway. . . ."

He goes over this in his mind, but as usual he can't initiate an exchange, and soon the issue recedes into the emotional murk surrounding it. And as it recedes he is both disappointed and relieved—disappointed because an argument may have helped clear the air, relieved because their marriage may not have survived such an argument. But now he feels that they are one step closer to the argument. And the need to clear the air and the size of the argument are both growing like tumors, pressing on his heart.

During this time I searched for the smallest indication that Marla was even remotely satisfied with life, that a future with me would be tolerable. At one point she said, "We should have a compost pile," and this reference to a future together floated me for two days. But the doubts were always there, and when I mentioned the compost pile again, she said, "We don't have room."

Those were hard days for me, days of despair. During this time I was convinced that I might never be happy again. Hell is when you would rather die than continue feeling what you're feeling.

No, wait. Hell is permanent. Which means it's when you believe that what you're feeling won't change. I know this isn't new, this view of hell. Even the idea that it isn't an actual place isn't new. But now, the way it was occurring to me, the sign above the cave tells you to abandon hope because this is the *definition* of hell. There's no red pit, no devils with pitchforks prodding you deeper into the flames. You are abandoning hope *by* entering. You enter spiritually. There isn't any cave. What you enter is the loss of hope. Hell is the permanent loss of hope.

Something strange happened around this time. It was on an overcast Sunday afternoon in the spring that I heard a sudden agitation of chirping in our backyard. By the time I made it to the deck the air was littered with bird cries. Twenty feet up in the fir tree in the back corner of our lot a juvenile raccoon was inching its way out a limb toward a nest. Two robins were flapping around it, frantically trying, I suppose, to turn the raccoon back or distract it into falling out of the tree. In the few seconds that I stood there, the raccoon reached the nest and started nosing around. I grabbed some pumice stones from our gas barbecue and threw them at the raccoon until I saw that they were landing on the neighbors' roof. By then it was too late anyway; the eggs were gone.

I know one thing about this event: If there had been a gun at hand, I would have shot the raccoon. I would have done so not because of the cluster of lives it was ending for the sake of a snack but because of the cries of the two parent birds. Any creature that hears such cries of pain from other creatures and continues with what is causing their pain deserves to die.

On the day after my interrupted meeting with Dave I considered getting the loaner back from Tim the mechanic. But no, I thought, all evidence must lead back to me alone. This wasn't a decision but a realization. It would defeat my purpose to involve an innocent person.

I can't describe that particular workday because I spent it internally—in my own head—trying to figure out a course of action. It was not a step-by-step formulation; other than deciding to not borrow Tim's car, I don't recall any continuum of "if I do this, then I have to do this" decisions, or even a mental list of goals. It was more like spending my time looking into the fog of my future, trying to discern a vague corridor I might take until it intersected with an even more vague corridor, and I would grope along blindly until I simply disappeared into the fog. I spent the day wandering through mental corridors in the fog.

If I had written down every concrete thought that came to mind, there would have been three:

1. Get caller ID.
2. Call a wrecking yard about tires.
3. Place street shoes in a sack by the front door.

That's what I recall thinking. What I did that day was call the phone company to order caller ID. After some back-and-forth the customer service rep agreed to set us up with only that instead of call waiting (which Marla refers to as *call rudeness*) and four other useless services. He asked if I wanted to order the little box, but after wrestling with him over the package deal I got stubborn and said I would get one from Radio Shack.

Then I called a wrecking yard listed in the yellow pages as Japanese Auto Parts.

A voice said, "JAPs."

"Are you open Saturday?"

"Yeah, that's when we do most of our business with the public."

I said, "I'm looking for tires for a Camry."

"Ones and twos and fours."

"I guess I don't know what that means."

"You can buy one for a spare, two to match on an axle, or a whole set of four. We got a ton for Camry. Rims too. Everything from styling stockbroker down to that teenage-gangster junk."

I hung up and asked John if he minded running the open tasting.

"If you line up the bottles, I'll pour. May I ask what's going on?"

"I want to be home by dark again. No big deal. I'll come in tomorrow to make up for it."

"You don't have to do that."

"I know, but I want to. I'll come in early."

He gave me a quizzical look, which made me feel I had already called too much attention to myself, gone too far outside my normal pattern. All I wanted was to have someone expecting me the next morning so that if something went wrong this evening, I would be missed. Otherwise it might be Monday before anyone thought to come looking for me. For my body.

I said, "I promised myself a long evening. Part of it is about the writing." This seemed to do the trick.

When I left the Deli, I drove to the Radio Shack across from the supermarket where I used to work and found a caller ID box for twenty bucks. At home I put a battery into the back of it and plugged it in with our wall phone. I took off my street shoes and placed them in a plastic sack by the front door. Then I tried to relax.

I had eaten at the Deli, so I couldn't distract myself with fixing dinner. I wanted to turn the clock ahead and have the Mazda idle down Juniper and pull in against the curb to park. The earliest this might happen was still more than four hours away. Four hours. A quarter of one thousand minutes. This arithmetic took me a quarter of a single minute. I would have to wait a thousand more of these time periods before the next thing happened. This might not have been the best time for me to be writing, but I had to do something, and writing killed time faster than anything else I could think of. I set our oven timer for three hours, then sat down to our iMac to reread the second draft of my explanation to Marla.

It was almost as bad as my first effort. I thought I had been explaining the situation, but evidently all I cared about was ducking responsibility, excusing myself from blame. Instead of "The Wreck," I should have titled it "Not My Fault" or "Poor Jim."

I started by trying to fix it sentence by sentence, replacing an awkward word here, deleting an unnecessary phrase there, but I soon saw that this was like trying to finish a crossword puzzle littered with incorrect entries; easier to start over. I deleted this entire document too and began again, this time by listing the facts as I had told them to John. Then I went back to fill in here and there where it felt thin. Finally I was able to admit seeing the van before I'd swerved all the way onto the shoulder. It was after this that I felt I was finally on the right track. I got lost in the work, and when the timer beeped this is what I had of a third draft:

Marla—I've gone numb (though not toward you), but I need to get something in the mail tonight. I've started and deleted two other efforts. This evening I promised myself to send whatever I got on paper, no matter how bad it turned out. Please forgive the writing. I won't ask you to forgive the content, but try to understand it.

The night those two guys tried to steal our Camry I awoke and went downstairs to look. When I saw what they were doing, I went back up and had you call the cops. Then I went out to get their plate number. When I got close enough, I saw that the truck was just sitting there with the doors open, engine running. I hadn't planned to take it, but I jumped in and drove away.

I headed toward the river, where I thought it wouldn't be found right away, and steered it into a ditch. I'm still not sure why, but I wrecked it on purpose. I started walking back until I realized you were alone, then I ran. When I got home, the cops had come and gone. We waited for the one cop to drive us down to the precinct, and then we talked to Sergeant Rainey and looked at the throw-downs.

What you don't know began at the police station, when you were with that other cop. Rainey told me some things about the car thieves that I didn't tell you. First, they were brothers, Larry and Wade Hood, with a history of violence. He also said that, whether or not I had taken their truck, they might blame its disappearance on me and try to get revenge. He said the cops couldn't do anything unless the Hoods did something first. And finally he told me that if I dropped the charges, the Hoods might forget about me, so I did.

A couple days later a guy I recognized from the throw-downs came into the Deli. He checked the place out and left. I watched his car as he drove away. It was a white Chevy Celebrity.

The next day I had to make a run out to a winery—this was during one of those stormy days the week after Halloween. I was at the light before the freeway on-ramp when I saw the white Celebrity in my mirror, and it was the same guy behind the wheel. Something in me changed. After we got on the freeway he stayed on my tail for a few miles. Driving conditions were bad, but I felt I had to lose him. I tried weaving in and out of lanes, speeding up and slowing down, but he kept on me. At one point I was in the fast lane, starting to pass a truck by driving on the shoulder, but there was a stalled van ahead, so I veered back, and the Celebrity didn't. The collision was huge.

This was the day you came out to the driveway and asked me what was wrong. I was just sitting there. I mentioned the wreck but couldn't say anything more about it.

Rainey called the following day to tell me that one of the car thieves, Larry Hood, had died in a traffic accident.

What I've been afraid to tell anyone is that I knew the van was there. It happened so fast I couldn't sort it out for a while, but if I'm being honest with myself (not the easiest thing here), I have to admit that I knew if I timed it right, he would run into the van. I didn't know it would kill him, but I think I hoped it would. This is what I couldn't tell you because I thought you would close up on me. Instead I closed up on you.

What I told you about driving around at night was the truth. The wreck happened so close to me that I couldn't get the sound out of my mind—it's what was waking me up. The only way I could get any sleep at all was to drive around until I was tired enough to nod off. It got to be a habit, cruising around and then dozing. One morning I overslept—again behind the wheel—and that same morning you moved in with Dave.

There will be more to tell, but even this took me forever to write, so I'll mail it now and send more when I can.

I found a font that allowed me to fit it single-spaced on one page, printed it, and wrote in ink at the bottom of the page that I loved her. Figuring in the previous drafts and the time I'd spent staring into space between sentences (time that John would say counted toward the final effort), it had taken me fourteen hours to produce the one page. I read it over and folded it into a business envelope, which I addressed to Marla at Dave's.

It felt risky, but I wanted to get it in the mail right away. For one thing it would give Marla something from me to read. But also, if things went bad tonight, the cops wouldn't find it in a search of our house for clues to why my body had been found in another part of town. I hoped Marla would see it as an explanation, but the cops would see it as evidence. Evidence, or a confession.

The Mazda hadn't arrived. It always came from the east, and the quickest route to the nearest mailbox would take me west on Juniper for two blocks, then south for two more—less than a three-minute round-trip if I ran. On the other hand, if I ran I might call attention to myself. Every decision I faced seemed to put me at war with myself.

The night was cold, good for clearing the head. We were deep into November now, a night some would call freezing, though technically it wasn't. It was the kind of night I used to enjoy because it foretold harsher weather to come. We were out of autumn and hadn't yet reached winter—a period of transition. There was no moonlight, just a weak glow in the overcast, the city lights bouncing back. Those were years of peace, when I used to enjoy this kind of evening, back when the greatest changes I felt were in the weather.

I had to keep my head in the present, so I broke into a jog. I didn't care about being conspicuous, only about getting to the mailbox and back. I had to remain goal-oriented, priority-driven.

At the corner I turned south and saw the mailbox beneath a streetlight, the humped blue receptacle standing like a *Star Wars* sentinel in the night. I was confused by a brief flash of panic until I realized it was because I could no longer see down Juniper; I could no longer monitor what was happening outside our house. I kept my head and walked deliberately the rest of the way to the mailbox, pulled open the steel gravity lid, and dropped in the letter. I let the lid clunk shut and walked back to Juniper.

I stopped. All was still. For a moment I considered the open field between here and home. As I stood there calculating the risk, the intersection on the other side of our house grew brighter with headlights approaching. I turned, backtracked one block to the street behind our house, and trotted down to the driveway of our backyard neighbors. I slipped through their yard and over their fence again, promising myself this would be the last time. I let myself in through our back door, again replacing the key in case I would have to go back on my promise, and left the lights out as I made my way upstairs.

Our bathroom window faces east, but you can get a view of the street if you stand next to the wall. I moved slowly toward the right side of the window. Through the small opening between the blinds and the frame I could see the Mazda, parked as usual with the driver's window down a couple of inches, cigarette smoke rising out. I couldn't say that the situation was perfect, but it was what I had hoped for. He was taking his usual beers and cigarettes as he watched my house. I pulled up a chair and sat while my heart calmed from my recent exertion. I watched him watch me. In this peaceful neighborhood, in the stillness of the civilized evening, we two troubled souls sat quietly in the dark, thinking sinister thoughts about each other.

I wondered what he was waiting for. What would tell him it was the right time to start picking those bones with me? When would I learn what he had meant by that?

Then came the real question: *Jim, what are* you *waiting for?* Which was all it took, asking the right question, for everything to make sense.

I went into the bedroom for the pistol under Marla's pillow. It was still in the ziplock bag, still loaded. I verified that the safety was off—I guess I preferred accidentally shooting myself to needing to pull the trigger in a hurry and not being able to. Going downstairs, I tried to tell myself not to panic. My wallet and keys were in the hall desk. I took my nylon jacket from the chair in the dining room and put it on, then shoved the bagged pistol into the left-hand pocket— the pocket Wade wouldn't be able to see from his car parked a little way up Juniper—and zipped the pocket closed. (I had to mentally refer to this guy as *Wade* or I wouldn't be able to continue.) The weight of the pistol pulled at the light jacket fabric, so I zipped up the front, which helped. I went to the kitchen for the dish-washing gloves and a handful of plastic grocery bags and put them as a single wad into my other jacket pocket. Last, I picked up the bagged shoes I had placed by the front door. Without hesitating—I didn't want to give myself a chance to reconsider—I went out the front door, locked it, and walked over to the Camry. It's not easy to act casual while trying not to glance in a certain direction, but I managed, cradling the pocketed pistol in my left hand to keep it from pulling on the jacket. The shoes, swinging in their plastic bag, probably made me look a little dorky, but I thought this might be good, distracting him from thinking about what might be in my other hand.

Holding the shoe bag in my teeth, I unlocked the Camry door, got in, and started the engine. If he lost me, it didn't matter, I could try again another night. What mattered was that he didn't suspect anything. As long as he felt in control of the situation, I was the one in control . . . or at least more in control than he was. I cautioned myself against overconfidence—the loser tonight would be the one who was the most overconfident. I turned on my lights and drove down Juniper as normally as possible, turning at 39th to follow my usual evasive loop around the block as I headed toward Fulton. As I went I unzipped my left jacket pocket and moved the bagged pistol to the floor beneath my seat, thinking that if a cop stopped me for any kind of traffic infraction, he wouldn't accidentally happen upon it as he flashlighted the interior of the car. My street shoes were fine on the passenger seat.

I took the same route I had taken the night I'd met Dave in the empty lot, thinking the repetition would work for me. It was several blocks before I caught the dark shape of the Mazda in my mirror, again moving in stealth mode, without lights. I wouldn't have been able to spot him without knowing he was there. He was a moving shadow. If it had been a windy night, I wouldn't have been able to see him even now. Which was good. I was able to remain calm, at least to a certain degree. Traffic conditions helped; driving was easy. Whenever I wanted to change lanes, all I had to do was signal and merge. At the first stoplight outside our neighborhood, the Mazda was two cars back. Now that we were among other cars, its lights were on, which was the new stealth mode. The light changed, and I drove on.

By the time I turned into the industrial area, he had fallen well back, and his lights were out again. I had to keep to the steps of my plan and trust that he would do his part. I reminded myself to not use the brake pedal when I got to the lot because the brake lights would come on—I would have to rely on the parking-brake lever. Then I verified that the dome switch was off so the light wouldn't come on when I opened my door.

Toward the end of a straight stretch I caught a glimpse of him a hundred yards back. I rounded the curve before the ditch where I had wrecked the truck and continued around the next curve. I pulled on the dish-washing gloves, then reached into the glove box for a small flashlight we keep there and worked it into my front jeans pocket. After rounding the next curve I sped up a bit to put more distance between us, then killed my lights. The night closed in on me, and I felt briefly claustrophobic, but within a few seconds my eyes adjusted to the dimmer light. I could make out the road, and then the break in the brush. Shifting into first and using the parking brake for control, I made the hard right turn into the empty lot, rolled to a stop, set the brake, and shut off the engine.

I got out of the car and pulled the pistol from the plastic bag. I worked my rubber-gloved index finger through the trigger guard and flexed a bit to get a comfortable grip. His car was moving slowly along in the dark, its engine barely murmuring, the tires crunching and popping on individual bits of gravel. I carefully walked to the entrance of the lot and stood behind the brush there. As his car continued to crawl toward me, I imagined his thought balloon in big black letters: *This is where I lost him last time.*

With only a few seconds to go, doubts started to leak in. Had I truly verified that this was Wade Hood? I felt I had, but I couldn't recall the steps. There was no time left to think it through. He was here; this was now. I pulled back the hammer of the pistol.

The nose of the car emerged from the edge of the brush, and in the semidark I saw the top of the primer-gray fender on the far side of the hood. The passenger-door mirror came into view, and then I saw that the window was down . . . and here my mind went blank. Imagine my eyes like unlit windows in an abandoned house. I stepped out and crouched with the pistol leveled toward the driver through the gaping absence of the passenger window, and even before I could make him out, I fired, and fired again. A shot came from inside the car, which continued at the same pace, slowly crossing into the other lane and coming to a stop in the ditch. It lurched once, and the engine died.

I approached from the center of the road, keeping the pistol aimed at where I thought the driver would be. There was no movement inside. Through the ringing in my ears I heard a hissing. I could see the shape of the driver slumped against his door. I felt in my pocket for the small flashlight, pulled it out, and clicked it on. When the beam struck him, he stirred and groaned but remained in profile. This was indeed the same guy who had confused me with his remark about confession in front of Arlene's.

I didn't see any blood. A pistol had fallen out of his right hand and joined four unopened cans of Pabst in the passenger seat. One of the cans had two holes in it, beer foaming out. His right arm was reaching forward beyond the seat as if groping for something that had fallen to the floor. I raised my pistol, aimed carefully at his head, closed my eyes, and fired. When I looked again, I saw a lot of blood. I aimed at what I could see of his chest beneath his right arm (again closing my eyes) and pulled the trigger repeatedly until I heard a click—three more shots, I believe—but this is more arithmetic than memory because the gun held six.

I walked back to the Camry, putting the pistol into one of the plastic bags I'd brought, and shoved it into my jacket pocket. I pulled off the dish-washing gloves, turning them inside out in the process, and put them into a second plastic bag and this into my other jacket pocket. Before I got into the Camry I looked back toward his car and saw a loose plastic bag in the road, where it must have fallen when I'd pulled my left hand from my pocket. Even though I couldn't feel any air movement, the bag floated like a ghost at an angle away from me, toward the opposite ditch. I walked over and retrieved it, then stood and scanned the area to see if I had left anything else around. I returned to the Camry and sat in the driver's seat sideways to keep my feet on the gravel. I took off my sneakers, put them into the loose plastic bag, and pivoted in the seat so that my socked feet were on the floor mat by the pedals. I slid the bagged shoes beneath the passenger seat, then pulled on my street shoes, tying them carefully.

Returning the way I'd come, I kept my lights on and my speed within the limit, signaling, obeying the signs. I parked in front of the house and left the jacket with the pistol and gloves stuffed under the passenger seat. I went inside and straight up to bed.

I actually got some sleep, but before I dropped off a casual thought concerning the six shots crossed my mental field: They had erased my memory of both the impact of Larry's car into the moving van and the sound of the one shot Wade had fired at his cigarette, and had done so without replacing them with their own sound. My head was strangely quiet.

aturday morning I felt pretty good. Not great, but better than I'd thought I would. At least I had enough energy to finish my few remaining self-assigned tasks. Before work I prepared a box of donations for the Goodwill station on Lincoln, filling it with random items from our camping supplies in the basement—utensils and plates and some dish towels—then walked the box out to the Camry. I pulled the windbreaker from beneath the seat, took the bagged pistol from the pocket, and put it in the glove box. I stuffed the windbreaker into the donations box, adding the dishwashing gloves, which I left inside out after removing them from their plastic bag. I shook my shoes from their bag into the box. I stuffed the empty plastic bags together into a corner of the box, assuming that some donations worker would either recycle them or throw them away.

Japanese Auto Parts was an easy drive to the southern outskirts of town. No other cars were in the parking lot. I took the pistol, still in its plastic bag, from the glove box and put it in my coat pocket, then went into the office. The guy at the desk remembered my call and said he had two different sets of tires that should work for my Camry. I told him that as long as they had tread and weren't Firestones—which was the brand I was changing out—they'd be fine. He looked at mine and asked why not keep those. I told him I didn't want to. He said, "I guess that's a reason." I had decided at the last minute not to lie, not to tell him about some invented uncle who'd had two blowouts with those same tires. I know what I look like to the average citizen, and what I *don't* look like is a suspicious character. If I had told him I had just shot someone and was disguising my tracks, he would have said, "Yeah, when I kill a guy I change my tires too."

Still, to keep from seeming eager or desperate, I dickered with him on the total and got fifteen bucks knocked off. While he had my car on jacks for the swap, I asked if I could look around the yard. He waved a hand toward where I would find the Camrys in the acres and acres of wrecked cars and told me not to get my greasy fingerprints all over his good merchandise out there.

I wandered off in the direction he had indicated, deep into the yard between two rows of Corollas stacked three high, then turned left and continued until I reached a farther sector marked "Datsun/ Nissan." The paths were paved with what seemed to be an equal mix of gravel and bolts and nuts with a mud binder, overstrewn with loose doors and bumpers and floor mats and windshield-wiper arms. Beneath the nose of an overturned hatchback, I used a hubcap to scrape out a hole in some softer mud. In a few minutes I was ten inches down. I pulled the bagged pistol from my pocket and shook it out of the bag into the hole, never having physically touched the thing. Then I pushed the gravelly mud back over it. I stood and reached with my foot to press down the hump and blend it with the surrounding ground; finally I pushed a battered trunk lid over it. I thought about how difficult it would be to use a metal detector in a wrecking yard to find a buried pistol. But if they used *dogs* . . . well, if they were here with dogs to find that pistol, I was already up a creek. On my way back through the rows of wrecked cars I used a broken antenna to poke the leftover plastic bag deep into the tailpipe of a rusted-out muffler.

At the wrecking-yard shop the guy was finishing the tire swap.

He noticed my dirty hands. "Find anything else?"

I said, "No, but it couldn't hurt to look."

"Am I going to have to check your pockets?"

I gave him what I hoped was a natural smile and paid out of the money left over from buying the pistol, which gave me a strange feeling of closure. I drove back to town, detouring long enough to stop by the Goodwill station—a semitrailer with its doors open and a temporary set of stairs leading up. A sad young woman in what was probably a donated coat took my box of eclectic offerings and placed it among a dozen similar boxes. It was already gone for good. She offered to write me a receipt, and I said thanks but no. It was a little before ten in the morning when I walked through the doors of the Deli. I was earlier for work than I'd ever been, but there wasn't anywhere else I wanted to be, and as I said before, a lack of routine helps conceal suspicious behavior.

Rainey didn't call until almost noon. When I heard the phone ring, I realized I had been expecting him all along—him or some other cop, which meant I had been hoping for Rainey. I was alert enough to the situation to see that this was at least in part why I had gone in early, so he would find me on his first try. I also wanted to have people around me even though I was hoping the exchange would be private, rather than a reading of my rights followed by the handcuffs. I had already left the island and started toward the back when Jason, our new man on sandwiches, answered and covered the mouthpiece of the receiver with his hand. I thanked him and took the receiver into the office.

"Hello?"

"Rainey here. I have some news."

"Good news or bad?"

After an odd pause he said, "It's complicated. This should be in person."

I left my own pause, then said, "Okay."

"It's not official, by the way. Are you free for lunch?"

"Sure. Where?" Not official. That could go either way.

He said, "How about there? What time do you break?"

I almost said whenever I wanted, but I didn't want to put him in mind of my scheduling freedom. Even though I had been hoping he would call, I was still afraid of him, of course—afraid of where this call might lead. Before I could respond he said, "Look, just stay there."

Five minutes later he walked in.

During this brief time I had a string of thoughts that ended uneasily. It started with feeling sure that Wade was the one in the car. But the word *sure* is a sketchy one. As soon as you use it, it no longer applies. If asked "Was Wade in the car?" and you're truly sure he was, you simply say, "Yes." If you have the slightest doubt, you might say, "I'm *sure* he was." And the more you emphasize the word, the less sure you are. You might still be willing to bet on it, but you wouldn't want to stake your life.

Rainey scanned the room until he spotted me at the island. I waved him over.

He said, "Can we sit? This time I want to sit."

I said, "Hang on."

I went into the back room to tell John that I had to meet with this guy.

John said, "Are you interviewing for another job?" He smiled.

I said, "No, he's a cop. I'm not sure what he wants. He's the guy who nabbed the two who were trying to steal our car."

"I thought that was over."

"Me too. I don't know what this is about."

He studied me and said, "Did you finally get some sleep?"

"I don't know. Why?"

"You look a little better than you have in a while. But maybe just different. Do you want us to bring you anything? A couple soups?"

"That sounds good."

"Go talk to him. He looks edgy." He poured two glasses of water, scooped in some ice, and handed them to me. "Put the man at ease."

Rainey took a seat at a table.

I went over, placed the water glasses on the brown Formica top, and sat. "What's the news?" I still thought he might tell me that an undercover cop had been shot.

He said, "Wade Hood is dead."

I said, "Wait."

"No, Jim, I will not wait. He was shot at close range through an open car window in that industrial stretch out where his brother's truck was found. He might be dead, but he is far from buried."

I didn't care about buried, only that he was dead. *Wade was dead!* I was so relieved that if Jason hadn't been carrying a tray with two bowls of soup toward us, I might have confessed right then.

Instead I said, "Here's lunch." I wondered about how he might be reading me, but all I got was a tangle of my own hopes, and my urge to confess faded.

"You said he was shot?"

"Someone emptied a handgun into him. He had his own weapon, which he fired into a can of beer riding shotgun—a wounded-guy reflex thing. What's interesting is where it happened."

"And where was that?"

"I already told you." His tone put me on red alert. He said, "Remember the truck that went missing the night they tried to boost your Camry? Where we found it was about where Wade was found dead this morning."

I wanted to ask if he thought it was a coincidence, but I didn't know how to inflect the question the way someone would if he didn't already know the answer.

Rainey continued, "It's an obscure area. The average citizen might drive past it every day and never know it was there. It's the kind of place where kids experiment with stuff they shouldn't, but the furthest your average joe might go would be to glance out the side window and wonder when some developer was going to move in with bulldozers and turn it into a goddamn Walmart. This puts the odds that the guy who stole the truck is the same guy who shot Wade at about a hundred percent. I've been in this line of work long enough to trust this level of arithmetic. The next most likely scenario is my alien theory. But your discomfort has never had anything to do with probes up your ass."

He studied the soup, then dipped his spoon and sipped. "You know, this is pretty good."

I didn't respond. He tried another spoonful.

He said, "I'm glad you've done away with that neutral stuff. Even though it probably means I'm on the right track, given the gravity of our . . . situation." He left an opening, but I was completely lost as to what might work for me and what might work against me.

He set down his spoon and said, "Jim, I play things at about third level. When I'm really on my game, maybe fourth level, but only maybe. Of course at fourth level, as soon as I think about being there, the whole thing collapses and I turn into a blithering idiot. I'm talking about the 'I think that you think' thing. About how a guy might be reading how I might be reading him. This usually gives me a sense of how to proceed. For example, I think that you think I'm not sure you killed Wade Hood. Most people would already be lost. There's this blank look like you get from a cow. Most bank-job guys coast along at about first level. They leave with the loot, and we find them three beers later in a tavern across the street. Not that bad, but pretty close. You, on the other hand, seem comfortable with at least two levels without even practicing. I hate to say so, but with a little work you might be better at it than I am. This makes you difficult to talk to."

He started to pick up his spoon again, then didn't. Instead he picked up the bowl, drank the rest of the soup, and wiped his mouth with the back of his hand. He said, "Which means I have to be direct. I liked it when we were adversaries. I enjoyed the verbal dance right up to when we found Larry underneath that van. But now we've crossed the centerline. We're talking about murder here. This wasn't a shootout or an act of self-defense or some kind of justifiable homicide. It was a plain old store-bought premeditated murder."

I just looked at him. *It wasn't murder. It was a removal.* I didn't care if he could read this thought. I welcomed him to read it and explain to me how a removal and a murder are or are not the same thing. Wade Hood was a rabid dog; shooting him was that kind of thing. I noticed that Rainey noticed that I hadn't blinked. I blinked with the small hope that he wouldn't notice that I had noticed. He was right about the levels. But it was the unusual intensity of the situation that had brought me there, and I hated it while he seemed to thrive on it.

He said, "As far as the law is concerned, nothing justifies this. That's what I came here to say."

"Okay. But I still don't—"

"Please let me continue. You'll get your turn in a minute. I'm not part of the investigating team. If I were, you would be in jail right now. Are you listening? Because this is important. If I were on the investigating team, you would be my only suspect, and my search would be over. The DA would be shaking my hand on a job well done, and the years ahead of you would be far worse than you can possibly imagine. That's if I were part of the investigating team. What I'm saying is, those years may still be worse than you can possibly imagine, but I'm not going to be a part of it."

I stared at my soup, unable to take the smallest sip. I tried to look up but couldn't.

He said, "The trust between us is gone. I protected you for a while there, but no more. Even now I might be recording this conversation, so if you're aching to confess—just to be able to talk about it—don't confess to me. Right now, if you say you shot Wade Hood, I will arrest you before the words cross this table. What we have between us now is distance."

My ears were so hot they hurt.

He said, "Jim, this isn't where I want to be. But the deal is, if I get called on the carpet for that business with the truck being abandoned out there, and it leads to this shooting—which it would, as sure as night follows day—I won't be able to explain my way out of it. Which would end my career. In fact, they might put me in the cell next to yours, and then I would be facing at least some of those bad years along with you. Hey, could I get some more water?" His glass was empty, and I hadn't noticed him take a single sip.

I said, "Hang on." I didn't have the strength to stand but was able to catch John's eye by holding up my glass. He raised his chin to show that he understood.

Rainey said, "Thanks. What I really want is a scotch. You too, I'll bet." He waited, then said, "It's your turn. Not about the scotch, obviously, but at some point you're going to have to say something. I'm not leaving until I hear you say something."

"I'm glad he's dead."

"That's a start."

I took a breath and managed to string together a small speech. "No matter what happens now, I'm glad he's dead." Rainey watched me with his full attention. I said, "He hunted me down, called Marla a cunt, and said something about using a soup can to cut biscuits out of her face. This was after she moved out."

He started to say something, then said, "Marla moved out?"

"Yes; we've been having some trouble over this whole mess. I haven't been able to sleep. I've been pacing, driving around at night, making her crazy. She moved in with her brother across town, which was a good thing because Wade was stalking me. You were right about his danger quotient. He tracked me down, used her full name, and called her a cunt."

"And the soup-can thing."

"Yes."

"He said this to you? That doesn't—"

"Her brother. I was hiding. If I hadn't been, I would be dead now. Dave and I were meeting because we were tired—all three of us were tired—of her and me being apart. Wade showed up, driving with his lights out. I hid, but I heard it."

"Driving with his lights out. What night, if you don't mind?"

"Earlier this week. It wasn't the first time. He was parking outside our house at night, just sitting there, watching. It got to be a regular thing. Always left a pile of beer cans and cigarette butts, Pabst and Marlboros. I couldn't sleep one night last week, so I was parked downtown and he drove by my car and mimed shooting me through my windshield."

"And where was this?"

"Outside Arlene's. It's one of those—"

"I know the place." He sat back and said, "So he followed you . . ."

I nodded.

After a moment he said, "Well, I'll be goddamned to hell. This is the first time since this adventure began that I just plain believe you."

"It's not the only time I've told the truth."

"I have no doubt. And I know this has been hard, but if you don't mind, back to this meeting. What did the brother—Dave, you said— what did Dave do?"

"He walked away, acted like he didn't know anything. Which he doesn't, by the way."

"So, Dave is also—"

"I just said he doesn't know anything!" I looked down at the table. "You have to trust me here, Dave is not an issue. All he has done this whole time is give Marla a place to stay. Leave him out of it."

"Okay, Jim, okay. Like I said, I'm not part of the investigating team. But I *would* be interested in where this meeting took place."

I kept looking at the table. I didn't know if looking at the table was real or an act. I had to look somewhere, and I couldn't look at Rainey. I stared at the fake wood grain in the brown Formica and thought about my staring and then wondered whether thinking about this made my staring an act. I was tired, but I thought mentioning being tired might work against me. I shook my head the way I thought I should.

"It doesn't matter where we met. None of it matters anymore." I truly believed it didn't.

We were quiet. From the corner of my eye I saw Rainey nod to himself. I regretted adding Dave to his list of people of interest, but it had come out of my mouth before I'd seen how it might be taken. On the other hand, I wasn't equipped to come up with a believable story that didn't involve him. And again, Dave was innocent, and Rainey wouldn't miss something as obvious as this.

Finally he said, "You're right; it doesn't matter. I was wrong about that son of a bitch, and *that's* what matters." He thought for a moment, rotating his empty water glass on the table as he looked out the window. "Well, I'm sorry for that. I'm sorry this thing exploded on you. I guess now we're going to find out what it will cost. One thing you need to know is where you stand with the investigating team. If they get it into their heads that you pulled the trigger, no matter how well you covered your tracks, they will probably find enough evidence to make an arrest. So don't give them reason to think about you."

"What if they go back to the night the Hoods tried to steal our Camry?"

Rainey thought for a moment. I waited for him to point out that I couldn't have come up with this angle in the supposedly brief time I had known about the shooting, but we were done with that. He said, "You should be okay there. Nothing in my report ties that to their truck being found in the industrial area. You might not appreciate how much trouble these guys were in on a daily basis, and it was easy for me to make the attempted theft of your Camry look like the other reports. We ran them in, you dropped the charges because of the hassle factor, and it's on to the next report. The trained eye won't flinch as it scans the paragraph of you in the book of Wade's life."

"What about your computers?"

"Our computers are somewhat limited. They may have all the necessary information, but asking the right question is what gets you the right answer. And in this situation you have to already know the answer in order to ask the right question."

"When he used Marla's name—"

He raised his hand. "Tell it to Marla, not me." When I sat back, he said, "Look. You never met my wife, Evelyn. You talked to her on the phone, and I've mentioned her from time to time—regardless, she is a good woman, and we've had some wonderful years together. In the way that all good women save their husbands, she saved me. I would do anything to keep her safe, and I mean anything." He shrugged. "That's the way some of us are wired."

I looked past him to let him know our water was on its way. He said, "Sometimes that attitude makes for lonely living."

John set the pitcher on the table. "There you go, gentlemen. Anything else?"

I looked at Rainey.

He opened his hands. "Not for me."

I said, "Thanks, John. I don't know how long I'll be."

Rainey said, "Not long. We're about done here."

John said, "Take what time you need." He retreated.

Rainey said, "Good guy."

I started to speak, but Rainey cut me off.

"Don't." He knocked once on the table. "Distance, remember? I still need distance."

"Okay. But all I want—"

"I know, Jim. It's all any of us wants. Who knows, you still might get it."

He refilled his glass from the pitcher and studied the ice on the surface. I waited for him to continue. He touched one of the cubes and said, "Wade was a rotten apple—you and I talked about this before. In fact, I recall saying that without Larry he wouldn't last two minutes on the street. I was right about that, at least." He smiled, still looking into his glass. "You probably know how much I like being right. Anyway, as I said, there will be a lot of suspects in this one, all more probable than you. But if your name does come up, it's a murder charge, and even though they know Wade was rotten, they're going to think that getting the guy who shot him will be removing a second rotten apple from our fair city."

"You're doing this to protect your career?"

"No, of course not. If I thought you were any kind of threat to society—"

"This happened once—it could happen again."

Rainey laughed, the first genuine laugh I'd heard from him.

"This? No, this couldn't happen again. There's only one person in the world who could've gotten it started, and you aren't him anymore. By the way, I'd like you to burn that card I gave your wife. Don't throw it in the trash, don't recycle it, just burn it. Same with those phone numbers I gave you. Go through and erase me completely. It would make me feel better—make my *career* feel better—if you were to do that."

"No problem."

He leaned forward. "The only real interest I have is finding out where the gun came from. You can't help me there, I know. And I suppose stopping that one source won't *really* change the flow, so I'm willing to drop it without a backward glance." He pointed at me.

"One more thing. You'll be relieved to know that there won't be any other Hoods crawling out of the sewer to find out what happened to Larry and Wade."

"Good. I'm tired of that family."

He smiled. "That reminds me, I have a question. Just between the two of us."

"Sure. I owe you."

"You don't owe me a goddamned thing, but here's the question. Do you know what happened to Larry? It's been bugging me like the dickens."

"On the freeway?"

"Yes. On the last day of his life Larry Hood went for a drive."

I sighed and felt the last of my defenses slip away. I told him about heading out to the winery and seeing Larry Hood on my tail. How I tried to lose him in traffic, but he stayed close. And how I sped up, jumped from lane to lane, but it was pretty snotty out, and then I saw the van on the shoulder. . . . Rainey watched me, waiting. Finally I said, "I dodged it, and he didn't. But the whole time before that—"

"Which is what shook you the next day when I showed you the copy of his throw-down shot."

"I thought you were going to arrest me."

He smiled. "You've survived a number of close calls recently. This isn't the way these things usually work out."

I shrugged. "I lost Marla."

"Yes, I want to talk about that. According to my calculations, we have one more piece of business, a question you never asked me, but I want to answer it anyway. It might help you get her back. Did you ever ask yourself why we didn't stick around that night, waiting for you to come home?"

"It did occur to me, but I was afraid to ask."

"Exactly. You thought it would force me to accuse you of taking the truck. Well, the answer is simple. She lied about looking out the window."

"That's why you didn't stick around?"

"Come on, Jim, you're good at this stuff. Think about it. Whatever she saw—whether it was you taking the truck or you running the other way—she knew you were safe from the car thieves. I asked her to call us when you got back, and she said she would. If she didn't know where you were—hadn't seen where you went—she would've wanted us to stick around. I could see that something was eating at her, and I assumed it was because you had taken the truck. But there was a *quality* to her agitation that didn't make sense, and I spent a good number of nights trying to figure it out. Then I got it—or at least I think I did. I actually sat up in bed and said, 'Aha!' like a scientist in the funny papers. Marla *stayed* at the window—you were already gone—and one of the Hood brothers looked back. I'll bet she locked eyes with the son of a bitch. Now that I think about it, that was Wade because he wanted to have a go at her face with a soup can." He rapped the table with his knuckles. "Which also means she could have identified him from the throw-downs. *She* was the one who faked me out. Shoot. You know, if I had seen some of this at the time, we wouldn't have gone so far into this mess. I'm not half the detective I pretend to be."

I said, "You're plenty."

He chuckled self-consciously and said, "Well, my wife owes me a foot rub. I should go home and collect."

"You're quitting early? It's not even one o'clock."

"Cops get days off too."

I nodded to thank him, and he nodded in reply.

He said, "I can offer to shake hands on this affair because anyone watching will assume we're simply closing an item of business." He started to stand, but I stayed in my seat, and he sat down again.

I said, "I have one more item for you to cross off your list. It's small. . . ."

"I'm listening. I'm not advising you to tell me more, but I'll listen."

I said, "It might not have been teens who beat the truck with a pipe."

After a pause he said, "Ah, adrenaline. I can see that. Turns a guy into an ape sometimes. Well, our decisions don't always make sense in retrospect." He sat there for a moment, then pointed at me. "So you couldn't have confessed to taking the truck that night to avoid all this because you knew it was totaled."

"That wasn't part of my thinking at the time."

"Decisions can be subconscious." He pushed himself out of his chair. "But now we're straying." He straightened his coat and offered his hand. I stood and took it. He said, "You're an interesting man, Jim Sandusky. I wish it could've been different between us. I hope you make it safely back to the planet." He left.

To keep the moment from seeming significant to anyone who might be watching, I collected the bowls and glasses and pitcher and carried them over to the dirty-dish bin. I went back and wiped down the table, then asked John if there was anything I could do to help. He looked at me for a long moment. I guess part of what he saw kept him from asking about the rest.

I didn't know what to do with myself, so I went down to the cellar and started sorting through some boxes of wine that I hadn't yet decided how to price or display. I didn't want to do much with them because I had a sense that later it would be impossible for me to guess why I had made some of these decisions. My underlying intent was to keep busy while not doing anything I couldn't undo later. My life needed more of this feeling.

Some unknown amount of time later, John called down to tell me that Marla's brother had come in.

"I'll be right up."

I heard feet on the stairs and Dave's voice: "Stay there, I'm coming down." I went over to meet him beneath the light at the bottom of the stairs, where the room has less of a cavernous feel. He handed me a crumpled column torn from a newspaper.

"Have you seen this?" It was more a demand than a question.

I smoothed out and read the short column:

HOMICIDE IN INDUSTRIAL AREA

A man was found dead in his car yesterday morning in the undeveloped yards east of the river. A truck driver for Denton Sand & Gravel discovered the body and called the police.

The car, a brown Mazda with a primer-gray left front fender, was stalled at an angle in the ditch. Police believe it had been traveling at slow speed with the windows down and headlights off. "This guy was on a combat mission," said one investigator. He added, "But so was the guy who shot him."

The incident is thought to have occurred a little before midnight.

Death was almost immediate, caused by six gunshot wounds to the head and body. The victim's identity will remain undisclosed until next of kin can be notified.

Police have no suspects at this time. Anyone having information pertaining to the shooting should contact the Homicide Department at the Northeast Station.

When I looked up, Dave said, "I just came from where we met the other night. It's all taped off. And that guy who stopped to talk to me was driving a Mazda with a primer-gray left front fender. The same guy who—"

"I didn't see the car. I was hiding."

He looked at me as if I were lying. "You don't get it. You were there, I was there, and he was there—all three of us—where this happened."

I said, "I got that part." I should have seen where he was going, but I didn't. And it wouldn't have mattered anyway; I'm sure I would still have given him the same dazed look I was giving him now.

Dave said, "You didn't ask if I killed him."

"What do you mean?

He snatched the clipping from me. "Just now. You didn't ask if I shot this guy."

"It's not something you would do, Dave. Even though you said you wanted to."

"That's not the point, *Jim.*"

"Then please get to the point."

He hesitated, then said, "I *did* want to—I even said so—but you told me not to get a gun. You said leave it alone."

"That's right."

"You still don't see."

"I'm tired of trying to figure stuff out."

He gave a sharp laugh. "No kidding! I mean, what's left?"

"This conversation. I still don't know what we're talking about."

"Sure." Looking down, he shook his head and said, "So why am I not relieved? I wanted to shoot this guy, and now he's dead—shouldn't I be relieved?" He kept looking down at the boxes of wine on the concrete floor. I waited. He said, "Jim, one of us killed this guy, and we both know it wasn't me."

"Dave—"

"You should have told me. Someone should have known."

"Sergeant Rainey knew. He was just here."

"The *cops*? How much trouble are you in?"

"None. He came to tell me it's over."

"This guy calls Marla a cunt, and the next day he's found shot to death, and the cops come in to tell you it's over? Do you have any idea how *unlikely* that sounds?"

"He knew this guy was after me. Look, part of what he said was that the investigating team has no reason to put me—or you, for that matter—at the scene of the shooting."

"Okay. That's good." Then he said, "But did he know about it going in?"

"No, he figured it out the way you did."

"See, that's my point. You should have told someone going in."

"I did what I thought was right at the time. All I wanted was for Marla to be safe. I couldn't take care of her, but you could. Now it's over and she's safe."

"Next time you're not leaving me out of it."

"Fine. It's a deal. Next time I'll give you—"

"Yeah, right, next time. Who am I kidding? And now I have this gun."

"Just give it back."

"It doesn't work like that."

"I thought you borrowed it from your friend."

Dave snorted. "That pussy? He didn't want to get involved— didn't want his *gun* to get involved. No, I had to go somewhere else."

"I'll buy it off you. Whatever you paid, that's what I'll pay you."

"There's no way Marla will let you have a gun in the house."

"No, I mean you can keep it, but you should be reimbursed."

"Christ, man, don't worry about it! *Reimbursed.*" Then he said, "Hey, if you're so responsible, why haven't you written to her about what happened?"

"I did."

He shook the crumpled clipping in my face. "Does it include this?" I blinked, and he said, "I didn't think so."

I said, "That hadn't happened yet." It took a moment for this to soak in.

He sighed. "Anyway, I thought you should see what they wrote."

"Have you said anything to her about it?"

"What? Have you lost your mind?"

My mind, I don't know. My soul, probably.

He looked at me for a moment and said, "She loves you, you know. She loves you like crazy. This is eating her up." He scratched his head. "Look, tell me whatever you want—truth, lies, I don't care. But you have to tell Marla the truth. You have to tell her everything, and it has to be the truth."

e was right, but I didn't have the energy to tell Marla anything. I sat in front of the iMac and stared at the blinking cursor as it waited for me to begin. I stared at it long enough for my heartbeat to align with the blinking. I was in sync with a machine as I spiraled inward. The only thing good about it was that I had no desire to drive anywhere.

On the wall above the computer I had taped the Rumi lines:

> *What was said to the rose that made it open*
> *Was said to me here in my chest.*

I thought about the man who had written these words, about his having lived some eight centuries earlier. The span of years made my own life seem random. Why was I alive now instead of last century or a thousand years in the future? The inquiry *Why am I here?* had taken on new meaning. I knew there was a difference between being alive and being aware you're alive, but I couldn't figure out what the difference meant. On the one hand, no critter seems more alive than a feral one; on the other hand is the idea that an unexamined life isn't worth living. What was the message here, "Be feral, but think about it"?

Maybe I didn't know what being alive meant.

Don't worry, it won't last. Nothing lasts.

Death lasts.

No meaning here either. Rainey was right; I should have gone down to the morgue and looked at a body to appreciate the condition.

Then I thought, *Rumi's words have lasted.* The words this man put on paper so long ago—in a distant land, in a foreign language—these words continued to live. Indeed, as they were translated into more languages and more people read them, they were growing stronger, gaining more life. This brought me back to my own efforts to convert thoughts to written words. I typed onto the screen: "Written words survive." This was a fact. It felt good to put a fact into written words. It was a step, to actually write something.

I reread the sentence. Not all written words *should* survive. I deleted it to save myself the embarrassment of having to face it later. Then I typed, "You killed Wade Hood."

This sounded like an accusation instead of a fact, so I changed it to "I killed Wade Hood."

Now it was confessional, almost like a suicide note. And it looked backward in time. I wanted to look forward. After a moment I erased it too.

Then I typed, "After the wreck I couldn't sleep."

I looked at these words for a while. They didn't look forward, but the thought they expressed was clear and safe and true, and they made you want to read the next sentence. Which, in a way, was forward-looking. I wondered why I hadn't written it before. I decided to quit while I was ahead, so I tapped "Save" and went up to bed.

I no longer felt relief about anything. Wade was dead: a fact. I had written a description of the wreck and sent it to Marla: another fact. I lay there thinking about the facts and wondering why I felt so empty. It took me a long time to see that at least part of it was the waiting. It wasn't my turn to do anything.

Dave was right, though; I did owe Marla another explanation. But how could I give her the next one without knowing how she felt about the first? I was beginning to believe that she might decide to leave me for good. And the longer it took for her to respond, the more difficult my waiting would be. (I was shocked to realize that I had mailed the envelope only the previous evening; she hadn't even received it yet.) I tried to convince myself that there had been no other way to proceed and that the anxiety I felt now was natural, something I would simply have to endure.

And of course her response to my letter wasn't my only anxiety. I was still facing the fact that I had shot Wade Hood. How I had gone about it was a series of steps, each logically (I thought) following the last and in turn leading logically to the next, but the fact of it lay out on the open ground like a toxic spill. And there were the cops, the *investigative team*, working as hard as they could to pick me out of the population. My anxieties were various and tangled.

At work the next week John remained steady as a ship. He knew I was going through some difficult times—I could tell by the way he talked to me, how careful he was with tone and wording. He kept to safe topics, but the subtext of everything he said was *You are among friends*. I wanted to tell him he didn't have to be careful, that I wasn't about to do anything rash, but this wouldn't have been a response to anything he had said, and I didn't know how to reply in subtexts. I did know that he knew more about where I was than I did, and that questions about existence and eternity were indicators, warnings of deeper issues. I was spending too much time thinking about these larger, darker questions.

He asked if I was still writing.

"Some. Mostly I stare at an empty screen."

"Part of the process. I think it's about transitions and plateaus. The transitions are the tough times, and you have to focus on climbing out of them. When you reach a plateau, you stop and look around and say, 'Wow!' And you write about what made you say it. Then you see some stairs carved in the stone and wonder where they go, and now you're climbing again."

"Really. I think I'm okay."

He said, "I have an image for you, something I came up with back when I was just out of the army. For a while I thought I was going crazy, which for me was darkness, as if light couldn't get inside my head. They sent me to this shrink who had me talk about whatever came to mind. Once I got going it just spilled out of me. What I eventually came to see was that all these words were in my head—this is the image—the *words* were blocking the light. In order to get sane, I had to get rid of the words."

"I can see that. Strange, but I can see it."

"I thought you might—and yes, it's strange. This was around the time I started reading poetry. Here I was, with this huge cloud of words in my head, and along comes Rumi, with maybe seven individual words in his. And each of his words was part of some small, essential poem. It was as if he could just pluck one from the air and put it on the page. So simple, yet so impossible. Obviously I have the Eastern thing going. You're probably picturing this guy with a pair of chopsticks picking words out of the air like flies, so I may have taken it too far. But the point is about the quiet up here." He tapped his forehead. "The lack of *busyness*. Might be something to strive for. It certainly was for me, once I understood it."

"I'll have to spend more time with that book." I wanted to keep it neutral because swarming words weren't my problem, and I didn't want to get into what my problem was.

He said, "If you figure out how he got where he ended up, let me know."

"I doubt I'll come up with anything."

"You might doubt that you'll come out of it at all."

If I had had the words, I would have explained to him that what was said to Rumi's rose had never been said to me, though the poem itself showed me that such a thing was possible. But it was Marla who brought me within proximity of such possibilities, such openings. If I had had the words I would have told John that Marla was to me what was said to Rumi's rose.

During this period the wine reps behaved differently as well. They kept to the business at hand, weren't inclined to linger and chat. Looking back, I see that they were simply reacting to how I treated them. I was all business, impossible to engage in casual conversation.

I had always found a desirable solitude in the island but never more so than at this time. It was a sanctuary even when I was helping a customer with a particular shiraz, say, or which regional rosé might complement grilled salmon. I could be direct and honest with them and still maintain my protective wall, which I guess means I was hiding behind my professional identity. After all, they weren't there to talk to Jim the Killer of the Hood Brothers. I was Jim the Wine Steward, and we talked about wine.

But if I wanted solitude, why not hole up in the wine cellar?

I thought about it, but John wouldn't have let me, not for long. He was aware of the warning signs I was giving off, and any attention from him would be personal rather than business. If I had started spending too much time in the cellar, he would have come down, pretending to see if I needed a hand with something but actually making sure I wasn't sitting in a dark corner staring at a handful of pills. When I was at the island, he could tell from a distance that I was functioning properly, and he would leave me alone. The kind of solitude I needed was more available at the island among customers.

Over the years I have noticed that some wine stewards grow obsessed with acquisition. They go internal and become difficult to deal with, for customers and owners alike. Imagine a Dickens character in a stone cellar examining row upon row of dusty bottles, his candlelit eyes greedy and more than a little mad, his twitchy fingers hovering above this bottle, then that, while he mutters to himself, "Mine! This too!" He resents the customers, who come in to trade money for what he has taken such care to collect, and he resents the owner of the shop (who is also the true owner of these dusty bottles), who can't afford to have so much money tied up in stock that isn't moving. Which means the wine steward can't celebrate what he has collected without calling attention to the fact that he isn't selling it. He has to hoard his satisfaction too.

Time is also a factor. A bottle of wine is a living thing. It ages, which means it has a period of improvement, then a period of maturity—this is when it is most drinkable—after which it begins to change and perhaps lose value. A vital aspect of the complete wine steward is a desire to share with the purchasing public. However important it might be for us to own a great wine, it's more important *to have owned* it, to pass it along to the final purchaser, the consumer, who will appreciate its great qualities while they are still great, which in turn helps finance the wine steward's next acquisition, the next great wine.

There is a little of the miser in any good wine steward, and there was probably more of it than usual in me during this time. I really did take dark pleasure in the cellar among the quiet, patient bottles, and this might have gotten bad if I hadn't realized it could, if I hadn't been watching myself, at least to some degree. I want to believe that being aware of some possibilities makes them impossibilities.

For a while, other than the sip-and-spit requirement of my job, I didn't touch alcohol. Which was good—but it was also passive. I could also say I didn't rob a bank or set fire to the grade school. On the other hand, the temptation to drink was real. I didn't drink because greater than the temptation to do so was a fear of what might happen to me with a wine habit. This was not the time to develop side obsessions, and while it was not the time to retreat into the solitude of a dark cellar, it would have been far worse to retreat into a binge. Granted, either way John would have come looking for me, but it's clear now that I didn't want anyone other than Marla looking for me.

I didn't drink because it felt good to resist an urge. It felt civilized. Resisting urges is part of being civilized.

In the middle evening, when I might have had wine and reflected on my life, now I sipped a mug of tea. The tea was old, having sat in the drawer beneath the coffeemaker for years, sealed in foil packets. Licorice had always been my favorite and continued to be, though when it ran out and I bought another box, it was too strong. Still, the warm mug of spiced aroma became a familiar friend while I sat there staring at the walls, not wishing I had something to do, not relieved I had nothing to do, just staring.

Cars passing the house were meaningless now. For a time I tried to guess which neighbor was pulling in, whether one door or two would click open and clunk shut, but I couldn't bring myself to care. They came and went, having nothing to do with me.

I remember thinking it was too bad I didn't have any physical energy because then I could have turned my focus toward something positive, such as jogging or biking or developing a routine at a gym. But I lacked the energy even to replace the sneakers I had donated. I thought about it, which was a step, but I couldn't get past the idea of someone noticing my new sneakers and asking about them. (I look back now and see that all I would've had to say was "Those other ones hurt my feet," but at the time this contrivance seemed hopelessly complex.) What I really needed energy for was to sit down to the sentence "After the wreck, I couldn't sleep," and add to it. Six words down, ten thousand to go. A *hundred* thousand to go. I needed to finish the next explanation, mail it, and trust that I would somehow win Marla back, but I couldn't get the seventh word out. I couldn't keep myself from thinking through the entire adventure that followed the wreck on the freeway, from driving around at night to shooting Wade Hood—and how this had cost me my relationship with Sergeant Rainey and yes, perhaps my soul—but I couldn't get a single word out until I knew where Marla was. Where her heart was. Writing the next sentence just to write it hadn't occurred to me yet.

Though I'm not religious in the organized sense, I do have a vague sense of a higher structure. I believe we're each born with a calling—not so much a purpose in life as something to which we are best suited—and if circumstances work out a certain way, we are a perfect fit for the specific situation. Only this far into it, I'm already in trouble. Not having kids has kept me from truly feeling my years, but I know that at least in a theoretical sense I am solidly into middle age, which means my "calling" should have been apparent by now. It doesn't make sense to have a religion to which you are an exception. But I really couldn't figure out how I fit into my own belief system. Maybe this is why I have to say that I have only a vague sense of a higher structure.

Religion is a way of explaining the unprovable to oneself, of making sense of the spiritual aspects of life. Our religion also guides us in our ethical behavior when instinct urges us to behave otherwise. And where religion fails to guide us, we as a society have developed a system of laws to keep us in line.

Laws to keep us from, say, killing a fellow citizen?

I considered raising this issue with John. His mention of an event involving a gunshot had me wondering what had happened to him in Vietnam. He successfully kept to himself any detail that might have given me a clue, but I had no doubt that he had his own meticulous understanding of how the universe works, and his gunshot must have figured in. Vietnam will always be sacred turf for a lot of servicemen, just as all wars have been and will continue to be sacred turf for many of those who were involved. Because I had never fought in any war, I didn't feel I had the right to intrude. But one day I hoped to learn some of the specifics, whatever he might be willing to share. Maybe hearing about his issues would help me learn how to live with my own.

On the other hand, I saw that our respective situations were different, perhaps fundamentally—his darkness was blocked light, whereas mine was an absence of light—and that it may have been impossible for either of us to understand the other's condition.

His concern for me felt good, though he seemed to suspect that I was still spiraling downward. And I respected his perception enough to wonder whether he was right. The look I sometimes saw in his eye made me think his event involving the gunshot had caused him, deep in his past, to embrace suicide as an option. I didn't want to end up just a brief local news item that some intrepid reporter traced back to the seemingly unrelated deaths of two sinister brothers.

Which brought me back to what had happened with Wade. I still didn't know how to make sense of it. When I looked at it a certain way, I felt I had broken a basic part of the social contract. It was murder, and I couldn't think my way past that bare-naked fact. Rainey's statement, "Nothing justifies this," ate at me, but not the way I expected it to. In the starkest definition of the word, I had *murdered* a man, but the fact that it didn't really eat at me was eating at me more than the murder itself.

I didn't know how to make sense of this either. Had I distanced myself from the idea in order to view it from a safe remove? Almost certainly. But I had been at safe removes before, and this felt different. Maybe there are different safe removes. Then I thought about it another way. After all, the social contract is a concept that helps keep the community whole, and there was nothing whole about Wade Hood sitting in his car at night, working through his cigarettes and beers as he waited for something to tell him that it was time to kill me.

Should I have settled all of this before I shot him?

Maybe I *had* settled it. Maybe I was now making my peace with the necessity of it, putting it into perspective, like a kid who's lost a tooth and now can't keep his horrified tongue from exploring the new raw hole.

hen you take primitive action to solve a modern problem, a part of you reverts. A part of your intellect and most of your emotional structure loses thousands of years of social development. You grow thick and stupid, and you scuttle backward on all fours into the narrowest crevice that will accommodate you, and wait in the dark as the moons cycle through. Perhaps you have the faintest notion that at some point you might crawl out again, emerge into the light of modern day. You still go through the motions of an approximated life—you work, shop, eat, sleep—but a vital part of you remains hunkered in the dark, waiting for some indication that your world is ready for you to re-evolve. When it does come (a few days later, though it feels like years), you sit up and stretch, and the hair on your knuckles recedes. You push yourself upright and find yourself dressed in socially acceptable clothing, and you gradually become aware that a hunk of molded plastic you once were able to identify as a telephone is annoying you with its electronic trill. You stare at it as you gradually become a person again. You check the caller ID box

and see that it thinks Dave Wick is on the other end. It dawns on you that it won't be Dave but instead his sister—who was once your wife—and then you remember that she still is. As you pick up the receiver you recall what certain grunted syllables mean.

"Hello?" I didn't recognize my own voice.

"Jim?" She sounded a million miles away.

I said, "I'm here."

"It's Thanksgiving tomorrow."

After a moment I said, "I guess it is."

It took her another moment to say, "How are you doing?"

"These haven't been the easiest days for me."

"Me either."

I said, "Did you get the writing I sent?"

"I did. You don't need to send any more."

"No, I want to. Working on it helps me sleep. It's just so difficult—"

"What I mean is, can you come get me?"

She was sitting with Dave on his porch, both of them bundled in heavy coats. The weather had eased, but it was still early winter, still cold. I could see in their posture now the children they had once been while waiting on dark mornings for the school bus. Marla's boxes of things were stacked behind them, with one armload of longer clothes on hangers draped over the stack. I mentioned her bike, and she said we could get it later. The three of us moved it all to the backseat of the Camry, working slowly, careful with everything, careful with each other. During the few minutes we took to get everything situated, I was trying to get a sense of where I stood with them. They were amiable and businesslike, as people dealing with strangers tend to be. They weren't being polite in general, but there was an element of politeness toward me, and I didn't feel a part of their family just then. As we said good-bye to Dave a part of me thought I might be back here an hour later, dropping her off again.

I drove in silence, hoping she would initiate the exchange so I would have a sense of where we were headed. We each had a false start, raising a finger to indicate the introduction of a thought, but then a hesitation and, as the moment was lost, more silence. Finally I felt I had to say something, if only to take a reading from the tone of her reply.

"Are you hungry?"

She said, "I'd like to get back home. Is there anything in the fridge?"

"I've been eating at the Deli mostly."

"Still, let's go home. We can shop later if we need to. And we need something for Thanksgiving dinner tomorrow."

I nodded. At least the car was moving in the right direction. We continued in silence for a while. I concentrated on traffic and route choices—which arterial to take and from it how to get back into the residential grid streets—but I was really just waiting for one of us to speak.

Finally she said, "There's more to tell."

"I'm trying. It took forever to get that first part written, and I didn't want you to have to wait. I'm getting there, though. Working on it has kept me home—which you'll be happy to hear—I'm not driving around anymore. Actually, it's kept me sane, even though the next part is tougher."

"Not that. I was serious about you not needing to write any more. What I mean is, there's more from my side of it. Something you don't know. Something I need to apologize for. If you give me a minute, I'll figure out how to say it."

"Take all the time you need, but I'm sure you don't owe me an apology."

She smiled. "I see how hard that writing must have been."

"I had a lot of time."

"Well, I think I should jump right in. It's about lying to you."

"Any lie you might have told had nothing to do with . . . well, any of this." It felt too soon to go deep. I could almost feel the car start looking for a place to turn around. "Besides, I told lies too. Remember, you caught me in some."

Marla said, "You were never unfair to me."

Unfair? That could mean a lot of things. It gave me a flicker of panic to think about some of them. "I don't know if I can hear this right now."

She said, "It's nothing like that."

"Nothing like what."

"There's no way you can know what I'm talking about."

I said, "Okay, then, how were you unfair?"

"I let you think you caused everything. That morning I went over to Dave's, I said some pretty nasty things, and some of them were unfair."

"The Hood brothers caused most of what happened. I caused the rest."

"I caused some too."

After thinking for a moment I said, "Does this have anything to do with Wade seeing you at the window?" There was a stunned quality to the silence that followed.

"How on earth did you come up with that? Stop the car! I need to know how you knew that."

I kept driving. "Not me. Rainey. He thinks you locked eyes with Wade." She turned to me. I said, "He put himself in your shoes and wondered what he would have done if his idiot husband had gone out to the street while a couple of car thieves were trying to steal their car. He said he couldn't have kept himself from looking out the window."

She turned forward again. "That makes it seem so obvious."

"Everything he says is like that. What got him thinking about it was, you didn't care about the cops taking off."

"I didn't care about what?"

"The cops taking off. That night two cops drove the car thieves down to the station, leaving one other cop and Rainey. When he told you they were heading back to the station, you said okay. If you hadn't known where I was—if you hadn't looked out the window to see where I went—you would've wanted them to stick around."

"He said that?"

"Pretty much."

She brooded. I drove.

Finally she said, "Did he go any further with it?"

"He says you lied about recognizing Wade in the throw-downs."

"Sure, but I mean about the window. Me being at the window."

"I don't think so."

"We didn't just lock eyes."

"What do you mean?"

"It was more than locking eyes. You know what? This time I mean it. I need you to stop the car." I looked over at her. She said, "Please, just park while I tell you this. I need to know you're hearing it."

A block later I found an open space, and eased in against the curb. She didn't say anything, so I turned off the engine. Finally I said, "So you didn't just lock eyes with Wade."

She said, "I froze. I couldn't look away. He had all this nervous energy, as if he had a bar fight going on inside his head. We stared at each other until the sirens broke it off, and then the other one—Larry, I guess—yelled at him. But before they disappeared up the street Wade looked back once more, and that's what scared me, that second look. He stood there—dead calm now—and pointed at me as if his hand were a gun. Then he pulled the trigger. I must have flinched because when I looked again, he was gone."

I said, "But that still doesn't mean—"

She held out a hand to stop me. "I didn't think it was so bad until I saw this." She pulled a folded newspaper clipping from a coat pocket. "I think this is what happened to Wade."

I snatched it from her, knowing what it was. "Dave said he wouldn't show you that."

"He didn't. The school takes the paper too. Part of my day is reading current news to the kids for discussion. When I saw this, I just knew."

I looked at the clipping. It had been cut out with scissors, leaving perfectly even margins, and it had never been crumpled. I said, "Well, you're right. That's him. That's the guy you locked eyes with." I held it out for her to take back, but she refused.

She said, "I have it memorized. It says he was shot six times."

I could feel my pulse high in my cheeks and around my eyes. I was about to learn whether or not I would lose the only love of my life. I decided not to base the rest of that life on a lie.

I said, "That's all the gun held."

When we got home, I parked and shut off the engine and sat there hoping she would make the next move. I didn't want to influence her or take anything for granted, so I stared out the windshield at nothing, trying to relax and at the same time pay attention. After a moment I looked over, and perhaps *because* I looked over, her eyes teared up. I couldn't read her because her face remained blank. Her cheeks reddened. She worked her hands into the pockets of her coat and then turned to look out the side window. Facing away from me, she said, "I'm sorry I made you do that."

"What do you mean?" I knew, but I needed to hear the words.

She said, "That thing with Wade. The newspaper clipping."

"You didn't make me do that to Wade. Wade made me do that to Wade."

"I need to start thinking about it like that." Her voice cracked. "My way is killing me."

Thanksgiving for us wasn't a holiday. Marla baked a chicken while I made up a batch of mashed potatoes and a skillet of asparagus sautéed in salad dressing. When the chicken came out of the oven, an apple pie went in. We raised a glass not to the pilgrims but to the fact that we were sitting at the same table. That we were alive and sitting at the same table and hoping for the same things we had always hoped for. Things that might be further away from us now than they had ever been, but at least they once again seemed possible.

At one point she said she felt awful about Dave having to keep the newspaper clipping from her. She understood it, but she hated putting him in such a position. And then she said she'd do the same for him, and yes, he would feel awful for having put her in such a position. She said that in some situations there was no right way.

In the next few days, when we were in close proximity—cooking (which we did together during this period) or figuring out why the television remote was getting stubborn on us—she would touch my hand, just reach over and make gentle contact for a moment before we continued with the task at hand. The first time she did this I didn't do anything in return except pause and smile downward, hoping she would see the smile. Later I thought I might have blown it by not at least returning the gesture. But then I thought I had done the right thing simply by not pulling away. I think she actually believed I might pull away from her. I didn't see why she would continue to hold herself responsible for what had happened to Wade. But assuming she did, what was she looking for now? I hoped it wasn't forgiveness because you have to put yourself above the other person in order to forgive them, and I wasn't about to do that. Acceptance made sense, especially from herself. But acceptance for what?

She had wished Wade dead. And like a kid (like the ones she worked with throughout the week), when she wished for this and then it happened, she couldn't help but feel responsible for it. As strange as it seemed, she believed that she had caused Wade to come after me, which in turn had caused me to kill him. I could see how this might hit her harder than my contempt for Larry Hood had hit me.

After this little epiphany I didn't wait for her to reach for me again; I came up behind her (she was at the sink exactly as she had been all those years ago when she'd decided she was through trying to get pregnant, which made this act one of the most difficult things I had ever done), and I slipped my arms beneath hers and around her ribs and nestled my face in her hair by her ear. Then I told her I loved her. She got soapy water all over the place as she turned to hug me in return. When she pulled away, her face was wet. She wiped her cheeks with the wrists of our new dish-washing gloves, then looked down and said, "Look what I've done to our floor!"

.   .   .

I started working on what had happened during those sleepless nights following the wreck. We would get home from work and chat while fixing dinner, then watch *Jeopardy* while we ate, and then I would spend a couple hours at the machine, trying to put the tangled mess of my recent history into words. Marla told me she really didn't need to see any more writing—or even *want* to—but I stayed at it. And, in fact, it got easier when I was writing for myself. I started a second file in which I took notes having nothing to do with my little adventure, just random thoughts that occurred to me about anything, my fingers rattling away at the keyboard like a foraging rodent. I slept well, the phone didn't ring, and I canceled caller ID. Every once in a while Marla would ask if I was okay, using a tone that told me she wasn't worried, just checking in. We didn't talk about the hard stuff. We weren't avoiding it or suppressing it. She seemed to trust me to talk about it if I needed to, and I trusted the same of her. And of myself.

Work became a job again—one that I enjoyed, but when I was there, I simply did the job. I didn't monitor the front door, and I could hear the phone ring without being viscerally aware of it, wondering who might be on the other end. We had another computer upgrade—John told me I should have an iBook for its greater memory and portability. "These things are really slick." He knew I was still writing about something important and private, and at least part of what he was doing was upgrading the machine I used at home. I let him—out of guilt, I suppose—because I had made such an effort to close off any other way he might help me out of my situation.

I reached a point where I no longer wanted to know the details leading up to his gunshot. In a fundamental sense I already knew everything I needed to know. Further details, while not meaningless, would have been useless to me. In understanding this distinction I also understood that he had no interest in where my own damage had come from. His concern was how I would deal with it. How I would get on with my life.

A week after Thanksgiving I was scheduled to meet Paul, the Stebbins Hill winemaker, for lunch across the river. He was planning to be in town anyway and wanted to hand off two bottles of what I had missed because of the wreck on the freeway. Out of what felt like whimsical curiosity, I gave myself enough time to circle past the porn theater on 10th. The old hooker wasn't there, of course; it was far too early in the day. Still, seeing the vacant area beneath the marquee left me with an unsettled feeling, an absence.

The following Saturday Marla and I had dinner downtown at a wonderful old Chinese restaurant called the Mandarin Palace. This was my idea, one of my better ones. We had eaten there one other time, when we were still living in the Agate House before we were married. We were surprised to find that the waiter we'd had then was at the cash register now, as if frozen since we had left him standing there so many years before. To my delight, he remembered us as clearly as we remembered him.

He said, "Good to see you again." He gave us a soft smile and said, "You should come in more often. Open every day, plenty of room." He seated us at the same table we had occupied before, handed us our menus, and moved off to see to other customers.

Marla said, "I'm glad we came here."

I said, "Just like the old days."

"Better." She put out her hand, and I took it. We sat like this while we looked over our menus.

I said, "I remember liking the sesame beef."

She said, "I liked all of it. That, the hot-and-sour soup, and the seafood broccoli thing, whatever it was called." We scanned down our menus to the seafood section and there it was: scallop shrimp with broccoli.

The waiter returned for our order and we named those three dishes.

"Same as last time. Be careful you don't get tired of it." He said this with the same soft smile, our gentle wiseass mandarin waiter with the perfect memory. He turned toward the kitchen before we could reply.

Marla said, "I've been meaning to thank you for sending me that page. The explanation."

"It was a mother bear to write."

"Well, it was what I had been hoping for, and I don't think I ever said so. It was exactly what I needed."

"It was what I needed too. To get it said. But I'm glad you don't want more."

"You're still working on something, though."

"Yes, but it's easier when it's just for me. I'm already on page forty-something, and that wreck hasn't happened yet."

"And as you said, it's keeping you home at night." She smiled. "I'm glad those days are behind us." She reached for my hands, and I reached for hers. She was assuring me that for her, those days were indeed behind us. She said, "But, there's something I want to talk about."

I pulled my hands back—I couldn't help pulling away—and folded them in front of me. "About those days?"

"About that piece of writing. The explanation."

"Okay, but I was hoping we wouldn't have to."

She reached and patted my arm. "This won't be bad. I promise." She withdrew her hand, giving me back my space.

I said, "Is this about me knowing the van was there?"

She said, "No, it's about closing yourself off to me."

"I don't remember that part." I couldn't tell if I was on overload, but I felt close and tried to fight it. I really couldn't think of what she was referring to.

"You were afraid to tell me about the wreck because I might close myself off to you, but instead you closed yourself off to me."

"Okay, yes, I do remember that."

"It's what you do. You close yourself off to me."

"Routinely? Am I closed right now? I really want to know."

"Maybe. There's the Jim I talk to and the Jim who sits just a little way off, making sure the one I'm talking to doesn't make any mistakes."

"Sometimes I'm not monitoring, I'm just watching. Sometimes I'm being defensive, but often it's just a habit. I'm not always trying to be perfect."

"Good. I can't have you perfect because I can't be perfect in return. But it's something you should know about, that when there's any *pressure* on you, you lock up while you work your way through it—through both sides of the exchange—and I have to wait to find out what was said. What was *decided*."

My thinking took me nowhere. "I guess I need an example."

"Remember when you donated the baby things to Goodwill?"

"Of course. And yes, that was a mistake. I completely missed the point."

"You're still missing the point. It was the right thing to do, to get that stuff out of the house because it was making me morose. But you should have talked to me about it first. Instead you thought it through on your own, both your side of it and mine, and out it went. You might be able to read my mind, but that doesn't help us unless I can read yours back. Which I can't. I don't care about the little stuff. If the dish-washing gloves are a problem, just replace them. We don't have to workshop what color we want. But we have to work together on the important things."

"Are you saying I started doing this after the miscarriage?"

"No, you've done it since the day we met, probably since the day you were born. The miscarriage was when I thought it might be a problem. For a while you seemed to think that unless you did everything precisely right, we would unravel."

"I guess that might be true." It was *exactly* true.

"So here's the deal; here's what I want. You can keep doing the internal thing—you will anyway, it's who you are—but if I ask about what's going on in there, you have to tell me something. Maybe not everything, but you have to give me a sense of where you are."

"I feel willing to talk, but I don't know how to get started."

"Start by not thinking about how I might reply. Take a chance and just say the thing. You can't imagine how good it will feel to me."

I thought about this, about how difficult it would be to just take that chance. I said, "Is it a burden? Me being like this?"

"Not one bit. Most guys have this hidden agenda about getting a woman into bed. At first you seemed more worried about rejection. Then you somehow turned that energy into an effort to keep us stable. Early on it puzzled me, but when I saw that I would have to *initiate* most of the time, everything got easier."

"Do you ever think about it? The miscarriage?"

She nodded and grew quiet. "At times. Especially when I see a kid about the age Brian would have been, I think about it. And sometimes it hurts. But miscarriages happen for biological reasons. More important, I love what we have now, and I would never trade this for some unknown life we might have had. For me, it's just something bad that happened to us a long time ago."

I said, "For some reason in the last few weeks I've been chewing my way through every little detail of it."

She smiled. "See? You need to tell your wife what's going on."

We took our time through dinner and didn't leave the restaurant until after nine. It was out of our way, but I decided to take the St. Stephen's bridge across the river. When Marla looked over, I said, "Just a little side trip." I turned up 10th. As we approached the porn theater, my heart rate increased, and sure enough, in the glow of the covered space beneath the marquee was my old friend Sally, looking as patient and comfortable with her place in the world as anyone I'd ever seen.

On what felt like a whim, though I'm sure it wasn't, I pulled into the no-parking zone, shut off the headlights and set the brake, but left the engine running. I asked Marla to wait.

"You're kidding." She studied me. "Really?"

"I won't be a moment."

She gave me a puzzled smile as she reached to poke on the emergency flashers. "Take all the time you want."

The hooker made a show of looking up and down the street as if I were putting her in a difficult situation, then said in her nasal, gum-chewing voice, "Sorry, honey, I don't do three-ways."

I said, "I wanted to thank you again for your help." I was standing ten feet away from her.

She stopped with the nonsense and nodded toward the car. "Is that the wife?"

"Marla."

She stooped to peer through the windshield. "She's a looker."

"Right up there with Monique."

She laughed and stepped forward, touching my chest with her finger. "See? You got your humor back." With Marla as her audience, she was pretending to put me in a situation I would have to explain later. As if I hadn't given myself enough to explain just by stopping.

I said, "Yes. That's part of why I wanted to say thanks. It's over."

She cast a doubtful glance. "Completely?"

"All better."

"Honey, I've seen worse and I've seen better, and you're not better."

I paused. "No, but that one problem is solved. That's all I meant."

She nodded and said, "Fair enough." Then she pointed at me with her thumb raised. "Did you keep any souvenirs?"

"Nope. I'm clean. And you are too."

"That's what I keep telling the boys."

I said, "In fact, I never physically touched it. I shook it out of the package into a hole and covered it over."

"That's what I like to hear." She nodded toward the car. "And now you got your life back."

"I think so."

"No more parking across from Arlene's?"

"Alas."

"Well, then. I suppose you should you run along before someone thinks we're conducting a piece of business."

"Anyway, thanks."

"I swear, the way you guys just up and disappear on me."

An emotion surprised me, and I didn't know how to reply.

She said, "Look, honey, I'm glad it's over. We don't need to hug." She made a casual turn and took a step away, her weary body doing this so beautifully that I wondered if the move had a French name. She turned again toward me. "What we had wasn't that kind of thing."

I stood there feeling as awkward as I'm sure she meant me to feel. You don't ask a hooker if she will miss having you around. And she's spent enough time in the world to see that it would be an empty effort to try to get together sometime in the future and catch up with each other. Finally I went around to the driver's side of the car. She smiled and gave me a little wave with her fingers, then stooped and waved to Marla too.

I got into the car, poked off the emergency flashers, turned on the headlights, and moved us back into traffic.

Marla said, "You meet the most interesting people in the wine business."

I opened my hands on the steering wheel in a helpless shrug and said, "Her name is Sally."

A little later she said, "I'll bet you a penny that was about a gun."

I said, "You're pretty smart for someone who fell off a turnip truck."

We continued in silence, watching the way the night city changed as we passed from beneath the tall, fluorescent-lighted downtown buildings out to the more randomly lit stretches north toward the river. Here the arterials meet the freeway in a tangle of overpasses, surrounded by big, boxy warehouses related to river and railroad commerce. We were on the St. Stephen's bridge, just having crossed the steel grate that opens skyward like double doors for the taller sailboats on their way to or from the upriver marina. The tires on the grate had been humming with an almost electrical insistence, and when we hit the asphalt on the other side, the car went quiet in a way that called attention to itself.

In the new quiet Marla said, "So how did you meet this Sally?"

ACKNOWLEDGMENTS

A special thanks to Jim Clark for fellowship, insight, and transcendent bottles of red from the back room; to Mr. Mike, another wine guy with a modest and generous heart; to Mike's friend, Steve Bloch, for short notice camera work; to Gail Hochman, for her keen ear and great tenacity in a difficult market; to Greg Michalson, for taking me on a second time, and providing the title; to Matt & Laura, for a few choice Kramerisms and guidance in the unappreciated world of teaching; to Tim Clifford's meticulous eye; to Officer Daniels of the Portland Police—any deviations from police procedure are my responsibility; to Connie Oehring, for her good comma sense—persisting errors are mine alone; but most of all to Marianne, my love, for making Marla's spirit possible, and granting me extended hours of solitude in my dusty cluttered office.